Praise for Laura Wolf

'If you liked *Bridget Jones's Diary* you'll love this. Also written in journal form, it's fast-paced and laugh-out-loud funny. And Amy is just as scatty and likeable as Bridget'   *Family Circle*

'Fast-paced, light-hearted and sure to put you off marriage for life!'   *Company*

'A laugh-a-minute read'   *Shine magazine*

'Very, very funny . . . Dry humour and pathos. Worth reading, even if you aren't getting married'
                                              Image magazine

'A brilliant, fresh and funny novel that will ring true for any bride-to-be and all her long-suffering friends'
                                    Wedding Venues and Services

'It'll make you laugh out loud'
                    New Woman (The Bloody Good Read Awards)

Laura Wolf lives in Los Angeles. She writes for television and films, and is also a compulsive writer of 'Things To Do' lists. Her first novel, *Diary of a Mad Bride*, is also available in Orion paperback.

Diary of a
mad
mother-to-be

LAURA WOLF

ORION

An Orion paperback

First published in Great Britain in 2003
by Orion
This paperback edition published in 2004
by Orion Books Ltd,
Orion House, 5 Upper St Martin's Lane,
London WC2H 9EA

Second impression 2004

A CIP catalogue record for this book is available
from the British Library.

ISBN 0 75285 897 1

Printed and bound in Great Britain by
Clays Ltd, St Ives plc

www.orionbooks.co.uk

For Charlotte, who made me a mother.
And for my mother, Susan, who made me.

ACKNOWLEDGMENTS

As always, many thanks to those who helped to support this book by offering advice, reading early drafts, or simply reminding me about prenatal vitamins: Albert Knapp, Elizabeth Marx, Lisa Moricoli Latham, Tracy Fisher, Jackie Cantor, Cori J. Wellins, Lolita Carrico, and, of course, Karl.

Diary of a
mad mother-to-be

february 10th

> MS. LINDER
> I see from your résumé that you have solid
> experience with the written word.

Twelve years of employment and all she's gonna give me is "solid"?

> ME
> Yes, for the last four years, I've been
> Associate Editor of *Round-Up* magazine.

> MS. LINDER
> *Round-Up*. Hmm . . . I haven't read that.

Which is precisely why it folded seven months ago.

> ME
> It was one of those insider publications.

> MS. LINDER
> Well, there's nothing "insider" about the
> *N.Y.R.T. The New York Refuse Times* has
> a thriving readership.

Here I am, Amy Thomas-Stewart, a magazine veteran, a college graduate, recipient of the Elm Street Junior High award for best penmanship, interviewing for a job on a sanitation newsletter. A municipal rag. Can I sink any lower?

Probably.

With *Round-Up* gone and my unemployment benefits dwindling, I've had to expand my job search into all areas requiring the written word: copyediting, fortune cookies, and marginal publications like *The New York Refuse Times*.

According to the receptionist they've had over 150 applications for this crummy job. It seems that as the magazine business shrinks, those of us who'd planned on making a living in it are literally being swept into the trash.[1] Which is the only reason I'm suffering through this job interview with a woman who's bitch-slapping my self-esteem with one hand while nursing her three-year-old son with the other.

That's right. I said *nursing her three-year-old son.*

Which would be a hell of a lot easier to ignore if the kid didn't keep interrupting our interview to demand "more." For God's sake, if you're old enough to make requests, you're old enough to open the refrigerator. And to top it off, the brat's a noisy eater. This, along with the image of my parents having sex, is something I do *not* need to see.

Which makes me wonder: What's the etiquette on public nursing? Am I supposed to ignore this? Applaud it? Do I maintain eye contact or do I plaster a warm smile across my face and act like this happens at all my interviews?

Desperate to make a good impression, I decide to play it safe and fix my gaze above boob level.

Of course, making matters worse is the fact that I'm actu-

---

[1] After all these years spent dreaming of a job at *The New York Times* (stop laughing, I'm talking about the Arts & Leisure section), how painful to be interviewing for a position with the *N.Y.R.T.* It's like God's little typo.

ally ashamed of my own discomfort. That's right, she's baring her boobs and yet *I'm* the one burning with shame. After all, I'm supposed to be a feminist. A woman's woman. Shouldn't I support working mothers? Applaud maternal power? Of course I should. There's nothing dirty, raunchy, or inappropriate about nursing. It's a *natural* act. Like shivering in the cold or lying about your weight.

Heck, I'm the first to admit that I'm clueless about raising a child, let alone weaning one. But dammit –

IF THAT KID SUCKS ANY HARDER HE'S GONNA RIP A LUNG OUT!

Generally speaking, under normal circumstances, this wouldn't have been such a horrible comment –

Had I not said it *ALOUD*.

And before you could even think the word *Medic!* she's snapping up her nursing bra and hissing a curt:

> MS. LINDER
> We'll call you.

Sure you will.

february 15th

Nowhere is unemployment more disastrous than in the area of romance. Sure, we get misty when "The Gift of the Magi" husband sells his watch in order to buy his wife a barrette only to discover that she has sold her hair in order to buy him a watch fob. . . . Ah, Love!

But in the Real World the exchange of useless items falls far short of a fancy dinner and a dozen roses. Which is what

3

Stephen and I did last year.[2] This year, struggling to pay our rent, we ordered in Chinese food. Which is not to say the evening was a total bust. The decadence factor associated with a meal as fattening as egg rolls and sesame noodles can make even the most pouty gal heady with delight. And a little horny, to boot.

Of course, most people would assume that being married to the senior partner of a software company would spare me the injustices of mounting bills and single-ply toilet paper.

Keep dreaming.

Stephen's company, along with all the other computer start-ups, is once again at the brink of bankruptcy. The computer project he developed around the time we got married bombed in the marketplace after a rival company introduced virtually the same product at half the cost.

But strained finances aside, after a year and a half of marriage I still think getting hitched was the best decision I ever made. Sure, the first year was taxing. Challenging. OK, fine, it was really *hard*. Suddenly those fights about nothing in particular carry much more weight. You can't just walk out and hit the singles bars.[3] Now if you want to walk out it's called Divorce, and in addition to requiring a lawyer and lots of paperwork, it'll cost you a ton of money.

So the bottom line on marriage? It's like any partnership – you need to get used to the other person's rhythms. Even if you've been with them for a while. But now, safely en-

---

[2] OK, it was lunch and three ginger blossoms. But ginger blossoms are my favorite flower and the restaurant was *really* fancy. David Bowie and Iman eat sushi there all the time.

[3] For the record, I've never actually been to a singles bar. I'm not even sure they exist. I suspect it's more of a code word for an evening spent with a bunch of girlfriends bitching about men.

sconced within our second year, Stephen and I have gotten into a groove, learned to compromise, to accept one another's idiosyncrasies, and to compromise.

Did I mention compromise?

Well, I should, because in marriage you compromise five times more than you get your way and three times more than you have sex. For instance, Stephen has learned to be silent when I try on at least eight different outfits before going out for the evening. And I've come to understand that he leaves dirty dishes in the sink because he has a chemical imbalance that prevents him from opening the dishwasher.

Additionally, I know that he will never, no matter how often I beg, remember to flush the toilet after peeing. Although to his credit he does put the toilet seat down, so in the world of potential mates it's safe to say I hit the jackpot.

february 18th

Mandy and I met for dinner this evening at our favorite Italian restaurant, Frutto di Sole. We've been regulars at this tiny West Village hangout, a cross between a grandmother's kitchen and a Neapolitan diner, since we graduated from college. Now in our thirties, I feel like we own the joint. Or at least the little table in the back by the fireplace. A feeling which is challenged every time the owner, Rocco Marconi, graciously kisses my hand then sneaks a peek down my blouse.

Still reeling from my *N.Y.R.T.* interview, I told Mandy all about my encounter with the kiddie milk bar. Mandy immediately felt my pain.

MANDY
Good lord, it sounds like a trip to the
petting zoo. Have these women no shame?
Whatever happened to modesty? Self-
respect? Perky breasts?

As I struggled to figure out how we'd gone from modesty to
perky breasts, Mandy, my more than slightly self-involved
friend, had already moved on. She was talking about an upcoming trip that she and her husband, Jon, are taking to
the Canyon Ranch Spa. Mandy insists that Stephen and I join
her. Never going to happen. But instead of saying that I'd
rather gnaw off my own limb than vacation with her
husband, Jon, I decided to focus on the fact that people who
are unemployed don't take spa vacations. Mandy wrinkled
her nose.

MANDY
Really, Amy. You should never say
"unemployed." It sounds so desperate.

In Mandy's universe – where the world is like a Cheever
novel with a tad less booze – it would be acceptable to do
nothing with my life if I were independently wealthy. But to
be jobless *and* broke is a socially shaming mixture akin to
wearing a see-through blouse without a camisole. The fact
that I'm goal-oriented and actually *want* to work is entirely
beside the point. Once again, I marveled at Mandy's ability
to live completely outside of reality.

It's a skill that's particularly pronounced later in the meal
as she starts talking about her mother.

It seems Mandy – who equates procreating with having a

6

really bad hair day – has begun taking desperate measures to silence her mother's incessant requests for grandchildren. And though Mandy's tactics are extreme, I can totally relate to her frustration. After all, what newly married hetero-sexual couple doesn't get the baby pressure?

> MANDY
> I thought about telling her that I had fertility problems. But that's too sleazy. So I told her *Jon* was sterile.

We should be so lucky.

> ME
> And she's still bothering you? Seems a bit insensitive.

> MANDY
> Tell me about it. Do you know she actually had the nerve to send us ten thousand dollars to go to a fertility specialist?

The nerve? I barely got that much for my wedding.

> ME
> So what'd you do with the money?

> MANDY
> How do you think we're paying for Canyon Ranch?

Check, please. And give it to her.

march 5th

My employment status is officially dire. Eight months after *Round-Up*'s demise, my association with New York's least-read magazine hasn't opened a single door. How awful to work for twelve years only to discover that you're still unqualified to do anything.

As visions of eviction notices dance through my head, I try to remember how lucky I am. I have my health. My friends. A wonderful marriage. If nothing else I can live on love. After all, love makes the world go round. Love is all you need.

Who am I kidding?

I can't buy name-brand pantyhose with love!

And all this free time is killing me. At first it was fun. Like an extended holiday. Only no one's around to share it with because everyone else is at work. Advancing their careers. Making something of their lives. So now I spend my days anxious, frustrated, and annoyed by my sister Nicole.

In less than two years Nicole, my vaguely younger sister, has gone from a married, suburban life with her college sweetheart, Chet, to leaving her husband, dating a younger guy, and wearing extraordinarily trashy clothes – most of which she finds tucked away in the back of my closet. In short, Nicole is finally living out her youth. Unfortunately, she's doing it from the middle of my living room.

Stephen and I live in a cramped apartment on Manhattan's Upper West Side. Sure, the building's got a pretty lobby and a shiny elevator. But no matter how many times the rental agent refers to our apartment as a "handsome two-bedroom," the fact remains that it's only 650 square feet. A glorified one-bedroom with a fairly large closet. Far too small for Nicole to spend every weekend sleeping on our couch after late nights of clubbing with her boyfriend, Pablo.[4]

At first I assumed Pablo was a rebound relationship after Nicole left her husband, Chet. A young sex toy easing her out of Mayberry and into Babylon. When their affair began he was an installer for the cable company and gave us free HBO – so I kept my opinions to myself. Besides, it was Nicole's life to live. Now, two years later, Pablo's been promoted to a desk job and can no longer get us free HBO. But it doesn't matter. I've really grown to like him. And no matter how you slice it, two years is too long to be a rebound.

And way too long to be sleeping on my sofa.

Especially since Stephen refuses to have sex when Nicole's around. He's says the walls are too thin. Great. First you spend high school evading your parents while groping in their living room. Then you spend college praying your roommate doesn't walk in on you. Isn't having sex in your own apartment one of the few inalienable rights of adulthood?

Apparently not.

Sure, it would seem logical for Nicole to exchange her apartment and job upstate for ones here in the city. After all, how hard could it be to find paralegal work in New York? But no matter how often I beg she refuses to get her own place in the city, or at the very least to convince Pablo to move out of his parents' house. "Isn't it about time? I mean for God's sake, the guy's twenty-five."

Nicole just shrugs. "Why should he? He saves tons of money this way. Besides, they treat him like an adult."

"Then why can't you sleep over there?"

---

[4] And yes, it's Stephen's bachelor couch. That plaid monstrosity that I've begged him to throw out since the day we got engaged. But no. Just like unsightly facial hair: No matter how hard you try, it just won't go away.

"Are you kidding? His parents would flip if they knew he was having sex!"

And for the record, I don't want to know about Pablo's sex life, either. So I've laid down the law. Nicole can sleep here, but she is NOT ALLOWED TO FORNICATE ON OUR SOFA. If Stephen and I can't have sex in our apartment, then neither can she. Which is why, after sneaking out of Pablo's bedroom, Nicole does the Walk of Shame back to my apartment every Friday and Saturday night.

This from a woman who used to spend weekends swapping meat loaf recipes and playing couples' charades.

march 12th

As materialistic, self-involved, and high-maintenance as Mandy is, she's been one of my best friends since college. And nothing, not even her off-the-cuff remark in 1996 about how bangs make me look like a man in drag, will ever change that. Our friendship will follow us to the grave.

A fact that has never been so greatly tested as when Mandy Alexander completely lost her sanity and married Jon Skepperman on the perfectly manicured lawn of her parents' country club.

On a certain level it made complete sense. Like Mandy, Jon comes from an old-money family and has a deeply rooted respect for tradition. People are on this planet to marry, earn money, and own Polo sport shirts in every available color. She's a real estate agent. Jon's a real estate lawyer. They're like two halves of a very disturbing puzzle. Except that while Mandy can be funny, charming, and an extremely supportive friend, Jon remains a pear-shaped man who runs like a woman and talks like a minor character from a Ronald Reagan biopic.

But Mandy loves him and I love her, so I keep my thoughts to myself. My interactions with Jon are brief, of necessity, and inevitably end with fantasies of me poking out his eyes with a ballpoint pen. Which is why I was surprised when he called me last night.

> JON
> Hi, Amy. It's Jon.

This can't be good.

> JON
> I was wondering if you're still living off the state.

Like I said . . .

> ME
> If you mean am I still receiving my unemployment benefits, to which I'm entitled after paying taxes for the last twelve years, the answer is yes.

> JON
> Must be humiliating. Just talking about it makes me uncomfortable.

Of course it does. After all, God never intended for jackasses to speak.

JON
Mercifully, I think I have a solution for you. A colleague of mine has a sister who works in public relations. She's leaving her job at a company called Brinkman/Baines, and they have yet to fill her position. It doesn't seem particularly challenging. You should look into it.

Please, sir, may I have another?

march 12th – 9 p.m.

ANITA
You're taking life advice from a guy without a pulse? You really have hit rock bottom.

My friend Anita is just as candid and uncensored as Mandy is. Only, while Mandy favors Emily Post, Anita is pure Courtney Love. No wonder they can't stand each other.

ANITA
That Jon has a job, let alone a law degree, proves that Western civilization is in decline.

Hard to argue. But the fact remains that despite Anita's best efforts, it's Jon, not she, who's provided the best employment tip I've had in months. So I insisted Anita stop bashing Jon long enough to tell me what she knows about Brinkman/Baines.

Turns out she knows tons.

As managing editor of *Teen Flair* magazine, she's had lots of interactions with the folks at Brinkman/Baines – a third-rate public relations firm specializing in minor celebrities and local politicians. Do you remember Glyniss O'Maley, the eleven-year-old who parlayed an attempt at the Guinness record for the highest number of consecutive cartwheels[5] into a recurring role on the soap opera *All My Sorrows*? In addition to being *Teen Flair*'s January cover girl, she's also a Brinkman/Baines client.

And Alexander Hastings, the candidate for city councilman who claimed to be thirty until a jilted girlfriend sent his high school yearbook to the opposition. The ink was still drying – the guy was eighteen. Brinkman/Baines helped him leverage the scandal by appealing to the youth vote. Last I heard, Councilman Hastings was spearheading a campaign to legalize marijuana.

Intellectual? Not really. Classy? Definitely not.

I immediately called for an interview.

march 15th

Deception starts early at Brinkman/Baines. For starters, there is neither a Brinkman nor a Baines. Brinkman is dead, and Baines has been on vacation since the company was purchased by a large media conglomerate ten years ago. Why a large media conglomerate would want such a small-potatoes enterprise is beyond me.

Which brings me to deception number two: While Brinkman/Baines is located in a fancy midtown high-rise, the

---

[5] She passed out at 250.

fat-cat atmosphere vanishes the minute you open the frosted glass door with the polished chrome sign. The shabby little office with industrial carpeting and yellowed cubicles is every bit the professional wasteland that *Round-Up* was. I felt right at home.

Except for the fact that every employee is under twenty-five.

You've never seen so many fashion T-shirts and college backpacks under one roof. The receptionist at the front desk with her professionally frayed jean jacket even had the nerve to snicker at my power suit.

Bitch.

Luckily, I was interviewed by the company president, Jack Nealy, who wore a blazer and corduroys. No tie. A bit jowly, with salt-and-pepper hair, I'm guessing Mr. Nealy's in his late forties. Jumpy and tightly wound, he's like a cross between Tony Blair and Robert Downey, Jr., after a long night snorting cocaine. During my interview he mentioned four times that he's got a master's degree in journalism. Three times that he hates slackers. Twice that the job requires enormous creativity. And I'm fairly certain that at least once, he farted.

And yet by comparison to my *N.Y.R.T.* experience, the interview went fairly well. Mr. Nealy kept his shirt on, and we both drank from cups.

march 16th

I just got my Visa bill – and with it such a frigid dose of reality that while dulling my pain with an espresso at Starbucks I filled out a job application.

march 18th

Out of nowhere, Stephen called from work and asked me to meet him at Fifth Avenue and Fiftieth Street. An hour later we were eating souvlaki from a street cart before spending the evening ice skating at Rockefeller Center.

This is why I love Stephen. Sure, it helps that he's tall and slender, with a beautiful smile that lists to the left. And that his sandy blond hair reminds me of honey and that his laugh is so incredibly joyful and embracing that it warms me from head to toe. Even on an ice rink. Yes, all of that is great. But what really sets Stephen apart is his sense of spontaneity.

While on the one hand he's as logical and rational as a software developer can be, he can also wake up in the middle of the night and decide that it's a perfect time for cheesecake. A train ride later we'll be at Junior's in Brooklyn snacking on some of the best cherry cheesecake money can buy – with five of our closest friends.

I know some folks would find this annoying. But for me it's essential. The perfect complement to my control-freak nature, which dictates that I triple-check details and plan *everything* in advance.

Thank God this obsessive behavior extended to my choice of husbands.

march 20th

Quick! Check for flying pigs and swimsuits cut for women with large butts because I actually got the job at Brinkman/Baines! That's right, come next week I'll be gainfully employed under the title of Senior Account Manager.

Is writing speeches and press releases for minor celebrities and local politicians what I envisioned myself doing at age thirty-one? Absolutely not. But since health insurance and a place to live currently outweigh my need for meaningful employment, I'll gladly take it. So what if Brinkman/Baines is a tiny third-rate company? They pay almost as much[6] as my job at *Round-Up,* and as far as I can tell they don't promote mass suicide or thongs.

So count me in!

Besides, it's not nearly as messy as selling my ova on the Internet. In fact, the only downside of this entire situation is that I actually have to thank *Jon* for helping me get a job.

march 21st

When it rains it pours. Anita gave me a big plastic shovel as a token of her enthusiasm for my upcoming foray into the world of P.R. Stephen was so happy that he agreed to have sex even though Nicole had unexpectedly dropped by and was snoring in the living room. And my father, the man who bandaged my knee when I fell off my tricycle, who never told my mother I got caught cheating on my high school chem final, and who's held his tongue during my extended period of unemployment, cheered with joy when I called to tell him that I'd gotten a job. He was so happy. Ecstatic. And relieved. So very relieved . . .

"Thank God. I thought you kids were going to hit me up for a loan."

Touching.

---

[6] As little.

16

Stephen and I had dinner tonight with his coworker Martin.

Before becoming a mother, Martin's wife was a professional chef with her own cooking show on cable television, so I was particularly excited about the invitation. Not to mention that I delight in telling *anyone* who will listen that I'm gainfully employed. Even if I don't start work for a week. And I have no idea what a Senior Account Manager really does. Details, details . . . The fact is there's a paycheck in my future and I was ready to celebrate. So, flush with the prospect of a two-income household, we bought a bouquet of flowers and a really expensive bottle of wine.

Unfortunately a case of Schlitz and a vial of Lithium would have been more useful.

Turns out an invitation to Martin's house includes a brush with death, otherwise known as his three hyperactive offspring. Each more insane than the next. Each with his or her own nut allergy. Clearly desensitized to the hysteria of his home, Martin actually had the nerve to ask when *we* were going to have children.

Excuse me? Was it something I said? Or perhaps it's my perfume. Have you mistaken my Calvin Klein *Eternity* for the scent of infant yearning? Because I KNOW you don't hear my "biological clock" ticking, since I'm only a youthful, almost teenage, thirty-one years old.

Which leads me to wonder why my childbearing plans are such a popular issue. It's bad enough when elderly strangers or my childless gay dentist asks, but there's something particularly insidious when the question comes from other parents. Yes, I'm constantly amazed by the way that people who have children push other married couples toward procreation. Well, I have only one thing to say:

Step away from my diaphragm, Mr. Mom!

Because some of us still relish sleeping through the night, walking around the house naked, and being able to buy peanut butter without worrying it's going to *kill* someone.

Trust me, nowhere on my marriage license does it say I have to bear children. Yet for reasons which are still unclear to me this hasn't stopped Stephen's grandparents and about eighty percent of the people I meet from asking about it.

Well, put a sock in it and on it and hand me another tube of contraceptive jelly, because I am in no rush to breed. I'm not even sure that I want children. Funny how no one ever considers that possibility. Sure, kids can be nice and cute and a welcome tax write-off, but right now I'm too busy living *my* life to oversee someone else's.

Which is not to say that I don't like kids. Or that I scoff at those who want them. Godspeed and safe passage for people who leave the altar and start cranking out offspring. I'm simply not one of them. And neither is Stephen. The desire to breed was not what motivated us to get married. Besides, anyone who's been to the zoo knows that you don't need a state marriage license in order to bear children.

So while I silently fumed at Martin's annoying question, Stephen politely responded with a noncommittal "Someday."

And it was all downhill from there.

That fabulous gourmet food I was looking forward to? A fantasy. While Stephen and I snacked on old carrots and store-bought onion dip,[7,8] Martin and Mrs.

---

[7] Served in the plastic container.
[8] With the price tag still on it.

Martin[9] struggled to wrangle their beastly children into submission so that the adults could eat. After an agonizing hour of Martin's daughter shrieking to watch *The Little Mermaid* and his sons biting each other in the corner, we finally sat down to dinner.

Or at least some of us did.

As we approached the table Martin, the procreation junkie, escorted me to the "Magic Chair." Assuming it was a chair intended for an honored guest, or perhaps the person in the room with the most painfully throbbing headache, I happily sat down. Unfortunately, as I made my way to sit Martin explained that Mrs. Martin, Martin's cousin, and his downstairs neighbor Marie all became pregnant after sitting in the Magic Chair. At which point Stephen, as if his ass were on fire, dove across the table and whisked away the chair – sending me crashing to the ground and prompting all three of Martin's hyperactive children to squeal with delight.

And for the record, no one gave a damn about my new job.[10]

march 25th

Today was my first day at Brinkman/Baines. Thankfully, the fact that most of the office staff is almost ten years younger

---

[9] Whose name we never did get due to her inability to engage in meaningful conversation for longer than two minutes before having to run off and stop one of her mangy brood from setting fire to the apartment or electrocuting a sibling.

[10] Or culinary standards. Dinner was overcooked fish and instant rice without the seasonings packet. Please, if I want a meal as mediocre as this, I'll go to my mother's house.

than I am doesn't appear to be a problem.

The *problem* is that they were all hoping to get this job.

That's right, everyone from Mr. Nealy's secretary to the four Junior Account Managers, who appear to be closer to administrative assistants than executives, all wanted to be the Senior Account Manager. Why? Because only the Senior Account Manager and Mr. Nealy work with the "celebrity" clientele.

Yes, it seems that for those recently weaned off *Tiger Beat*, the prospect of interacting with celebrities, even those who routinely appear in infomercials and on *Hollywood Squares*, is the stuff that dreams are made of. Even if the job doesn't come with a secretary or an expense account. Which it doesn't. So while I'm wincing in horror at my proximity to people who surgically enhance their boobs as well as their lips, cheeks, and butts, my coworkers are seething over lost opportunities. Plus the fact that I get my very own cubicle.

And what lofty feats do I accomplish to earn this cubicle?

My first assignment was to write a speech for the actor Doug Tucker. You know the guy. He's the first one killed in all the action movies. Usually because he says something stupid. Judging from the interviews with him I've read, it's pure type-casting. Well, he's one of the accounts I manage. That means that he's paying big bucks to have Brinkman/ Baines bolster his public profile. To that end my predecessor finagled him the job of official spokesperson for the National Organization for Penile Erectile Dysfunction. Ironic, since I've always thought of Doug Tucker as an enormous prick. In any event, Doug is set to host the annual NOPED fund-raiser next week, and it's my job to make him sound intelligent and charming. A hefty challenge.

This year's fund-raiser is a Ping-Pong tournament. My

opening line?

"Gentlemen, keep your balls in the air!"

At last. My life has meaning.

april 1st

In an effort to spend my first paycheck before Brinkman/
Baines even prints it, I joined Mandy for a manicure at her
favorite nail salon.

The only difference between Nail Couture and the other
hundred nail salons in Manhattan is the cost (double), the
decor (vaguely tasteful), and the accents (French versus
Korean – except anyone with a semester of high school
French knows that the closest these *nail clinicians* have gotten to France is the Au Bon Pain baguette shelf in Grand
Central Station). But Mandy's a sucker for anyone willing to call her *mademoiselle,* so Nail Couture hits the spot.
Besides, she was eager to relax and after a brush with death
during an aromatherapy session last year – caused by an
allergic reaction to Bach flower essence – it's the paraffin-
scented altar of Nail Couture at which Mandy now wor-
ships.

So I tagged along for the ride.

And while pretty nails are fine and dandy, what I was
really looking forward to was being cleansed. That's right.
Rinse my hands a thousand times because after a week at
Brinkman/Baines my innocence is shot and I'm head-to-toe
in filth.

Turns out public relations is one part fact gathering and
ninety-nine parts bullshit. Hence Anita's shovel. That creativity Mr. Nealy kept harping on during my interview? Of

course it's essential – you have to completely fabricate stories, histories, lives, and actions. And I'm not just talking "spin" but flat-out lies. Falsehoods without a shred of fact. I am completely immersed in bullshit.

Sure we suspect the world is filled with lies and deceit, but after all these years spent editing articles based on facts and reality – the financial motivation behind an outer-borough cemetery, the hidden dangers of chin lifts – to actually be inside the evil empire that manufactures reality is overwhelming, sickening, and yes, dear God, *YES*, the teeniest bit arousing.

I'm sure it's far less base at larger P.R. firms, or at those with a more sophisticated clientele – authors, scientists, Vegas showgirls . . . But Brinkman/Baines is strictly a bottom-feeder. I'm getting paid to put words into people's mouths, to create their personalities, and in some cases to suggest professionally advantageous dating partners. I'm not so much a muck-raker as a muck-maker. It's a power that is both awesome and perverse. As if I've suddenly become the Wizard of Oz. Liz Smith. Or Bill Gates. With one small caveat: Screw up, piss off the client, or embarrass the firm, and I'm on the street faster than the newest designer drug.

So is it any surprise that I was desperate to be cleansed? Of course not.

Besides, Mandy deemed it a virtual health hazard not to.

MANDY
I know you've been hard at work, Amy,
but really, no one should walk around
with that much cuticle.

22

april 7th

Tonight was our monthly dinner with my family. Unfortunately, Stephen had a late business meeting in the city and couldn't join us.

My parents and maternal grandmother live upstate in my quiet, suburban hometown, a place so boring that just going there gives me the shakes. The highlight of the town's social calendar is the Baked Chicken Contest sponsored by a local chapter of Weight Watchers. Last year's winner featured Velveeta cheese and salt. This is why Nicole, who moved back there when she married her lovely but painfully dull ex-husband, now spends every weekend on my couch – casual sex is much tastier in the city.

Coincidentally the town where Stephen grew up – and where both his parents still live – is only a few miles away. Although more affluent, his hometown is also quiet, quaint, and perfect if you're preparing to die. And yet despite their proximity we rarely combine our family dinners. It's a defense strategy, because both our families are crazy. Although it takes a while to notice. Like the way poison ivy looks pretty enough to touch but makes you scratch for weeks. So combining our families is a risk we're only willing to take on major holidays and funerals. And even then it's a dicey proposition.

My parents, Bob and Terry Thomas, are practical and reliable people. My father is middle-management at a grocery store chain, and my mother is an elementary school teacher. They've lived in the same house for the last twenty-five years and have only redecorated once. Dinner consists of whatever is currently in the refrigerator, and is always served promptly at six-thirty, just after the local news. Although we're all older and wiser, to varying degrees, there's a reassuring sameness to these dinners. Sure, the participants have changed over the years – Nicole's ex-husband is no longer there,[11] Stephen's usually here, and since moving in with my parents, my grandmother's joined us. But for the most part it's the same as it was when Nicole and I were kids.

Right down to the conversation.

No matter what happens in our lives or in the world around us, our family dinners inevitably serve as a forum for family gossip. The joys and tragedies. The triumphs and humiliations. Uncle Leo had a suspicious mole removed,[12] and Cousin Lydia's dating a man who's been in prison. It's like an alternate-universe version of my meals at Frutto di Sole with Mandy and Anita – only without all the sex talk. And no matter how much I complain about my monthly pilgrimage upstate, I truly love it. It reminds me where I came from,[13] and how important family is. Even if some of them are insane.

That's right. For anyone who's ever thought that "normal" people actually exist, my family is here to shatter that illusion. In their own practical and reliable way, my parents are nuts. My father has an unnatural attachment to the television show *Diagnosis Murder,* and after thirty years on the job my mother is completely unable to see a runny nose without wiping it. No matter whose nose it is. Nicole's recent life transition from Betty Crocker to Mary Magdalene speaks for itself. And then there's Gram.

My octogenarian grandmother and I had a picture-perfect relationship – until I decided to get married. After a series of manipulative remarks, passive-aggressive gestures, and out-

---

[11] Which is a good thing since I don't think his new wife would appreciate it.
[12] Benign.
[13] Or how far I've come, depending on the day.

landish acts, I finally realized that my sweet, loving grand-mother was unwilling to allow the pendulum of attention to swing from herself to me. Having a granddaughter usurp her role as the family focus was simply too much for her to bear. Hence she did everything in her power to prevent my marriage from happening. Yes, that five-foot-tall[14] powerhouse staged a variety of attention-stealing coups, including an eleventh-hour pronouncement that she, and consequently we, were Jewish and thus had no business proceeding with a marriage in a Presbyterian church. And when I decided to go ahead with my wedding, she declared me an anti-Semite and stormed out the door.[15]

Meet her in a dark alley and you wouldn't bat an eyelash. In the context of a family therapy session – she could be deadly.

But time heals all wounds, and yesterday's star is today's flash in the pan. So when the hoopla surrounding my wedding died down and Stephen and I settled into being just another married couple, Gram and I mended fences. After all, the woman sewed my Brownie patches.

It was against this backdrop that I learned my great-aunt Lucy had had a minor stroke.

My great-aunt Lucy is really a cousin several times removed who lives in Wisconsin. When I was a kid I spent the summer with her and fell in love. Despite being in her sixties at the time, she was vivacious, permissive, and totally captivating. Her behavior defied that commonly associated with senior citizens, as well as with any member of my immediate family. To this day she is my favorite relative.

---

[14] Five foot two in her fashion-forward orthopedic shoes.
[15] To a bingo game where apparently God was not on her side as she went on to lose that month's Social Security check.

So to learn that she'd had a minor stroke was both infuriating and devastating. First off, "minor stroke," like "minor surgery," doesn't exist. No matter what the medical texts say. Especially when you're eighty-nine years old, as Lucy is. And while I was relieved to hear that her prognosis is good, and vowed to call her first thing in the morning, the very thought of losing her chilled me to the bone. Having Lucy in my life has truly been a gift.

So few of my friends have the luxury of older relatives. Even my relationship with Gram, although stormy and not nearly as meaningful as my relationship with Lucy, has helped to shape the person I am. The bottom line is that elderly relatives benefit everyone, especially children.

And it was this very thought that changed the rest of my life.

It occurred to me, after some quick math, that if I'm thirty-one years old and Stephen and I have kids in a few years, by the time those kids are my age their grandparents will be in their nineties! And Lucy will be over 120! My heart began to pound.

Where had all the time gone?

I felt like Rip Van Winkle waking up from a decades-long sleep only to discover that everyone was gone and that I was OLD. Suddenly thirty-one was a lot closer to middle age than to my teenage years. Why was I just realizing this now? Sure, I was no math major in college, but this is simple addition. Even a preschooler can add!

But there was more. Oh, so much more! The desire to share. To nurture. The infinite yearning to hold and never, ever let go.

And there I was, with every thought I'd ever had about childbearing rushing over me like a tidal wave, leaving me drenched in an unmistakable reality:

I WANT A BABY.

It was all I could do not to shriek in horror and delight. An action which undoubtedly would have disrupted our meal – although it may have put an end to Nicole's droning on and on about her exciting life as a single woman. As if anyone really cares.

But no, I kept my life-transforming desire to myself, knowing that before I went public, I had to discuss it with Stephen. After all, an egg without a sperm is nothing more than an omelet waiting to happen.

Still, I could think of nothing else – all throughout dinner, dessert, Nicole's monologue about her new fitness routine, and Gram's carping about anorexic supermodels. And I continued to think about it during my walk to the train station, the trip home, and my taxi ride to our apartment. The desire to have children has been hovering at the bottom of my mental "Things to Do" list since Stephen and I met. It's like knowing you're going to eat the entire pint of ice cream but instead of plunging in, you gingerly skim the edges until the bottom of the carton is undeniably visible. You're basically waiting until the time is right and it's safe to act. After all, we've always said we'd have kids – Someday.

Well, Someday is here.

It was the most liberating sensation I'd had in years. Far from being shrouded in burden or dragged down by responsibility, the idea of becoming a mother felt *empowering*. Invigorating! And as I approached our apartment building, I considered various ways to broach the subject with Stephen. After all, it's not the sort of thing you just come out and demand. It's got to be mutually agreed upon. So I decided to tread lightly.

Very lightly, remembering Stephen's reaction to Martin's "Magic Chair" and the swollen coccyx I nursed for the following two weeks.

But if there is one undeniable truth about me, it's that patience is not a virtue which I possess. And by the time I arrived at our apartment door I was ready to burst.

So I did.

With a flick of my key I swung open the door and stormed into the living room. Stephen, who was sitting on the couch in his boxers eating leftover Chinese food straight from the container, jumped into the air. It probably took a few years off his life, but there was no time to apologize. I had to speak my piece.

> **ME**
> Either we're having a baby or getting a
> cat! And since our lease says no pets, I
> guess it's a baby!

With soy sauce dribbling down his chin and onto our tan throw pillows,[16] Stephen looked up at me and said,

> **STEPHEN**
> We could move.

Bastard.

> **ME**
> No! I want kids. I know I said I could
> wait, but I can't. Not anymore. My time
> has come. THIS IS MY TIME!

[16] Note to self: Ask dry cleaner if soy sauce stains.

Clearly stunned by my sudden declaration for children, Stephen grappled for something he could actually comprehend.

> STEPHEN
> Are there any dumplings left?

And this is how we began the discussion about the biggest decision of our collective lives. A discussion that lasted well into the night and remained unresolved.

Around two A.M., we declared the topic T.B.D. and went to sleep as best we could. But in truth neither of us got much sleep. I know because Stephen spent most of the night tossing about without a hint of snoring. And while I don't know what he was thinking, I couldn't help but think how ready I felt to have children, and how very, very much Stephen disagreed.

april 11th

I know these past few days have been tough on Stephen. To suddenly insist on a baby would shock even the most secure man. But Stephen's not like other men. Far from staid or inflexible, he's impulsive. He'll go somewhere because he likes the sound of its name. He'll hear a song and buy the album. He'll see a beautiful beach and convince his wife to have sex on it. He *is* Mr. Spontaneity. So after his initial shock wore off I really expected him to jump aboard the baby bandwagon.

But no.

He still doesn't think he, or we, are ready to have kids.

And although he's completely wrong, I understand that he thinks he's right. And that he's confused. And nervous. Well, I'm nervous, too. After all, I'm the one who's gonna have to carry the baby. Not to mention birth it.

But do you see me running out and spending THOU-SANDS of dollars?

Of course not. Hell, it's been more than eight months since I bought new shoes! And yet tonight I came home to find a set of Harley-Davidson keys sitting on the coffee table. Despite the fact that the future of Stephen's company is uncertain, and that we're still digging ourselves out of credit card debt, Stephen had channeled his spontaneous nature into purchasing the quintessential male toy.

For Christ's sake, if he was so desperate to regain his youth, he should have bought a blow-up doll. *That* we could afford.

> ME
> You don't even know how to ride a
> motorcycle.

> STEPHEN
> I can learn.

> ME
> Terrific. And where do you intend
> to go on this motorcycle?

> STEPHEN
> Larry and Mitch are riding to Nova Scotia
> this spring. I thought I'd join them.

Larry and Mitch are two of Stephen's longtime friends. The kind of friends you hope your partner will outgrow but never does. So while most of Stephen's friends are interesting, intelligent, and fun, Larry and Mitch are like that red wine stain that never comes out of your carpet. Only in this case it's closer to bong water – which means in addition to staining, it also smells really bad.

Larry's an ambulance-chasing attorney who advertises at bus stops. And Mitch walks dogs. That's right. A thirty-four-year-old dog-walker. And he's not doing it to pay the bills while he pursues his art or some other such noble reason. He's doing it because it's a cash business, which means that he doesn't pay taxes, and because it helps him meet "chicks." Trust me, the guy needs more than a herd of canines to attract women.

So Larry, Mitch, and Stephen riding motorcycles to Nova Scotia? It's the Flight of the Imbeciles. Besides, it doesn't take a genius to know you can't put an infant seat on a motorcycle.

> **ME**
> You really want to go to Nova Scotia?
> Fine. Start harvesting your sperm. You
> never know when you might injure
> yourself in a crash.

> **STEPHEN**
> Is that all you love me for?

> **ME**
> No, I love you for your brains, which is
> why I'm asking you to protect your pecker.
> And while we're on the topic – no

bicycling, hot showers, or Jockey shorts. I
once heard they decrease sperm motility.

STEPHEN
This is crazy.

He's grinding us into poverty and *I'm* crazy?

STEPHEN
We're not ready to have kids.

Here we go again.

While I'm the first to agree that having children needs to
be a mutual decision between two people, and that it should
be carefully considered and discussed, after four nights of
discussion I was talked out. We simply weren't getting anywhere. Stephen's arguments remained the same:

1) I've only just gotten a new job. Which, as I was quick to
remind him, meant that we now have full medical benefits.
2) His job is unstable. A fact which won't change unless he
leaves the company he helped start – which he won't – so
to wait for stability is futile.
3) We live in a 650-square-foot apartment. So what? There
are places in Africa where that's considered a hotel.
Besides, to postpone children because of Manhattan real
estate is ridiculous.

And for the next three hours we sat on our unrelentingly
ugly plaid sofa, with Stephen clutching his motorcycle keys
like a toddler's blankie as I tried to convince him that there
is never a perfect time to have kids. That there will always

be some aspect of our lives that is not ideal.

And that if "Someday" doesn't eventually arrive, it becomes NEVER.

april 13th

We just got back from a family dinner at Stephen's mother's house upstate. The minute I unlocked our apartment door Stephen made a beeline for the medicine cabinet, desperate to be anesthetized. Of course he claims his discomfort stems from the stuffy train ride back to the city, but I know better. Stephen's cranial discomfort has everything to do with his mother's stimulating new "hobby."

Almost four years since her divorce from Stephen's father, Mrs. Abigail Stewart is, as the advertisement goes, *alive with pleasure.*

Initially stung by the dissolution of her thirty-five-year marriage, and then shocked by the almost immediate coupling of her ex with a former schoolmate of Stephen's, Mrs. Stewart went through alternating phases of fury and fragility. One day she wanted to burn down her ex-husband's new bachelor pad,[17] the next day she'd spend hours bemoaning life's empty promises. It was both awkward and sobering to be experiencing the joys and optimism of our new marriage against the backdrop of her disillusionment.

But now, with her hefty divorce settlement finalized – among other things she got their gorgeous suburban New York home with multiple bathrooms and a clay tennis court – and having reclaimed her independent self after thirty-five

---

[17] With her ex and his new girlfriend in it.

years of sublimating it to a man who appreciated televised golf tournaments more than her home-cooked meals, Abigail Stewart's gotten back her land legs.

Or more accurately – her bed head.

Yes, my mother-in-law is experiencing a personal renaissance and is determined to let everyone know *all* about it. Having found the mother lode of eligible men at her new country club, she is juggling them in a fashion that would make Mick Jagger blush. And while I'm impressed by her fortitude, her children aren't nearly as pleased.

Stephen's attempts to be supportive of his mother's joy are thwarted by his impulse to run and hide whenever she uses the term "intimate relations." Stephen's spoiled little sister Kim spends her time fretting about a possible second marriage and the effect it might have on her inheritance. And Tom, Stephen's unpleasant, sex-addicted older brother,[18] flatly refuses to join their family dinners. Thus proving that every bad situation has a silver lining.

Unfortunately, with all their discomfort I think Stephen and his siblings are missing the bigger picture: We should all hope to be that "alive" when we're his mother's age. So while Stephen massages his temples and tries to act like none of this is happening, I say *"Vive la Sex!"*

As long as it isn't *my* mother.

april 14th

I got my Visa bill today and for the first time in several months

---

[18] Apparently my assumption that his libidinous behavior was inherited from *Mr.* Stewart was wrong.

I didn't panic. I was able to pay almost a quarter of the balance – a first since I lost my job at *Round-Up*. Near-solvency feels good. And I feel good. So good in fact that I bought Nicole a new pillow for her ongoing romance with my sofa.

Besides, I've finally woken up and smelled the roses. Who cares that Brinkman/Baines isn't my ideal job? I love working, and I can actually do this job really well. I'm a talented writer and I'm creative. I can devise angles to work, and scams to run. I can spin bad news into good. I can even make complete idiots seem vaguely intelligent. So enough bellyaching about professional tracks and corporate ladders. Dammit, I'm in a groove. I'm cruising! I'm writing some of the best crap ever spoken by third-rate players to an empty house. Professionally speaking I'm back in the game, albeit the league is full of shills.

Plus, it finally occurred to me – OK, Stephen pointed it out while we were watching *The Matrix* for the hundredth time on DVD – that no legitimate employer will ever hire me if I don't excel in a job as crappy as this one.

It's like making a lousy batch of Rice Krispies treats. If you can't do that right, then who's gonna hire you to make a soufflé?

april 15th

After staying up all night with Stephen struggling to finish our taxes, and debating whether or not to have a child, I arrived at work to discover that I've been assigned a partner. News to me. Suddenly the Brinkman/Baines food chain has gotten a bit fatter with two Senior Account Managers now working under Mr. Nealy. Myself and a guy named Eddie.

As if tax day weren't painful enough.

Apparently I wasn't the only one caught off guard by this hire. While two of the four Junior Account Managers were in the tiny office kitchen drinking themselves, one Diet Coke at a time, into artificial-sweetener–induced comas, the other two were bitching on their phones at volumes that far exceeded the privacy factor afforded by open-air cubicles. And to be fair, I can see their point.

Many of them have been here since the day they graduated college – which is also their liability. Even though the content of what I do may be drivel, the quality is not. Good writing and the skills that accompany it are honed over time. And, generally speaking, over a succession of jobs. So unfortunately, most of these twenty-something club kids will have to move to other companies, or continue dabbling in designer drugs and duds while working with colorless politicians on a Junior Account Manager's salary. Which, considering how poorly I'm paid, must place them barely above the poverty line – or, more accurately, still living off Mom and Dad.

As for Eddie, he's an extremely friendly man somewhere in his mid-thirties. I distrusted him on sight.

Call me paranoid, but there's something strange about Eddie. I'm just not sure what it is. Which is too bad, because we'll be working side by side while sharing accounts. That's right, all my clients, including Doug Tucker, the face – or, more appropriately, the head – of Penile Erectile Dysfunction, can now rely on both myself and Eddie to help promote their careers. And no, it's not Eddie's pretty-boy looks, waxed eyebrows, and gently feathered hair that make me uneasy. Or the fact that he's the kind of guy who fights with his girlfriend for mirror time. Because he probably could be a male model if he weren't five foot six. And honestly it has nothing to do with the way he claps his hands together when excited. Although that *is* odd. No, it's something more intangible that gives me pause.

But, given my level of professionalism and my respect for teamwork, I went out of my way to be overwhelmingly polite to him. Besides, I'm a veteran of workplace warfare. I spent three of my four years at *Round-Up* dodging professional backstabbing and corporate shenanigans from a he-bitch named Barry. Hence, I am a seasoned office warrior. Able to thwart takeover plans, deflect snide public remarks, and diffuse incendiary e-mail trees in less than a single afternoon. So in the event that Eddie's got any nefarious intentions for me, he's got another thing coming. While promoting trust and an open line of communication with a smile, I shall be vigilantly watching my back because, although we're equals, the need for two Senior Account Managers has yet to be proven. And there's no way I can afford to be edged out of this job.

After all, there are those nice folks at Visa to consider.

april 28th

Just in case I wanted more child-related anxiety in my life, Brinkman/Baines readily supplied it.

It seems Glyniss O'Maley, the girl who tried to cartwheel herself into the *Guinness Book* and landed on *All My Sorrows,* has tumbled into a rehab center in Minnesota. That's right, the plucky eleven-year-old has developed a taste for toot and it's my job, or rather mine and Eddie's, to put a positive spin on the situation.

I may be good, but this is ridiculous.

Making matters worse is Eddie's less than stellar ability to focus. This is the first assignment that Eddie and I have shared. And it's a whopper. Necessitating all the energy and attention that two supposedly creative people can muster. And yet while I sit here banging my head against the computer trying to put a happy face on a preteen who's been dusting her breakfast cereal with cocaine, he's buffing his fingernails with a chamois file.

I really want to start this professional relationship on the proper foot. To build a sense of trust and partnership. And up till now our limited interaction has been nothing but cordial. But if this Ken doll thinks I'm going to do his work for him, he's been sniffing way too much hair mousse!

april 29th

By yesterday afternoon the best suggestion I had for Glyniss the coke fiend was DENY, DENY, DENY.

No, Glyniss wasn't tucked into a Minnesota hospital bed with a bad case of the shakes. No, she hadn't been fired from her job for unprofessionalism. She'd simply decided to move on. And in a carefully worded statement issued through her representatives at Brinkman/Baines, Miss O'Maley would express her eagerness to expand her horizons by pursuing more challenging roles, perhaps on stage or in film. But first she was taking an extended vacation at an undisclosed location.

Eddie, on the other hand, wanted to milk the situation for all it was worth.

Turns out that while Eddie's here at work, his VCR is

at home recording *All My Sorrows*. He's a huge fan. And according to Eddie, Glyniss's character Lizzie is the quintessential girl next door – sweet, wholesome, innocent. In short, a prime target for a catastrophic downfall. Eddie's spin? To accurately represent the pressures to which so much of America's youth succumbs, Glyniss had hoped to expand her character and had begun researching the world of teen drug use. Unfortunately, during her research Glyniss herself had fallen victim to this terrible fate. She was currently nursing herself back to health in order to return to work and warn the world.

It was perfect. A cautionary tale about lost innocence and drug use. Glyniss would garner the sympathy of her viewers, thus strong-arming the soap opera into corroborating the story and rehiring her. Her onscreen role would become more challenging, which would raise her chances of being nominated for a Daytime Emmy award. And *The National Enquirer* would have a field day with the entire story, thus ensuring our client enormous publicity. Hell, the kid could get her own talk show out of this mess.

I had to admit Eddie's idea was inspired. And to his credit, he received my praise with humility and good nature. So when he began teasing his hair in the middle of our discussion I did everything I could to block the words "Evil Genius" from my mind.

may 2nd

I've discovered that Stephen's reluctance to have kids is partially based on total and complete fear, and partially on economics. With two of us, he feels comfortable sharing the financial burden. We both earn paychecks, we both help to pay the bills.[19] But throw children into the mix and everything changes. Our expenses will increase, and for a very brief period I won't be able to work. Then there's day care, summer camp, braces, and higher education to worry about. The very thought causes Stephen to hyperventilate.

It's funny that no matter how evolved we like to think we are, when push comes to shove – we're not. If you were to ask me, I'd say Stephen is an egalitarian, forward-thinking man. And yet here he is saddled with the Breadwinner Complex, which necessitates that Dad earn a paycheck and support the family. And when I reminded him that I want to work he said it didn't matter. That somewhere between his nuclear family upbringing and his hours spent watching *The Brady Bunch*, he's been hardwired to a world where Dad takes care of the family by wielding a mighty wallet. Anything less is both failure and certain doom.[20]

So while I was supposed to be writing a puff piece about how Representative Blanca Fernandez is a longtime supporter of animal rights despite the fact that she was captured on video taunting a gorilla at the Bronx Zoo,[21] I was instead focusing my P.R. talents on an emotional appeal to the rational side of my husband's computer-programmer brain – specifically, that a father's love is more important than a

---

[19] Including that damn motorcycle bill which we'll be paying the installments on until our kids can ride it to college.

[20] I considered pointing out that despite his father's financial success his nuclear family had experienced a complete and utter meltdown. After all, his dad was living with Stephen's old classmate and his mother was sleeping her way through the social registry. But I refrained.

[21] Who retaliated by tossing excrement at his tormentor, thus proving that gorillas are remarkable judges of character.

father's money and that he has love in spades.

may 5th

After extensive consideration, sleep deprivation, and soul-searching, Stephen and I have officially agreed to have a baby.

We've also agreed not to tell anyone until the stick turns blue.

I have never been so excited, or nervous, in my entire life. Luckily Stephen's spontaneous side seems to have kicked in, so instead of being nervous he's focusing on the immediate: the process of *getting* pregnant.

We're gonna need a new box spring.

may 6th

Since we're officially trying to conceive, and I want to be as responsible as possible, I went for a checkup with my gynecologist. Except my gynecologist is not on the Brinkman/Baines medical plan. In fact, my fabulous new medical plan only has ONE ob/gyn on the entire island of Manhattan. And since I rarely travel to the outer boroughs as it is, there's no way that I'm doing it pregnant. And that's not a snobbish point, it's a practical one. I can afford a taxi-cab home from a doctor's appointment in Manhattan. But I can't afford one home from the outer reaches of Brooklyn, the Bronx, or Queens. And forget Staten Island. The ferry ride alone would kill me. So with all due respect for my yet-to-be-conceived child I immediately made an appointment with Dr. William Eiger, of Manhattan.

Thankfully his offices are clean, his staff is efficient, and his manner is both gentle and professional. There's only one problem: His speaking voice is inaudible.

Flat on my back with my feet in the stirrups I found myself repeatedly yelling down between my legs for Dr. Eiger to please repeat himself. But it was no use. This seemingly lovely man in his early sixties with soft gray hair and sparkling blue eyes was clearly unable to project his voice past my ankles.

So I gave up. And dubbed him the Crotch Whisperer.

may 7th

With my procreation light flashing, I thought it was time to seek guidance – especially since I can't hear a word my obstetrician is saying. After exhaustive on-line research, I spent my lunch hour at the bookstore, where I bought what is unanimously considered to be the pregnancy bible, Baby How, Baby Now.

Baby How, Baby Now has been guiding women through the pregnancy journey for generations. Its cover features a pencil drawing of a beautiful, slender woman with long hair wearing a peasant blouse and khakis. Leaning against a tree, she's looking down, touching her bulbous belly in awe.

It's so peaceful you can almost hear the birds singing.

Inside its tranquil cover *BH, BN* is structured like pregnancy – by months. After presenting an overview of the conception process, it takes you through each month of pregnancy, offering both medical and practical information as well as helping to prepare you for what to expect. By the time I returned to work I was halfway through the passage about conception.

And at the brink of a panic attack.

Since when did it become so hard to get pregnant?! A two-day window of opportunity? A variable potential for success? How could I be thirty-one years old and not understand how ovulation works?!

The minute I returned to the office I sat at my desk and cursed the fact that I don't have a door on my cubicle. I've been a professional woman long enough to know that in the business world the term "working mother" is synonymous with "retiree." Regardless of a company's official maternity policy, the unwritten rule, and often the unconscious assumption, is that the woman's professional life is coming to an end. Which it's not. After all, you can't end something before it begins. So the last thing I want is for Mr. Nealy, or worse, Eddie, to know I'm trying to get pregnant. And ditto for my Gen-Y coworkers. If they snickered at my power suit, God knows what bodily function they'd employ to acknowledge my pregnancy.

So I did what any mature person would do. Tucking *BH, BN* under my shirt, I went to the bathroom and read it in the stall.

may 7th – 11:30 p.m.

Sometime between my trip to the toilet stall and an afternoon meeting with a prospective client, my head began to spin.

The details, the information, the tips, the odds . . . getting pregnant was suddenly more complicated than counting calories. According to *Baby How, Baby Now,* it's completely normal for it to take as many as six months to get pregnant.

Six months!

I can't wait six months. I could be dead in six months.[22] This is ridiculous. Even if I were to spontaneously conceive while standing here at my kitchen counter it would take me nine months to have the baby, plus three months of maternity leave and God knows how long to regain my size eight figure.[23] So there's no way I can handle six months of simply *trying* to get knocked up. It must be done in ONE.

This is the challenge that I presented to Stephen over our dinner of frozen pizza and salad. After detailing the intricacies of conception and my general level of concern regarding our ability to get pregnant as quickly as possible, I showed him *Baby How, Baby Now.*

Which immediately freaked him out.

Instead of comforting me and assuring me that everything would be okay, as I assumed my rational, logic-oriented husband would do, Stephen had a painful flashback akin to a bad acid trip without the entertaining visuals.

When I was planning our wedding I turned to a book entitled *Beautiful Bride.* Over time *Beautiful Bride,* with its instructive passages and detailed advice, went from being my inspiration to being my tormentor, ultimately pushing me over the edge into outright hysteria. In fairness to Stephen, I did become utterly obsessed with its advice and a dronelike disciple of its rules. And now, years later, Stephen was gripped by the fear that it was happening all over again.

---

[22] Did I mention that patience is not a virtue which I possess?
[23] OK, fine, size ten.

Only this time, instead of affecting our choice of ceremony it was going to affect our sex life.

Which is why he gasped when he saw *BH, BN*. Springing away from the dining table he toppled a lamp which shattered on the floor and made a huge gash in his right foot. There was blood everywhere. But he didn't notice – he was preparing to make the sign of the cross because his fear was greater than his pain.

Poor bastard.

Doesn't he realize that I'm older and wiser now? That my actions are based on reason rather than emotion? After all, were we not at that very moment eating a low-fat, wheat-free pizza?

I rest my case.

But Stephen wasn't satisfied. He begged me to throw away the book. I refused, reminding him that since conception was such a difficult process, we'd need all the help we could get. Sensing a losing a battle, he turned away from *BH, BN,* and toward pragmatism: If conception was so difficult, then perhaps my one-month goal was overly ambitious.

Oh, please. There is no such thing as "overly ambitious," so I immediately chose to ignore his negativism. After all, what does he think we are? Amateurs? Ha! Sure the odds may be stacked against us, but we've got three essential things working in our favor:

1) We own *Baby How, Baby Now*.
2) We're good at having sex.
3) We're smarter than sperm.

may 8th

I went to work today with a renewed sense of mission. And an ovulation kit in my purse. If complete morons can get pregnant, then why not me?

But first I've got to prepare a list of talking points for Representative Fernandez's visit to a truckers' convention.

may 10th

As suggested in *BH, BN*'s conception chapter, I've started to take prenatal vitamins. Loaded with every imaginable vitamin and mineral, they're designed to keep my potential child healthy, boost his/her intelligence, and ensure that all vital organs are in the right place.

And for anyone wondering, doubling the dose will not ensure entrance to Harvard or a great set of legs.

That's right, I checked.

may 12th

According to the five individually wrapped ovulation sticks from the drugstore, I'm ovulating at this exact moment.

Unfortunately, Nicole's in the other room drooling on that new pillow I bought for her.

She was supposed to go clubbing with Pablo tonight. But Pablo had the nerve to get food poisoning from a hot-dog stand, which means that WE had the pleasure of Nicole's nonstop company. And no matter how hard I tried to convince her to go home, she refused. Desperately holding out hope for some weekend nooky, she insists that Pablo will be better by tomorrow – just in time for his folks to go to a ballgame, thus leaving them an empty apartment in which to frolic.

Get a life.

Sure, I could just tell Nicole that Stephen and I have to have sex tonight. That we're trying to conceive. But I won't. This is a private matter between me and Stephen. I even hid *Baby How, Baby Now* in the back of my underwear drawer so she wouldn't see it. And yet none of this helps me convince Stephen to have sex while Nicole is here.[24]

So I do the unthinkable.

I wake Nicole up in the middle of the night and tell her that Stephen is in the bedroom suffering from an acute case of gastroenteritis. He simply cannot stop crapping. While I help him with unspeakable matters in the bathroom, could she run out to the all-night grocer and buy some medicine?

Much to my amazement she actually hesitates. Every weekend we give her food and shelter and pretend to listen to her endless stories of personal liberation, and she hesitates at my request for a nocturnal medicine run? The nerve. Especially foolish when you consider that our 650-square-foot apartment only has ONE bathroom.

Realizing I have to tighten the screws I remind her that she's out of cigarettes and could pick up another pack.[25] She's sold. And moments later she's out the door, leaving

---

[24] Which is ridiculous, because he's a MAN – and how many men do you know who turn down sex because someone might hear them? Especially a man who's indulged in beach sex! Clearly this is the flip side to the husband who puts the toilet lid down . . . he's got a modesty streak.

[25] A nasty habit that she resurrected after splitting from her husband. As if being single and smoking are synonymous.

Stephen and me a solid fifteen-minute window in which to conceive our child.

As the front door closed I triumphantly entered the bedroom.

> STEPHEN
> It's one in the morning. Where's she going?
>
> ME
> I asked her to get me some juice.
>
> STEPHEN
> And she actually said "yes"?
>
> ME
> Of course, silly, we're sisters.

Climbing into bed I had a brief moment of regret. My actions had been so crafty, so manipulative, so . . . Mandy. Luckily, that moment passed the second my allegedly dysentery-beset husband wrapped me in his arms and kissed me.

may 19th

I spoke with Lucy tonight. I was dying to tell her all about our decision to have a baby and how at this very moment I may in fact be pregnant! But I held my tongue. Not wanting to count my chickens before they fertilize.

Only weeks after her "minor" stroke, Lucy is clearly on the mend. She's boisterous, opinionated, and outspoken.

Very outspoken. So much so that she's been asked to leave the senior center where she lives. This is her second eviction in two years – which supports my position that Lucy is the last person meant to be in geriatric housing. But unfortunately, at eighty-nine she's no longer able to live alone. The cooking, the cleaning, not to mention the little things like getting a sweater down from the top shelf of a closet have become overwhelming. So about a year ago she moved into a local senior center. She was asked to leave that first center after organizing a campaign for NC-17 movies in the recreation room.

Who could blame her? A veteran of World War II (WAC) and a lifelong supporter of the First Amendment, the banning of movies based on their content strikes her as un-American.

Besides, she's got a thing for full-frontal nudity.

Now she's been asked to leave another senior center for encouraging the distribution of Viagra to all male residents. Apparently her demands for the performance-enhancing drug have sparked an uprising among the center's female population – something about storming the center's pharmacy and a sit-in at the director's office.

And you wonder why this is my favorite relative?

may 20th

Lily.

That's what I've decided to name the slender, pregnant woman on the cover of *BH, BN*. With her long wispy hair, her willowy body, and her gentle awestruck gaze she strikes me as the quintessential Lily. Soft. At ease. Natural.

That's exactly how I want to be when I get pregnant.

may 23rd

After spending several days trying to convince myself that I pulled a muscle, got food poisoning, am nervous about the future of gun control – it's time to acknowledge that my cramps are premenstrual.

I am not pregnant.

Which is completely crazy. How can I not be pregnant? I charted my menstrual cycle. Used an ovulation test. Forced my husband to wear boxer shorts!

At this rate I should be able to will myself into pregnancy.

And to think I went two entire weeks without alcohol for absolutely no reason. Something must be wrong. These days even fifty-year-old women are getting pregnant. Of course, thanks to fertility drugs they're giving birth to small nations – triplets, sextuplets, even octuplets . . . Either way, they're getting pregnant and I'm not.

may 28th

I've now read the *BH, BN* conception chapter three times and the statistical possibilities of getting pregnant seem more daunting than ever.

How do all those teenage mothers do it?!

According to *BH, BN,* Stephen and I should be having lots of sex on my prime ovulation date and some sex, but not too much sex, on the days surrounding it. Except nowhere in its index does *BH, BN* offer a definition of too much sex. And please, it only takes a second to consider the Catholic Church versus Wilt Chamberlain to realize that "too much" sex is a relative term.

Meanwhile it appears that I'm doing my job at Brinkman/Baines very well. Perhaps too well.

Brinkman/Baines frequently garners publicity for their celebrity clients by fabricating scandals, then writing press releases in which the clients issue "No Comment." It's like manufacturing cheese so you can sell lactose intolerance pills.

Proving that truth is stranger than fiction, a scandal that I planted about Doug Tucker, the actor/National Organization for Penile Erectile Dysfunction spokesman, fathering a love child with a stewardess turns out to be true. And now the real flight attendant, who works for Skyways Airlines, is convinced that he's publicizing their affair for personal gain and has broken her silence to sue him for child support. Lots of child support.

And while you'd think NOPED would embrace Doug as the ultimate penile success story, they're cutting him loose from his contract. Doug in turn has fired Brinkman/Baines, and while Eddie just shook his head and buffed his nails, I received a very stern warning from Mr. Nealy: no last-minute scandal changes without first clearing it with the client.

You see, originally we had Doug being caught copulating with a fellow airline passenger in a first-class lavatory, extreme turbulence being the reason they tumble, half-naked, into the aisle. But clearly I have baby on the brain, because that story seemed too pat. So I added the love child without first consulting Doug, who was on location in Canada shooting a film about a global epidemic of gay killer bees.

And they say *I'm* out of line.

june 8th

Tonight was our second Big Ovulation Night. After double-locking the front door, I slipped into some sexy lingerie and dabbed pumpkin spice on all my nooks and crannies – anything to get Stephen hot and crank up that sperm count.

Medically impossible? Not according to an article I read on the Web. Seems that of all the scents in the world, pumpkin spice is the sexiest to American men. Must be something about pilgrims, Puritanism, and NFL football. Either way, it doesn't matter. I'm desperate.

Besides, if you'd seen the size of my lace undies you'd say wearing them was medically impossible, too.

june 14th

I made an incredibly exciting discovery today at work. And it has nothing to do with massage guru Abe Hamen's "Famous Fingers" or where celebrity twins Jeanie and Joanie Reese buy their matching outfits. Oh, no. It's far more exciting than that. It turns out that the media conglomerate that owns the lowly Brinkman/Baines also owns *Focus,* an award-winning magazine that covers New York's cultural and political life. It's like *Round-Up*'s better-dressed sister with a college education. To work at *Focus* would be a dream come true – even if Antonio Banderas isn't involved. But the most exciting detail? They occasionally recruit staff from within Brinkman/Baines!

Hallelujah! The light at the end of my professional tunnel might not be the flames of Hell after all.

june 18th

We had dinner with Jon and Mandy tonight. It's the first time I've seen Jon since I got the job at Brinkman/ Baines. Somehow I'd been lucky enough to avoid him. But tonight there was nowhere to hide. I had to face my demons, and thank him for helping me get a job.

For this type of humiliation, I should be getting dental benefits.

june 22nd

Today is our second wedding anniversary. To celebrate, we went to see a movie at the same theater in Times Square where Stephen first proposed to me. Admittedly, at the time, I was less than thrilled with a marriage proposal delivered while waiting on the concessions line for a Diet Coke and Gummi Bears. But since then I've come to cherish that moment as the beginning of something extraordinary.

So off we went for an evening of romance and a feature film – a sci-fi flick about a team of astronauts who slaughter extraterrestrials while trying to colonize Mars. Can ya feel the love?

Afterward, honoring the tradition where twenty-five years means silver, and fifty years means gold, Stephen and I exchanged . . . cotton.

Whoever came up with this system clearly designed it with long-term payoffs in mind.

Luckily both Stephen and I thought beyond Q-Tips and gym socks. He gave me an exquisite Hanro nightie and I gave him an official Knicks towel, which Latrell Sprewell used to wipe his sweat during the 2001–2002 season.[26]

Now *that's* romance.

june 24th

As I sit here devouring a bowl of instant mashed potatoes while doubled over in menstrual pain, I am exasperated by the fact that we still haven't conceived, and incredulous that our next opportunity falls on July 5 – squarely in the middle of Stephen's company retreat. At this rate we'll be buying adult diapers before the baby's.

And as Stephen continues to insist that my expectations for an immediate conception are unrealistic, and that it will probably take us numerous months to attain our goal, I've begun to question his dedication to this plan. After all, the longer it takes the more sex he gets.

Meanwhile work has begun to heat up. Summer is the proving ground at Brinkman/Baines. New television shows are publicized and summer movies are released, and our bottom-scraping clientele need all the help they can get. With the intense demands for clever quotes, provocative press releases, and creative spins, this summer will be an opportunity for me to prove myself not only to Mr. Nealy but hopefully to the powers-that-be at *Focus* magazine.

Ever since my gaffe with Doug Tucker and his mile-high liaison, I've been acutely aware that Eddie's been getting the meatier assignments. And although he acts innocent, if not a bit aloof, I can tell he knows it, too.

---

[26] Thank you, eBay.

june 26th

I wonder if Lily had trouble conceiving.

june 27th

This year Stephen's company retreat has a "rustic" theme and is designed for families. There'll be cookouts and relay races and all sorts of backwoods fun. As a partner in the firm, he has to go, and so do I. As a woman desperate to get knocked up, I refuse to even think about it. But Stephen's promised that it won't interfere with our attempts to conceive. We'll have our own cabin and plenty of privacy. So I've reluctantly agreed to join him.

Who knows. Maybe we'll learn something from the birds and the bees.

june 28th

The more I think about it, the more I can't believe that I'm not pregnant. I did everything *BH, BN* said. And that includes taking my armpit temperature –

Just say "ahhh."

After all those years trying NOT to get pregnant, who knew it'd be this hard? Trust me, if I'd known this before, I would have had a lot more fun in high school.

Adding to my frustration is that we've had a breach in privacy. Stephen told Mitch and Larry about our intentions to start a family – despite the fact that we vowed not to tell a soul until our stick turns blue. Traitor.

And not for a minute do I equate Stephen's breach of privacy with my having secretly told Anita about our grappling with the issue of children, our struggles to conceive, and my purchase of *Baby How, Baby Now*. After all, confiding in Anita is closer to religious consultation than snitching. So what if the preacher prefers premium liquors to holy water? She even invoked the word "God" several times during our conversation. As in, "God, you can't be serious." And, "My God, have you completely lost your mind?"

So really it's Stephen who's out of line here. Which he must know or else he wouldn't have tried so hard to assuage my anger. As if repeating Mitch's remark about having sex upside down to increase our chances of having a boy was going to make me feel any better. Fat chance. Clearly Mitch has spent way too much time watching those dogs hump.

And while Stephen thinks the remark is funny, I think the only laughable thing about that statement is the depth of Mitch's ignorance. The rest just makes me queasy. I mean, the last person I want meddling in our sex life is Mitch.

Besides, didn't Stephen say he doesn't care if we have a boy or a girl?

june 29th – 1:30 a.m

I just finished watching a two-part television special about infertility on a cable station I didn't even know we got.

I'm now completely certain that I'm infertile.

june 30th

The only explanation I can come up with for my not being

pregnant is that I'm not worthy. That all this conception trouble is some pagan fertility goddess punishing me for having bad thoughts about babies who cry on planes.

And in movie theaters, and restaurants, and supermarkets . . .

So I had dinner with Anita in hopes of confiding my persecution by the pagan fertility gods and of getting drunk. Sure, there was every chance that Anita, the queen of noncommittal relationships, would once again dismiss my desire to have kids as suicidal, but that was a risk I was willing to take. Besides, I had no choice. She's the only respectable person who knows we're trying to conceive.

Thankfully, instead of passing judgment she offered reason and some sensational red wine.

> ANITA
> Relax and have a drink. If God were going to punish you, she'd punish you for encouraging Mandy to take singing lessons.

She has a point.

july 2nd

Suddenly the topic of infertility is everywhere. Either it's in the news, on the radio, or a friend of a friend is having trouble conceiving after *years* of trying. That's right. Blocked fallopian tubes, hormonal imbalances, the potential for sterility caused by computer-generated electromagnetic fields . . . Not to mention some oil secreted by the peel of a banana which can lead to decreased sperm counts. No matter how you slice it there's bad pregnancy mojo everywhere I turn. True, I don't actually have any of these problems.

Yet.

As far as I know.

But it's hard not to take these things as omens. Bad omens, for me and my chances to procreate. Which is crazy, because all I want is a simple, old-fashioned pregnancy. Is that too much to ask for?

Apparently, the answer is yes.

july 4th

So far, Stephen's company retreat has been a pleasure. However, it seems he neglected to read the memo about cost-cutting measures. Because while the food is great, the people are fun, and the rural Connecticut location is idyllic, there are NO DOORS in our cabin and we're sharing it with *two other couples*! And since we're neither exhibitionists nor avant-garde performance artists, these are hardly the ideal circumstances under which to conceive a child.

Although Stephen votes to skip this month's prime date, a.k.a. tomorrow, as far as I'm concerned we haven't got a choice. We made a plan. And if you make a plan, you stick to a plan. Otherwise it's not a plan. It's a suggestion. And the mere suggestion of sex won't be nearly enough to impregnate me.

july 6th

Yesterday was our big day. Not wishing to shock our bunkmates, I devised a list of semiprivate, alternate locations where we could fornicate: the woods, the rental car, and an unmarked shed behind the local diner. Stephen refused them all. I was beside myself.

Wasn't he the one who was so gung ho to have sex on the beach during our honeymoon? Sure, I can sort of understand his discomfort at having sex within earshot of Nicole. But sex in an unmarked shed? It's the height of anonymity!

But no. The retreat is a work-related event, and he can't jeopardize his professionalism.

Unwilling to give in, I finally convinced him to have late-night sex in our cabin bathroom. After all, it has a fairly solid door.[27] And by three A.M. everyone else was sound asleep. With a skillfully worded pitch that made our potential late-night rendezvous sound like a live-action version of the *Kama Sutra*, Stephen finally agreed.

Sadly, the reality was not nearly as enticing. Even I had to admit that the cold linoleum floor, the unsanded walls, and the fly strip sticking to the back of Stephen's head were not exactly mood enhancers. So in an effort to get Stephen's motor going I began to whisper words of encouragement in his ear.

ME
You're such a stud. A big stud. Like a
young Brando. An old Rick Schroeder . . .

Stephen just wearily shook his head. Tired? Or wishing this would all go away? Too hard to tell.

---

[27] The only one in the entire place.

STEPHEN
Thanks, Amy. But right now the only stud
I feel like is Seabiscuit.

Well, giddy-up, partner.

july 9th

Some sadist did a study that was reported in every national newspaper about the difficulty of conceiving in your thirties. Apparently my clock may have stopped ticking without my knowing it was even running! Great. And the longer I wait, the longer they say it's going to take me to conceive – if I *ever* conceive. Just thinking of this makes me ill. My fear of not getting pregnant quickly is now completely eclipsed by my fear of never, ever, having a child.

A fact which really hit home when Angie, the Gen Y receptionist who snickered at my power suit, announced that she was pregnant and would be leaving Brinkman/Baines to follow the remaining members of the Grateful Dead on tour. I'm still uncertain what one thing had to do with the other but, poof! She was pregnant. And poof! She was out the door.

Bad mojo, mojo, mojo . . .

All Stephen has to say on the topic is that I'm overreacting and should enjoy the experience of trying. It's just a matter of time.

Of course he's not concerned. As long as men can scratch their nuts they can make sperm. Well, tick-tock, tick-tock, Mr. Casual. Go peddle your breezy outlook somewhere else.

I immediately called Anita, who was busy editing an

article on idols. Topping the list? Britney Spears. After all, Anita does work for *Teen Flair*.

> ANITA
> Relax, Amy. The group that conducted that study is run by men eager to screw you and me out of jobs by literally fucking us. Probably the same bunch of guys who are paying us seventy-five cents on their dollar.

> ME
> So you don't think it's a valid study?

> ANITA
> I think it's equal parts medical and conspiracy.

> ME
> Like freezing Walt Disney's brain?

> ANITA
> No. Like all-natural bust enhancers.

Ick.

july 10th

Anita's right. One study shouldn't send me into a panic. There's no reason Stephen and I won't be able to start a family. Besides, even if we can't have kids, we're still a family. The adult kind. With lots of dry-clean-only clothes and junk mail.

And I'm not just talking about Stephen. I'm talking about my extended family of Lucy, Gram, my parents, and maybe even Nicole – if she ever returns my dark blue skirt with the side slit.

Furthermore, I don't think you need a biological relationship with someone in order to consider them family. After all, I definitely consider Mandy and Anita part of my family. And then there are the millions of adopted or inherited families. Even the Brady Bunch didn't fall from the same tree. And just because people are biologically related doesn't necessarily ensure happiness. Hell, look at the Jackson Five. And don't get me started on those Guccis!

Anita's absolutely right. I need to relax about that stupid study and about my entire pregnancy crusade. If it happens, great. And if it doesn't, well, I'll have to be fine with that, too. Besides, Stephen and I have been incredibly happy thus far without children.

Who's to say that we can't stay that way?

july 18th

I'm late.

july 19th – 12:30 a.m.

Okay, I've tried to be cool about this. But after waiting all these months I've blown straight past cool and careened into hysteria. After all, I could be pregnant!

I woke Stephen up to discuss the matter further.

> ME
>
> Don't you want to talk about this?!

> STEPHEN
>
> Sure, just as soon as the sun rises.

> ME
>
> How can you be so blasé?

> STEPHEN
>
> I'm not blasé. I'm asleep.

> ME
>
> But I'm twenty-four hours late!

Stephen shook his head and rolled over.

> STEPHEN
>
> Wake me when it's nine months.

Nine months? Maybe he didn't understand. So I turned on every light in the bedroom.

> ME
>
> This isn't some dinner reservation I'm late
> for. This is the potential for having the
> proper mix of sperm, egg, and fertilization,
> from which an entire human being can form!

> STEPHEN
>
> Okay. Wake me in eight months.

I was not amused. This was big with a capital "B" and he was sleeping? I'm like clockwork. Have I mentioned that? I'm a highly organized individual. Type *triple*-A, and don't be fooled. I'm not the least bit ashamed of it. Sure, others may scoff at my intensity and desire to be on time, etc., but they're the ones who show up late to weddings and forget to pay their bills. I'm organized right down to my period.

Which is *not* here.

july 19th

Manhattan in heavy rain. You'd think it was Bombay during monsoon season. My regular subway line was suspended due to flooding, and the buses were so packed that I couldn't even get on the first four that arrived at my stop. I was beside myself.

Didn't the New York Department of Transportation know that I still hadn't gotten my period and that a newly purchased box of home pregnancy tests was tucked in my shoulder bag just waiting to be used?

Bureaucrats!

When I finally got home I threw my umbrella on the floor, kicked my shoes in the air, and ran for the bathroom without greeting Stephen. Rude as it was, it was physiologically necessary. It was already eight P.M., and in preparation for my big test I'd forgone peeing since noon. I was officially ready to burst. A few minutes longer and I'd have urine spewing from my ears.

Hovering over the toilet I frantically opened the box and was stunned to discover ONE test stick. In my haste I'd purchased a "single test" box. No wonder it was so cheap.

Damn my ill-timed frugality! Coming to my senses I realized it didn't matter. This wasn't a group activity. One was all I needed.

After a quick glance at the instructions, and something about the stick turning blue, I immediately went to work – peeing on my hand, the floor, and my left foot, only to have that little stick blankly stare back at me, dry as badly permed hair.

Determined to learn once and for all if I had a bun in the oven, I carefully placed my dry test stick on the back of the toilet and headed for the kitchen, where I proceeded to drink every available liquid that didn't come with a skull and crossbones warning.

An hour later, like a frat boy at a chugalug party, I made my way to the bathroom. Thrilled, excited, and nervous. Perhaps too nervous. Because while peeing on my stick, and trying not to soak my hand, my foot, or any other body part, I managed to drop the tester directly into the toilet.

I immediately stood up and stared at the test stick – my ONLY test stick – now floating in the toilet bowl like an unmanned canoe.

We can put a billionaire in space, decode the human genome, and give Chelsea Clinton a successful makeover, but I couldn't manage to take a simple home pregnancy test. I was incredulous.

And hysterical.

So I did the only thing I could think of – I burst into tears. Moments later Stephen hesitantly knocked on the bathroom door. "Is everything okay in there?" I just continued to cry. No doubt terrified by what he might find, he cautiously opened the door. Through my tears I began to babble. My test. My pee. The canoe. He looked around the room.

"What canoe?"

I pointed to the toilet. "The canoe, dammit! Can't you see the damn canoe?!"

Clearly I was cracking under the pressure. The anxiety of wanting and worrying had all become too much. I was now seeing watercraft in the toilet bowl.

With sympathy in his eyes, Stephen leaned down and plucked the test stick out of the toilet bowl and tossed it into the garbage. After rinsing his hands, he wrapped me in his arms and gently kissed my tear-stained face. He reminded me of how happy we were, and that a baby would come when it came. He said that as much as he wanted a baby, he didn't want it at the expense of our sanity. We were in love, and that's what mattered most. He reassured me that everything was going to be okay. Then suggested that I take up a hobby – perhaps racquetball? – to relieve my tension.

Through my tears I nodded in agreement, knowing that he was right.[28] And as I rested my head on his shoulder I happened to catch sight of the test stick lying at the bottom of the garbage can – glowing bright blue.

For what felt like an eternity I just stood there. Frozen. While simultaneously having an out-of-body experience. Floating above the scene, I was looking down at me, Stephen, our broken towel rack, and my bright blue test stick.

Then suddenly I was shrieking with joy, causing Stephen to jump back – startled and deaf in his left ear. Reaching into the garbage I clutched the urine-soaked test stick to my bosom.

ME
We're going to have a baby!

---

[28] Except about the racquetball. I have nominal hand-eye coordination.

STEPHEN
Let me see that.

Taking the stick from my hand, Stephen held it up to the light.

STEPHEN
It might be an optical illusion.

ME
No, it's blue!

STEPHEN
It can't be blue.

Test stick in hand, Stephen marched out of the bathroom and into the living room light. Seconds later I heard a scream.

I'm not wholly convinced it was joy.

july 20th

Stephen and I spent most of the evening huddled around our test stick. Bright blue, and now beginning to stink of old urine, we couldn't take our eyes off it. The more Stephen said, "This is so weird," the more it occurred to me that if he and I can be parents to someone smaller than a bread box, then weird is just the tip of the iceberg.

By daybreak I was dying to tell EVERYONE. But who to tell first? Anita? Mandy? Or my mother?

After serious consideration over a celebratory chocolate croissant, I decided that the first person to hear this incredible news should be my mother. After all, she gave me life. She deserves to be the first to know. Besides, isn't this the type of news that mothers dream of hearing?

Unfortunately, a quick glance at *BH, BN* put the kibosh on telling anyone until the twelfth week of pregnancy – the point at which the chance of miscarriage significantly decreases. I completely see the wisdom in this advice.

But the twelfth week?!!

Along with patience, silence is another virtue which I do not possess.[29] It was near impossible for me to wait two weeks before telling my mother the news of my engagement. And to keep quiet regarding my honest feelings about Jon for lo these many years has often brought me to the brink of insanity and beyond. But to wait three months before telling anyone that I'm going to have a baby may actually cause me to COMBUST.

Desperate to channel my silenced excitement into productive action I attempted to make an appointment with the Crotch Whisperer, only to learn that he was booked until next month. After minutes of ranting (mine), followed by a response peppered with mid-range invectives (the receptionist's), we agreed that I would come in tomorrow for an official pregnancy test. Which is just fine with me, because even though doctors have more advanced methods of determining pregnancy, according to *BH, BN* those overpriced Popsicle sticks are pretty darn accurate.

Besides, it's a lot easier to read a home pregnancy test than the Crotch Whisperer's lips.

---

[29] And yes, there are several more virtues outside my grasp, but we needn't go down that road. . . .

Great news. Not only am I pregnant – or at least I think that's why the Crotch Whisperer gave me a thumbs-up – but due to some mystical pregnancy math I'm already *four weeks* pregnant! I even had the Crotch Whisperer write it down so I could be sure.

After all, I'm a novice in the art of lipreading.

Four weeks! A whole month. One ninth of the entire process! This pregnancy will fly by in no time, and come next March 29th we'll have a baby!

I immediately entered the date in my Palm Pilot.[30]

On my way out of the office the nurse handed me a pamphlet on nutrition, which I read at the bus stop. I knew all about no caffeine and no alcohol but I was surprised to learn that with the exception of vegetables, pregnant women are advised to avoid raw foods. Well, big whoop. The state health code and better judgment preclude both Frutto di Sole and our local Chinese restaurant from serving anything raw, so I wasn't worried, until –

It hit me. And I gasped.

People on the street turned to stare as I clutched my heart in shock. It was the shock of a woman realizing that she can no longer eat SUSHI! Suddenly eight more months seemed like an eternity, because although I can't afford to eat it that often, next to sesame noodles and a good *risotto di mare,* I'm a sucker for spicy tuna rolls.

---

[30] Note to self: Cancel bikini wax on that day, reschedule teeth cleaning for the following week.

I can't stop smiling. Flush with the fiery energy of keeping a secret, I spent the whole day grinning and *dying* to share my news. To stand on my desk, to lift my mid-1990s computer console in the air, and to declare myself "Full with child!" But I resisted the temptation. After all, *BH, BN* advises against early announcements, and lifting that enormous console would probably kill me.

Not to mention the fact that I've got my career to consider. Which is not to say that I've completely separated my work from my pregnancy. On the contrary, I spent a good twenty minutes in the bathroom stall reading, then rereading for further clarification, Chapters One and Two of *BH, BN*. I now understand how I'm suddenly four weeks pregnant. Turns out they[31] start counting from the first day of your *last* period. Not your missed period. Or the point at which you conceived.[32] Does it make sense? Absolutely not. I suppose that's why medical school costs so much. Fabricating an entire system of logic and lies is a costly business. Just ask any Brinkman/Baines client.

On a wholly unrelated note, *BH, BN* states that morning sickness usually starts between weeks two and eight. I'm already at four without a projectile vomit in sight. Looks like I'm in the clear!

If only I could tell someone!

---

[31] The doctors, the medical board, the fertilized eggs – who the hell knows.
[32] Which will forever be kept a secret from this child. After all, who needs to know they were conceived in a log cabin with no doors, several fly strips, and an audience?

july 24th

I now understand how those people muttering to themselves on street corners got that way: They had a secret they couldn't tell and it drove them CRAZY!

july 25th

Stephen and I had sex last night for the first time since learning we're pregnant. It was a disaster. After all these months of gung-ho lovemaking, Stephen was suddenly overwhelmed with concern. Would having sex hurt the baby? Would his penis knock the baby in the head? Would our child have a dent in his/her cranium from Daddy's member?

My first reaction was "Don't flatter yourself!" Luckily, I kept that sentiment to myself. Instead I referred Stephen to Chapter Two of *BH, BN*, which explains at length how and why sex, especially this early in a pregnancy, cannot hurt a baby. Among other things, the baby is protected in an amniotic sac, a bubblelike cocoon that faces far bigger threats than Stephen's penis. Thankfully this put Stephen at ease and we were able to get back to business.

It's amazing how the prospect of sex can allay even the most neurotic of male fears.

july 26th

Anita called me at work to tell me that a colleague of hers from *Teen Flair* is dating a guy who works at *Focus,* and he says that a senior writer was just fired for fabricating quotes for an article on the National Endowment for the Arts.[33] This means that there's a job opening at *Focus*!

I decided to apply immediately. So instead of working to get Manny Zamon, former boy-band pinup turned (overly) dramatic actor, into the local gossip columns, I went to work updating my résumé.

First order of business: how to make eight months of unemployment appear productive.

july 28th

Eager to stay one step ahead of the game – and to avoid all inklings of chaos which might negatively impact my professional or personal life – I've scoured the first few chapters of *BH, BN* with a fine-tooth comb.

And thank goodness, because it's become clear that there are tons of things that have to be done before the baby arrives in March. We've got to find a pediatrician, a crib, a stroller . . . It's endless. And though it's early in my pregnancy I'm well aware that if you're not organized, things spin out of control. That goes for everything from having a baby to packing for a weekend trip. And how better to avoid all that unpleasantness than with a list?

Luckily I'm the list queen. And yes, I know that's an extension of my control-freak nature, but it keeps me sane.

Additionally, lists help to keep others on track as well. Between his lackadaisical approach to conception and his spontaneous purchase of a motorcycle, I can already tell

---

[33] Although immensely inappropriate in journalism, a sign of natural ability for the P.R. world.

that Stephen will need some help to stay focused on our baby preparations. For while he's a fabulous husband, a talented computer programmer, and will be a loving, caring father, the truth remains that despite his logical mind he's got the planning skills of a nudist in Antarctica.

So, plain and simple, a list is a practical item. Like support-support hose. And travel-size shampoos. And with the help of *BH, BN* I've made a list of my own. And though it may appear daunting, I'm not the least bit afraid. After all, I'm an extremely efficient person. I was four weeks pregnant practically overnight. Who knows how much I can accomplish in eight months. In fact, I'm pleased to announce that I've already done four of the following sixty-three things, and an additional four have no relevance to us since the closest we get to religion is our fanatic love of carbohydrates.

> Things to Do
> 1. Find ob/gyn
> 2. Get prenatal checkup
> 3. Get prenatal vitamins
> 4. Find physical exercise
> 5. Decide childbirth method
> 6. Join childbirth class
> 7. Buy crib
> 8. Buy bassinet
> 9. Buy crib mattress
> 10. Buy crib bedding
> 11. Buy changing table
> 12. Decide cloth or disposable diapers
> 13. Buy diapers
> 14. Buy diaper bag
> 15. Buy diaper pail

16. Buy crib mobile
17. Buy layette
18. Buy stroller
19. Buy infant bathtub
20. Buy baby monitor
21. Buy infant swing
22. Buy night-light for baby's room
23. Choose color for baby's room
24. Paint baby's room
25. Buy pacifiers
26. Buy dresser for baby's clothes
27. Buy infant-size hangers
28. Create medical emergency kit
29. Prepare emergency phone lists
30. Decide nursing or formula
31. Buy nursing supplies or formula supplies
32. If nursing, decide to rent or buy breast pump
33. If nursing, buy nursing bras
34. If nursing, buy nipple cream
35. Decide on legal guardian
36. Prepare wills
37. Plan estate
38. Create college fund
39. Begin Kegel exercises
40. Buy first-year memorabilia scrapbook
41. Decide whether to learn gender
42. Choose name(s)
43. Choose hospital
44. Take tour of hospital maternity ward
45. Find pediatrician

46. Appoint someone to organize baby shower
47. Make invite list for baby shower
48. Register for baby shower
49. Buy thank-you notes for baby shower
50. Select birth music
51. ~~Prepare for appropriate religious ceremony~~
52. ~~Book venue for religious ceremony~~
53. ~~Arrange for priest, rabbi, or *mohel*, etc.~~
54. ~~Buy baby's outfit for religious ceremony~~
55. Buy maternity clothes
56. ~~Decide who will be in delivery room with you~~
57. Prepare baby announcements
58. Prepare overnight bag for hospital
59. Make birth plan
60. Schedule maternity leave
61. Make phone list for announcing baby's birth
62. Buy baby's take-home-from-hospital outfit
63. Decide on postbirth child care

It's amazing how many of the items start with the word "buy."

july 29th

I showed my Things to Do list to Stephen. At first he bristled, citing my "excessive" list for our wedding. But I quickly reminded him that *that* list had been based on information from *Beautiful Bride* – a book which was without a doubt authored by the Devil himself. But *this* list was informed by the most popular pregnancy book on the market. A book which has guided mothers through the pregnancy journey for over three generations. Sure, a quick glance at items #27 and #36 did little to boost his confidence,[34] but acknowledging his dearth of experience with children, let alone preparing for the arrival of an infant, he promised to defer to my and *BH, BN*'s better judgment. Smart man. Especially since I'm the one doing all the reading and research on the topic while he goes about his life like nothing new is happening.

Can you say DENIAL?

Underscoring Stephen's sense of denial is his request that we don't make any preparations for the baby before Nicole moves out. No painting the room, no buying furniture. But to be honest, this is probably a reasonable request when you consider that the baby's "room" is currently being used as a storage closet, with a window that's painted shut.

But I'm not worried. Especially since I have no intention of going nuts and obsessing. Life's too short. We don't need, nor can we afford, a thousand cute outfits, stuffed animals, and toys. This isn't the next Dalai Lama, a von Trapp child, or the heir to the British throne we're talking about.

Just a wonderful little baby to call our own.

august 1st

We had a crisis today at work. The Reese twins, Joanie and

---

[34] Although I did assure him that the answer to #56 was my husband.

Jeanie, have had a falling-out and are refusing to speak to each other. Thus making it very difficult to promote them professionally. You see, in the case of the Reese twins the sum of the whole does NOT equal its parts – it vastly exceeds it. Without each other the gals are virtually useless. Even by Brinkman/Baines standards. This is because they are wholly without talent. They're not singers, or actors, or dancers. They're not even models. They're just two incredibly cute twenty-something girls, with four incredibly fake boobs, who have somehow managed to tap into every male fantasy about identical twins and propel themselves to the status of "celebrity." They're seen at movie premieres and major sporting events, on game shows and talk shows, and they're *always* in the Thanksgiving Day parade.

Except Jeanie has suddenly decided to become a vegetarian. Without consulting her sister, she's disposed of all their leather clothing and fur-trimmed boots.

Vive la Meat.

One problem. I've spent months securing them the position of the Twin Mountains Prime Beef cover girls. It's a plum assignment with immense publicity. And a job that officially starts with their hosting the National Twins Convention *tomorrow*. In *Chicago*. Which means that they had to be on a plane by nine P.M. tonight or the whole thing – the convention and the beef company – would go to Hell in a handbag. A leather handbag.

Only now, Jeanie, the born-again Veggie, is refusing to represent a beef company because it "promotes the slaughter of innocent sheep." Yes, that's an actual quote.

After informing her sister that beef comes from cows, not sheep, Joanie – the possessor of the twins' brain – was furious. Why these women can't argue about normal sister things like borrowed skirts and missing nail polish is beyond me. Instead they're arguing about the ethical implications of owning a rawhide sofa.

So at seven P.M. I found myself in the twins' apartment begging them to reconcile. At eight P.M. I was wedged between them in the backseat of a limo heading for Kennedy Airport – blocking bitch slaps with my purse. At eight forty-five P.M. I was brokering the final stages of a truce while simultaneously dragging their carry-on luggage to the Delta Airlines security checkpoint.

By nine-ten P.M. I was watching their plane take off with one eye while wistfully considering the airport bar with the other. If ever I needed a drink, now was the time.

But of course I couldn't. Because Chapter Two of *BH, BN* clearly states the dangers of fetal alcohol syndrome. So I settled for a bottle of water.

And on the bus ride back to the city[35] it occurred to me that there was no way I could pull a crazy day like this, where I ended up on the Van Wyck Expressway at ten o'clock at night, once I had a baby.

Which led me to another quandary: How will Brinkman/ Baines react to news of my pregnancy? After all, I've only been there a few months. And I'm going to need maternity leave. Not to mention more reasonable working hours. Will they give me flextime? Will they fire me? Is that legal? I can't lose my job now. I need the medical benefits!

Unable to discuss this with anyone due to my twelve-week vow of silence I immediately called Stephen on my cell phone. Deeply engrossed in the final chapter of the latest Dick Francis novel, Stephen devoted a fraction of his atten-

---

[35] No beef-sponsored limos for us lowly P.R. gals.

tion to talking me down from the precipice of hysteria.

He reminded me that it's illegal to discriminate on the basis of pregnancy, and that as long as I was able to perform my job there was no reason to fire me. And certainly, he insisted, I could write trashy copy and promote idiocy with or without a child.

I still wasn't convinced. "What about last hired, first fired? Could they use that?"

"Wasn't that guy Eddie hired after you?"

Hey, that's right. Maybe my pregnancy will make them fire Eddie. "But what if I suddenly get morning sickness and barf all over the office?"

Stephen laughed. "You don't have any morning sickness. Besides, you can't be the first person to vomit at a P.R. firm. Have you read the crap you guys write?"

august 2nd

Something's up. Eddie started to look at me differently today. I swear he grinned – no, *beamed* – in my direction.

He's also become highly solicitous. Perhaps he also wants the job at *Focus* and has decided to suck up in order to orchestrate my downfall. Why else would he suddenly be so chummy?

Unless of course he's just a freak. Which is always a possibility.

Either way, instead of intercoming me with questions about Glyniss O'Maley's appearance at the mall in Short Hills, New Jersey, or Abe Hamen's celebrity-studded infomercial to promote his new line of citrus-scented massage oils, Eddie's suddenly taken to walking over to my cubicle.

To sitting on the corner of my desk. To volunteering to reposition my computer at a more ergonomic angle. He's like some sick hungry dog sniffing for something to eat.

Well, heel, Cujo! Heel! Because my career's not a doggie treat. And that job at *Focus*? *I'll* be snacking on that tender morsel.

That's right. I'm up to Eddie's challenge – no matter how many styling brushes he owns.

august 3rd

Apparently having a taco lunch was not such a good idea. By two o'clock my stomach was flip-flopping like a Romanian gymnast. Eager for some relief, I was about to take an antacid when I noticed the warning label: Do not take if pregnant.

Why the hell not? I immediately consulted *BH, BN,* only to learn something shocking: Antacids contain aspirin, and pregnant women are discouraged from having aspirin because it poses a risk of birth defects.

Are they kidding me? I can't forgo aspirin for the next nine months. It's a dietary staple! One of the five major food groups – meat, dairy, pizza, carbohydrates, and aspirin.

Everyone knows that!

august 5th

After reviewing my Things to Do list it occurs to me that I have no idea what a "layette" is.

august 7th – 1:15 a.m.

I was startled to wake up alone in the bed. No one stealing my covers or snoring in my ear. Just the strangest sound coming from the other room.

Grabbing my robe, I made my way to the living room to find Stephen curled up on the sofa, weeping over a pint of Ben & Jerry's ice cream. Chunky Monkey, to be exact. Rushing to cradle him in my arms, I asked what was wrong.

He just wailed. "I can't spend the next eighteen years changing diapers!" Then, opening wide, he shoveled another spoonful of his dairy pacifier into his mouth.

The poor guy. In addition to having a panic attack based on irrational fears he's officially been reduced to a *girl*.

august 8th

In the middle of our afternoon staff meeting I began to overheat. Flushed and sweaty, I quickly progressed to nauseous. What the hell was going on? Had my lunchtime chicken salad been left in the sun? Had my low-fat chocolate chip muffin exceeded its expiration date? And that's when it hit me: Sweaty, flushed, nauseous . . . this was morning sickness.

Except it was *four in the afternoon*!

While Mr. Nealy had departed early to meet with a client, I was keenly aware that Eddie, four Junior Account Managers, and our college intern all stood between me and the conference room door. So I struggled to act calm. But after an inadvertent dry heave all eyes were on me. Unwilling to reveal my pregnancy, I turned to my young, hipster colleagues and cooed an apologetic "Guess I partied a little too hard last night."

Five hipster heads sympathetically nodded with knowing looks. Eddie was too busy checking out his reflection in the window to respond.

That evening I scoured *BH, BN* for some plausible explanation of what had occurred. Turns out that "morning" sickness is a vicious misnomer. Far from an A.M. event, morning sickness is a *twenty-four*-hour ordeal.

That's right. You could have morning sickness at eight o'clock at night. Which yes, technically speaking, is morning . . . *halfway around the world.*

august 9th

After spending all night hunched over the toilet I had only one question: "Why would anyone want to be bulimic?"

Sure I'm ambitious and I pride myself on excelling, but really, it was never my desire to be the Super Puker. What's that in the sky? It's a bird! It's a plane! It's Super Puker! Able to hurl semidigested food at the drop of a hat. To spray bits of yesterday's lunch across the living room floor. All I need is a latex jumpsuit and a cape.

Silly me. I really thought I'd evaded morning sickness. According to *BH, BN*, it starts between the second and eighth week of pregnancy; I'm already at the end of the seventh. But no. Looks like I got in just under the wire. And trust me, whenever it ends it's gonna be one hell of a photo finish.

Unfortunately, *BH, BN* says, there's nothing to prevent or stop typical morning sickness. You just vomit when you need to and eat what you can. There are, however, a few things to soften its blow: ginger tea, toast, rice, and bananas. So after work I went to the supermarket to buy these things in bulk because I can't afford another round of nausea like the one I experienced at the office.

While paying for my purchases, and trying my best to think happy, nonnauseous thoughts, I noticed the cashier's name tag: Dagmar. Perhaps I don't get out much, but the name Dagmar conjures up smoky black-and-white movie images for me. Most of them featuring Marlene Dietrich in dressing gowns trimmed with ostrich feathers. All of which couldn't be further from the woman behind the cash register. Short and heavyset, her long brown hair was struggling to recover from a really bad perm. Which is not to say she wasn't attractive. Because in a strange Fred Flintstone way she was actually pretty. But her name raised the bar of expectation so high that no matter what she looked like, if she wasn't a sultry Dietrich, you were bound to be disappointed.

In short, her parents screwed her from Day One by saddling her with a name that she could never live up to.

This is something I've been considering a lot recently – the awesome responsibility of naming another human being. Will they like their name? What if they hate it? And what if some eponymous criminal rises to fame and tarnishes that name forever? How bummed were all the Sirhans?

Then there's the identity you hope to impress upon your child through the choice of a name. You want your kid to be attractive, smart, respectable. Think about it. We constantly form opinions about others without ever meeting them. What comes to mind when you hear "Lola," "Rex," and "Herman"?

That's right – tart, closet homosexual, and dork. Admit it.

And what if you name a kid Susanna and she lisps? Or Ralph and the kid's so ugly he makes people want to puke. So what's in a name? Plenty. Just ask Dagmar.

august 10th

I got a call this afternoon from the human resources director at *Focus*. She thanked me for submitting my résumé and for all ten of my calls to follow up on its progress. Extremely friendly, she assured me that as soon as they're ready to start interviewing I'd be hearing from her.

Apparently they have yet to resolve certain employment issues with the guy who's getting fired. Which probably means that he's suing for wrongful termination or to have his contract paid out. Either way, this could take a *long* time.

august 16th

Even with morning sickness I go from day to day, moment to moment, doing my thing. I talk to clients, pick up our dry cleaning, and cuddle on the sofa with my husband to watch more late-night television than I would ever admit. And yet, all the while, my body is actively taking some spare biological matter and transforming it into a completely new human being.

It's the ultimate in multitasking.

Sometimes I just stop what I'm doing and marvel at both the miracle and the enormity of the job. Someone who will be able to walk, talk, and operate heavy machinery is currently in my stomach. Like a major organ, a recent meal, or a huge bowel. And come March 29th that someone will come *out* of my body.

It's a mind-boggling concept. An incredible feat. And an awesome responsibility. No wonder it's a task entrusted to women.

august 17th

Eddie's shift in behavior continues to worry me. No longer content with limited contact and the occasional cubicle visit, he's advanced to idle chitchat on a regular basis. A pursuit which has significantly cut into his nail-buffing time. The weather, my weekend plans, the daily coffee flavors at the café downstairs . . . He wants to hang out and talk about it all.

Which is especially dangerous since I can't afford to let him see me getting sick – an event that happens at least once a day, anywhere between the time I arrive at the office and the time I go home.

Morning sickness, my ass.

And everything makes me sick. Brushing my teeth in the morning. Drinking water in the afternoon. Reading, writing, raising my arms above my head . . . And don't get me started on *eating*.

So when it hits at work I try to be as casual as possible while assuming my secret identity of Super Puker.

Unfortunately, while I can manage to escape Eddie, I can't shake Stella. Stella, one of our Junior Account Managers, is a major pothead. And every time I make my stealth escape into the bathroom – ducking behind cubicle walls, tiptoeing past

Mr. Nealy's office, and skirting the new receptionist as she's completely consumed by an Internet chat room devoted to fans of half-pipe skateboarding,[36] I find Stella either locked in a stall lighting up a joint or balancing on the sink in her three-inch heels, struggling to disable the smoke alarm.

During our first two encounters we acted like we didn't notice each other. But by the third time it was too awkward. So I went for levity.

> ME
> We have to stop meeting like this.[37]

Stella just stared at me, her big brown eyes like two Ring-Dings floating in space.

> STELLA
> Wow, is that puke on your shoes?

Wiping splattered bits of lunch from my sensible leather pumps, I tried to be cool.

> ME
> Yeah, uh, guess I had too many beers last
> night.

Stella bobbed her head up and down. And up and down. And up and down some more. As I began to wonder if Stella was bouncing to the beat of a song I couldn't hear, or if she had simply lost all feeling in her extremities – her head and

---

[36] Whatever the hell that is.
[37] Note to self: Levity lost on person who's stoned out of her mind.

brain included – she pointed to the burnt remains of her joint and uttered in a scratchy voice,

> STELLA
> It's for medicinal purposes.

Oh, yeah? What health plan is she on?

august 18th

Stephen accompanied me to my appointment with the Crotch Whisperer this afternoon. Now eight weeks pregnant it was our first ultrasound of the baby and he wanted to be there for the occasion.

It was also his first encounter with the infamous doctor. Determined to hear every word the Crotch Whisperer said, Stephen made a point of standing very close to him. Too close. The Crotch Whisperer, that highly professional man in his early sixties with gray hair and bright blue eyes, clearly thought Stephen was coming on to him – and took three steps back for every step that Stephen took forward. At a certain point it looked as if he'd be conducting my examination from the room across the hall. Luckily Stephen finally got the hint and resigned himself to my nightmare of reading the guy's lips.

Although I knew that the ultrasound would be quick, simple, and utterly painless, the minute the nurse rolled the video monitor into the room I became tense. Despite *BH, BN*'s description of the process, I still had no idea what to expect. I knew I'd be "seeing" the baby, but what exactly did that mean at this point?

Would it look like a baby? Would she/he be holding up a

"Hi, Mom" sign or flashing a big thumbs-up for the camera? Or maybe I'd misunderstood the receptionist who scheduled the appointment. Perhaps we'd be screening *Flashdance*. After all, there was suddenly an awful lot of video equipment in the room.

Luckily my wandering mind was soon ground to a halt as the process began. With the Crotch Whisperer between my legs, Stephen by my side, and the nurse fiddling with a bunch of knobs,[38] an image appeared on the screen. The image of my soon-to-be child. That's right. My kid looks like a bunch of fuzzy black-and-gray swirls – a stormy night sky after a few martinis.

I glanced at Stephen. He, too, looked underwhelmed.

But before we could express our disappointment, the Crotch Whisperer began tapping on the screen. At first I was annoyed. Of all the times this guy could dust the monitor, he chooses now? *Hello!* He could at least wait until I get my underwear back on!

That's when I realized that the speck he was tapping on was MOVING.

Stephen inched closer. "What the hell is that?"

The Crotch Whisperer smiled and moved his lips. From my fully reclined position I couldn't hear a word. But obviously Stephen had heard loud and clear. His eyes grew wide, and a look of incredulity spread across his face as if he'd just been told that the undulating speck was the garden beetle I swallowed when I was five.

What had the Whisperer said?!

"Would someone *please* tell the woman in the stirrups what's going on?"

---

[38] The monitor's, not mine.

The nurse frowned. As if my inquiry were the nagging of yet another whiny mother-to-be who needed to be coddled because she wasn't paying attention. Looking me straight in the eye, she spoke slowly and deliberately as if English were my second language. "It's the heart."

And that's when I burst into tears. My baby's got a heart!

august 18th – 11 p.m.

Until now I'd based my belief that I was pregnant entirely on faith – a few tests, a lot of nausea, the Crotch Whisperer's inaudible pronouncement that I was pregnant. For all I knew it could have been some enormous ruse by Stephen to make me spend less money on sushi.

But now, having seen the heartbeat, it's all become so real.

Nothing in life prepares us for the experience of being pregnant. No sex ed or biology class can express the thrill and shock of *seeing* your baby's heartbeat. For the first time I can really relate to *BH*, *BN* Lily's sense of awe.

I just wish we could talk about it. We'd take walks in the park, shop for cribs, go to the salon where I'd encourage her to get a hipper, more contemporary hairstyle . . .

But no. She's busy hanging out under her tree, and I'm stuck talking to myself.

august 20th

Pregnancy math stinks. Sure, I was thrilled to learn that by some mystical calculation I was suddenly four weeks pregnant. But after considering my due date things just didn't seem right. It was too far away. So I got out a calculator and opened *BH, BN*.

What I learned was shocking. Pregnancy math is like voodoo – it gets you when you least expect it. There are forty weeks of pregnancy. Otherwise known as TEN months. The popularly touted figure of nine months must have been part of some pro-pregnancy campaign back in the Middle Ages.

Sure, an extra month is a small price to pay for something so wonderful as a baby, but since my days are now measured by sprints to the bathroom it might as well be a year.

I immediately turned to Stephen – my partner, my lover, the father of my child – for sympathy. Instead I got pragmatism.

> STEPHEN
> Technically speaking, forty weeks isn't really ten months, since each month has approximately thirty days, or just over four weeks, which makes forty weeks closer to nine months and two weeks.

And before I could reply, "Oh, goodie, then you carry the baby," I was running to the bathroom to toss my lunch.

august 25th

Pregnancy makes me so tired that I completely fell asleep at my desk today. After what was probably fifteen minutes I awoke in a puddle of drool with an impression of my keyboard mashed into my face.

This wouldn't be such a big deal if it hadn't already happened four times this week.

september 1st

Apparently the pregnant body assumes a variety of superhuman powers that the average person would never dream of.

This evening, while waiting for the subway, I was suddenly overwhelmed by the stench of broccoli – and it made me want to gag. At first I thought I'd mistaken someone's cheap cologne or fetid body odor for the vegetable stink. A reasonable possibility considering it was rush hour and lord knows smells commingle among throngs of weary humanity. But no. After a moment or two I became quite certain that I was, in fact, smelling broccoli.

And yet a quick scan of my immediate surroundings revealed no vegetation. A cup of coffee, half a bagel, the remains of an old Twix bar lying on the ground . . . but no broccoli.

Then I noticed a man eating something from a takeout container that appeared to be green. One problem. He was standing *across* the platform on the downtown side of the station. That's right, I was smelling something across two train tracks. A distance of at least twenty feet!

But that's impossible!

Isn't it?

I immediately turn to *BH, BN* – which I've begun to carry in my purse – for an explanation. Apparently a heightened sense of smell is a normal development during pregnancy. Great. As if being the Super Puker weren't enough, I now possess olfactory powers which far exceed those of the average human being.

And let me tell you, "heightened" doesn't begin to describe the situation. It's closer to bionic. If it were the 1970s I'd have my own television series.

After all, we're talking the ability to sniff foul odors from over twenty feet. To find the needle in the haystack – using only my nose. To play "Guess what I ate for lunch" without even looking.

Simply put, I've got DOG NOSE.

september 2nd

With this recent development of Dog Nose, I've begun to suspect a cover-up. A grand pregnancy cover-up undoubtedly orchestrated by MEN. After all, if women knew these things before we got pregnant, how eager would we be to conceive?

Outright lies? Casual omissions? Or necessary evil in order to perpetuate our species? It doesn't matter. Either way, women are NOT getting the straight scoop on the pregnancy experience. And while I'm thrilled by my pregnancy, and yes, like my *BH, BN* cover girl Lily, I feel an incredible sense of awe for what my body's accomplishing, I can't help but feel a bit duped.

Well, the gig is up. I'm keeping track. And making a list.

> Things No One Tells You About Pregnancy
> 1. No sushi
> 2. Twenty-four-hour morning sickness
> 3. Forty weeks (ten months) of pregnancy
> 4. No aspirin
> 5. Dog nose

september 3rd

I called the Whisperer's office this morning to schedule my next appointment. Before hanging up, the receptionist said, "In case you're wondering, you're having a boy."

I was stunned. How the hell did she know that? Was it the ultrasound? I thought back to the monitor with its cloudy mass of black-and-white swirls. It was like *Where's Waldo*, only with penises and vaginas. Where could a sexual organ be hiding?

But it didn't matter. Because Stephen and I had decided NOT to learn the baby's sex. We wanted to be old-fashioned and wait for that much-documented delivery-room moment where the doctor exuberantly declares, "It's a boy!" Or, "It's a girl!"[39]

In a need-to-know world where everything from Julia Roberts's shaving habits to Kennedy's last words are constantly revealed, we were eager for a surprise. A fact that we'd made clear during our last visit.

So why was this woman blowing it?! Didn't obstetric receptionists receive special training on the subject of gender-secrecy? Wasn't there some "keep your trap shut" clause in their employment contracts? Loose lips sink ships, babe. If this were war she'd get us all killed!

Luckily, instead of bitching her out, I opted to tread lightly. "How do you know it's a boy?"

"Oh, I don't actually *know*. At least not medically speaking."

"Then what are you basing it on?" Astrology? Astronomy? The agrarian crop cycle?

---

[39] Although, given the Crotch Whisperer's muted tones, I'll probably have to crane my neck and look for myself.

"Nothing specific. It's just a sense I get."

A sense? What kind of sense? Am I walking a certain way? Leaning to the left? Giving off some male odor like Aramis or Brut? The whole thing was crazy.

Or was it?

september 4th

Morning sickness is like being stalked by a psychotic. You walk around with terror in your heart and one eye on the nearest exit.

Like today, for instance.

A group of us had gathered to brainstorm about what to do with our client Alexander Hastings, the barely pubescent city councilman. He'd recently been spotted at a rock concert in Central Park drunkenly stage-diving into the audience. Stella, Councilman Hasting's point person at Brinkman/Baines, didn't understand what all the fuss was about. Of course, being a twenty-something pothead made clarity of thought, let alone assessment of popular opinion, a challenging act for her. Sensing that this might not be a time when her youthful perspective would come in handy, Mr. Nealy had summoned Eddie and myself to the meeting.

It was crucial that we put a positive spin on this event before the councilman was dragged through the mud by his challengers in the upcoming election. Was he really drunk? Or just youthfully exuberant? Was he interacting with his constituency or letting loose with some friends? Perhaps it was a symbolic gesture for his upcoming campaign – "Councilman Hastings Stays on Top of the People."

It was around the time we came up with that gem that

94

my stomach turned over. Coincidence? Maybe not. In any event, my stomach was convulsing and I could feel my gag reflex prepping itself for formidable action. Without thinking, I swallowed hard and rubbed my head.

Unfortunately, Stella chose that moment to have a viable synaptic reaction. "Hungover again?"

Faced with jeopardizing my career by revealing to Mr. Nealy that I was pregnant,[40] I decided to run with Stella's lead. Feigning embarrassment, I mentioned that I'd been out late dancing. Then I casually threw out the name of some club that I'd heard Nicole mention. As an elder (relatively speaking) member of a hip P.R. firm, I figured it couldn't hurt to seem *au courant* in front of my boss.

Unfortunately, of all the clubs in this city I chose the one Stella was certain had closed two weeks earlier. "My roommate said the entire place is boarded up."

Shut up!

But before I could dump my bottled water on Stella's head, Eddie jumped in. "That was the old venue. It reopened down in Nolita. Right off Houston Street. You should check it out."

I was floored. This would have been a perfect time to humiliate me, not to mention make me look like an idiot in front of Mr. Nealy. But instead of sleazing his way to Office Favorite, Eddie – my pretty-boy coworker – had played the role of Knight in Shining Sateen and saved my butt. Will wonders never cease?

The answer is no.

Because after our meeting, Eddie followed me back to my cubicle, where he leaned in very close. For a moment I

---

[40] Which I couldn't possibly do since I hadn't told my mother yet!

thought he was gonna try to steal second. Instead he quietly whispered in my ear, "I don't mean to be intrusive, but are you pregnant?"

My jaw dropped. My mind whirled. And my ability to lie, an art I had honed throughout my childhood years in order to ditch school, break curfew, and date seniors, suddenly failed me. Without realizing my lips were moving, I heard myself say yes. After all these weeks of silence my secret was out of the bag. Had I not been talking to *Eddie,* it would have felt wonderful.

But before I had a chance for regret, Eddie began to clap his hands excitedly together like Flipper on speed. Or a windup toy with a broken spring. No matter what the analogy, it's an odd activity for a man old enough to shave.[41] When he finally wound down, he insisted on buying me lunch.

At a lovely sandwich shop only four blocks from our office, Eddie repeatedly congratulated me on my pregnancy. And though my first thought was that Judas was preparing to rat me out, there was something about the way he kept clapping his hands and hugging me that made me think this was sincere. Between his stellar save during our meeting and his insistence that we put our heads together and strategize ways in which I can keep my pregnancy a secret until I'm ready to go public, I was soon convinced that Eddie was sincerely happy about my pregnancy.

Hell, he even told me how great I look.

Maybe this is a reward for the horrible experience I had at *Round-Up* with Barry, the back-stabbing coworker who'd smother you to death behind the file cabinets if he

---

[41] Or in his case, wax.

thought it would help his career. Maybe Eddie, a male-model–wannabe with feathered hair and tinted lashes, was my new office girlfriend. It could happen. Heck, he actually recommended a place to buy prenatal vitamins in bulk.

Who would have guessed that the first person I'd share the most incredible news of my entire life with would be a guy I'd known for barely five months?

september 5th

Despite my fierce morning sickness, I had my first craving today. And no, it wasn't pickles, or ice cream, or peanut butter. It was American cheese. That yellow rubbery substance that comes in individual slices wrapped in plastic.

It's the Pink Champale of cheeses, and if it's any indication of this baby's personality, she/he is going to be a class act, because I'm eating the stuff by the pound.

september 6th

Eddie's been amazing. While continuing to maintain my privacy, he's been providing me with all sorts of great pregnancy advice. From prenatal vitamins to special ginger teas from India. He must have a *ton* of sisters.

But the best tip so far was the name of a prenatal yoga studio – a place on the Lower East Side called Balanced Breathing. I've never considered myself a yoga person; in fact, I'm kind of disgusted by the whole yoga phenomenon – pampered white people getting in touch with their inner Indians – but Eddie says it helps to keep your joints limber for delivery and your attitude positive forever.

How can I say no to that?

september 8th

For eleven long and torturous weeks I've been silent about
this pregnancy.[42] Well, I can wait no longer. If I don't start
telling people immediately, I will definitely explode. After
all, this is the best news I've had in my entire life. Is it really
so surprising that I want to share it?

Of course not.

So with this in mind, Stephen and I cleared our calendars
so we could go upstate to tell our parents the news in person.
Because this is the type of thing you share face-to-face. And
the first face I wanted to tell was my mother, since she was in
labor with me for either six quick or nineteen agonizing
hours – depending on how pleased or annoyed she is with
me when she's recounting the tale.

To ensure that my entire family would be there, we took
the afternoon train and arrived at my parents' house just as
the Midwestern broadcast of *Diagnosis Murder* was about
to begin on my father's new satellite TV. This gave me a
chance to speak with my mother privately while Stephen
joined my father in my childhood bedroom, which is now
his den – although my bunk bed remains and the back of the
closet still smells like Cheez Whiz.

Don't ask.

Thanks to my dog nose, I could also smell the evening's
dinner – tuna casserole – cooking in the oven, and yesterday's

---

[42] If you don't count Stephen, Eddie, the Crotch Whisperer, and his nurse.

dinner – fried chicken – rotting in the garbage can. Nice.

Never a fan of television, my mother was in the kitchen grading a spelling quiz she'd just given to her fourth grade class. It didn't look good. Apparently the word "truck" had stumped about half the class, while the word "yellow" had eluded everyone – including the transfer student from the Philippines who was rumored to be a child genius. Irritated by such disappointing results, my mother sat at our old dinette set tapping her big red pencil against the Formica tabletop. I momentarily considered postponing my announcement. Did I really want news of my pregnancy soured by a bunch of ten-year-olds who were too stupid to spell "truck"?

Before I could ponder this further my mother turned around, greeted me, and offered me a cup of coffee. Even under the best of circumstances, I know better than to accept a cup of my mother's coffee. But lord knows what it might do to my unborn child. Especially in the afternoon, since it's virtually guaranteed that the bitter, overbrewed sludge that she made in the morning is now the bitter, overbrewed mud coagulating at the bottom of the pot.

Fact: Even under extreme conditions – like tropical heat or nuclear winter – coffee is not supposed to coagulate. Ask any chemist.

"Thanks, Mom, but I doubt my doctor would approve."

I grinned from ear to ear, figuring my no-caffeine stance was the perfect lead-in to my joyous pronouncement.

Wrong.

Gathering up her papers, my mother slid her big red pencil behind her ear and frowned. "Why, Amy? Because he owns stock in Starbucks and would prefer that you spend the price of an entire meal on a cup of the very same coffee

99

you can get here for free? I swear, the way people waste their hard-earned money on overpriced designer coffee, you'd think it was brewed at the Fountain of Youth."

So much for the perfect lead-in. And for the record, anyone with a sense of sight, smell, or reason knows that my mother's coffee is, at best, the anti-Christ to Starbucks's.

Which is not to say that she's a bad person. Because she's not. She's a truly lovely human being. Warm, thoughtful, and caring. But she lives in a world ruled by practicality where extravagant expenditures simply don't compute. This goes for everything from culinary matters to weddings.[43]

Peeved, and unwilling to waste any more time debating the worth of gourmet coffees, I cut straight to the chase. "Actually he'd disapprove because I'm pregnant."

It may not have been the most dramatic delivery, but it got the point across. Seconds later my mother had tears streaming down her cheeks and was rushing to hug me. "Oh, sweetie, that's wonderful news!"

Although my mom and I love each other, we're not that close. We're not the type to talk endlessly on the phone and share the mundane details of our daily lives beyond those imparted during our family dinners. As a result, I approach these "mother-daughter" moments with great expectations. As if their level of emotional effusion should equal that which is absent from our relationship the rest of the time.

And sometimes, I'm disappointed.

Like when I told my mom that Stephen and I were getting married. Sure, she was happy, but she didn't really seem

---

[43] And transportation. After driving the same car for fifteen years, she finally bought a new one last month. The star of the Economy Class, it gets great gas mileage, was voted "most reliable" by *Consumer Reports*, and has absolutely NO options. I rest my case.

moved. In fact, minutes after I had told her about our engagement, she was scrubbing the grout between the kitchen tiles. Granted, I'm no fan of housework, but I defy anyone, Heloise included, to call this a celebratory gesture.

But today, with the news of my pregnancy, my expectations were not only met but exceeded.

Repeatedly welling up with tears, my mother asked me all about my due date, my thoughts, my excitement, and my fears. And as my answers came pouring out I felt cloaked in my mother's maternal warmth, a sensation unparalleled by any other. And even though our decision not to learn the baby's sex elicited a dismissive "That's ridiculous," it didn't matter. My mother and I were bonding.

Until she suggested that I wait to tell my father the good news, "Just a little while. Maybe a month."

A *month*? Was she nuts? I'd kept my mouth shut for eleven weeks only to lug my butt upstate to tell my parents this fabulous news face-to-face, and now she wanted me to wait another thirty days? Not going to happen.

"But why? Don't you think he'd like to know? Won't this make him happy?"

"Of course he'll be happy. It's just that he's feeling a bit sensitive these days" – and here's where she lowered her voice – "about his *age*."

My parents are only in their late fifties. I was completely confused.

"What are you talking about? Is he having some type of midlife crisis?" I cringed as the image of my father wearing a cravat and soliciting young women flashed across my mind. It was like looking directly into a solar eclipse with your eyelids taped open.

My mother scoffed, "For goodness' sake, Amy, give your

father some credit."

"Then what's the problem?"

After carefully glancing around the room, as if some confused federal agent might have wire-tapped our suburban home, she said, "Your father was replaced by a younger man at work."

"Since when?"

"Eight months ago."

What?! My father had been canned from a job he'd had for ten years, at a company he'd been with for over a quarter century, and it took her *eight months* to tell me?

Apparently, my father's managerial job at the supermarket chain was folded into another job held by a younger employee – rendering my father expendable. He'd been cut loose with a pension and early retirement benefits. But no pride. It was awful. Having recently been unemployed myself, I felt particularly empathetic. Except I had the benefit of knowing that somewhere there was a job for me. But almost sixty years old with limited computer skills, and no interest in acquiring more, my father had effectively been put out to pasture. No wonder he'd gotten satellite TV. My only solace was learning that Nicole hadn't been told, either.

But it was precisely because of this awful revelation that I insisted we tell my father about my pregnancy. Sure, it didn't come with a desk or a secretary, but becoming a grandfather was an invaluable position with lots of responsibility. My father had a right to know, and the sooner we told him the sooner he could brush up on those nursery rhymes. My mother finally relented.

At that moment Nicole walked into the kitchen, a Victoria's Secret bag dangling from her arm. Big surprise. She took one look at my mother and me and knew that something was up. "What's going on?"

"I'm pregnant and Dad got fired." And before she could respond, or show me her sporty new thong purchase, I was halfway to the den to tell my father the good news.

Good news, which definitely raised his spirits. He even turned off *Diagnosis Murder* to give me and Stephen hugs. Casually glossing over his recent "departure" from work, he expressed his excitement at the prospect of being able to take his grandson to the park to play ball. Clearly the thought that we might have a girl never crossed his mind. I guess after having two daughters himself and being canned from his job, he figures God owes him. So Stephen and I just smiled.

In fact, everyone was smiling. My mom and dad because they were going to be grandparents. Nicole because we have yet to tell her that she can't stay with us anymore. Even Gram, who came home from an afternoon game of bingo, was thrilled by the news. At first I was worried that another high point in my life might inspire her to drastic measures. But as it turned out, I didn't need to worry. Far from the attention-stealing octogenarian she became when I got married, Gram literally rose to the occasion – lifting a cup of my mother's lethal coffee in the air and proposing a heartwarming toast in honor of our child-to-be.

Buoyed by such a welcome reception, we convinced Nicole to drive us a couple towns over so that we could share the news with Stephen's family. We were on a roll.

When we arrived at Stephen's stunning childhood home, Mrs. Stewart was examining fabric samples with Stephen's little sister Kimberly. Although she's in her mid-twenties, Kim will forever act like the baby of the family. She's spoiled, petulant, and self-absorbed. So it was no surprise to learn that she'd harangued her interior designer mother into decorating her apartment – as well as paying for it. Judging from the samples laid out on the coffee table, an array of god-awful prints would figure prominently in the decor.

It was a stunning display of passive-aggressive behavior. My mother-in-law was to be commended.

Perhaps because her eldest son is a chauvinistic moron, because her only daughter is materialistic to a level that rivals Mandy's but without any of the grace or charm, or because her husband of thirty-five years was inattentive, Mrs. Stewart has spent the last six years lavishing her nurturing instincts on Chuffy – a fair-haired Chow who's fed at the dining table and travels in Mrs. Stewart's handbag. Even Stephen, who could easily be considered the model child, is only a fraction as loyal to his mother as Chuffy is. And though I was certain that once Mrs. Stewart's romantic life went into overdrive her attachment to Chuffy would wane, interestingly it appears to have had the opposite effect. So it was no surprise to find Chuffy snoozing at Mrs. Stewart's feet, a petite cashmere throw draped over her back to ward off the September chill.

Yes, all the Stewart ladies were present for our big announcement.

Mrs. Stewart was very pleased. Not thrilled. Or wildly ecstatic. But definitely pleased. So much so that she immediately went to the kitchen to fetch a bottle of Prosecco and some almond cookies to celebrate. Sure, had it been *my* first grandchild I would have run dancing throughout the house and returned with the best bottle of champagne I could find. But I've learned the hard way that you can never predict the reactions of others. Nor should you expect anyone to react in the same way you would. Trust me, it's a recipe for disaster. So sparkling white wine from Italy was just dandy. After all, I'm eleven weeks pregnant – I couldn't drink it, anyway.

For her part, Kim had only one thing to say: "*You're* going to be a mother?"

What the hell was that supposed to mean? And why did she sound so incredulous? It was as if we'd said I'd be competing in the Olympic pole vault. Or modeling for *Vogue*. Why was the thought of my being a mother so shocking?

Kimberly and I have had a strained relationship from the start. When Stephen and I decided to get married, his grandmother gave him an emerald ring to use as my engagement ring. It had been in their family for four generations, and offering it to me was the ultimate gesture of acceptance and love. Except it left Kim nearly deranged with fury. After insinuating that her grandmother had plunged into senility, Kimberly informed me that the ring was rightly *hers* and that I should hand it over immediately.

I told Kimberly to kiss my ass.

But this was different. This was our child, our family, my ability to MOTHER that she was questioning. So I turned to my dear sister-in-law and smiled. "Yes, that's generally what happens when you have a child."

And then, because I simply could not resist: "I guess your days as the family baby are numbered."

Ponder that, you little wench.

Apparently she did, because seconds later the blood drained from her face and she was asking her mother for some "pocket" money.[44] Loaded with cash and fabric swatches, Kim made a beeline for her car and was gone within seconds –

[44] Which she actually got! All two hundred bucks of it!

her glass of Prosecco barely touched.

Oddly, no one seemed to mind.

Reaching for an almond cookie, Mrs. Stewart gently stroked Chuffy's back and remarked on how excited Stephen's grandparents would be to hear the news. Stephen and I agreed. Then, almost as if she were asking us to pass the cookie tin, she nonchalantly requested that we not mention the pregnancy to anyone else she might know.

Excuse me? Even Stephen was taken aback by this.

Mrs. Stewart immediately attempted to assuage our shock. "Don't misunderstand. I'm very pleased with the news. Really, I am. But you know how it is . . ." She grinned. "Being a grandmother might take the 'shine' off my image as a dating prospect."

Good lord. This was Nicole in thirty years.

Stephen, ever the good child, readily agreed. Then tossed back his glass of Prosecco. And Kim's. Fearing that the term "intimate relations" was only moments away, he politely said our good-byes.

Outside the house, rubbing his temples to ward off his impending headache, Stephen opted not to visit his father. He'd had all the celebrating he could handle. Instead we called Mr. Stewart from the train station as we waited to go back to the city. Thrilled by the news, Mr. Stewart invited us to dinner the following week.

Good enough for me.

september 9th

Right after calling Mr. Stewart from the train station I called Anita and Mandy and told them to meet me this morning at a diner that is equidistant from all our apartments. In my excitement I arrived a half-hour early. Already beset with a hefty dose of morning sickness, I went ahead and ordered dry toast, herbal tea, and a slice of American cheese. Sipping my tea and scoping out the quickest route to the bathroom, I excitedly considered how to tell my two closest friends they were about to become honorary aunts.

When they finally arrived, Mandy was grumpy and Anita was hungover. I momentarily reconsidered the whole honorary aunt thing.

MANDY
Is that American cheese you're eating?
How disgusting.

She started wiping down her cutlery with a napkin.

MANDY
I can't believe you dragged me to this
dump so early in the morning. I'm going
to need another tube of eye-firming gel
just to get through the day.

ME
My apologies to your baggy eyes.

MANDY
Fatigued. Not baggy.

ME
Whatever. I have something important to
tell you.

ANITA

Great. But first I'd like to mention that I'm
going to become a mother.

What?

ME

I thought you were against having
children.

ANITA

Not against, just ambivalent.

ME

And now you're pregnant?

ANITA

Not yet.

MANDY

Of course not. You don't even have a
steady boyfriend.

ANITA

And I have no intention of finding one.
I just need to buy some sperm.

Mandy gasped. Then frantically signaled for the waiter.

MANDY

Double espresso!

And a whip! I couldn't help it. I was both stunned and annoyed. After all, this was supposed to be *my* big announcement.

> ME
> Well, guess what. I *am* pregnant.

Again, Mandy gasped.

> MANDY
> Are you sure?

> ME
> As sure as a Popsicle stick and a thumbs-up
> can be.

> MANDY
> Oh, Amy!

Springing from her chair, Mandy wrapped me in her arms, her eighteen-karat-gold Tiffany bangle wedged against my larynx. Now *that*'s the spirit!

> MANDY
> I'm sooo sorry.

Huh?

> MANDY
> But don't worry. I know a fabulous doctor.
> He's licensed, talented, and, most of all,
> discreet. My cousin Elise used him when
> she had her accident.

As I struggled to extricate myself from her clutches, my head reeled from oxygen deprivation and fury. I'm the first person to support an individual's right to choose. To make their own decisions regarding their body. But I HAD chosen. Hell, I'd worked my ass off for this.

Anita shrieked with amusement.

> MANDY
> How dare you laugh at this!

> ANITA
> Tell her, Amy.

> ME
> This wasn't an accident.

Mandy immediately recoiled. Then hissed.

> MANDY
> *Et tu*, Brutus?

> ANITA
> Come on, Mandy. Everybody's doin' it.

> MANDY
> Shut up.

> ANITA
> Well, I for one congratulate you, Amy. I
> think it's grand. In fact, it was after we
> discussed your having kids that I began
> considering it for myself.

MANDY
Wait a minute. You sought lifestyle
counseling from *her*?

Here we go.

ME
Maybe. I don't know. Perhaps I mentioned
something in passing.

MANDY
I sincerely doubt that a "passing" remark
was enough to send Madonna over here
searching for a turkey baster. If you ask
me, you're both insane.

ME
Insane? I thought you'd be happy for me.

MANDY
Oh, please, Amy. It's a baby, not a Prada
luggage set.

ME
This from the woman who once warned
me to hurry up and get married so I
wouldn't have to get kids through a mail-
order catalog?

MANDY
I never said that.

ANITA
Sounds like you.

MANDY
Didn't I tell you to shut up?

ME
Three years ago. Frutto di Sole. I was
drinking Chianti and you were nuzzling
with Jon.

MANDY
Well, that was then and this is now.
As in *now* my mother can say,
"Even Amy Thomas is having a baby."

She turned dismissively to Anita.

MANDY
Thank God she's never met you.

ANITA
Come on, Mandy. You of all people
should appreciate my decision. After all,
it's the ultimate shopping experience.

MANDY
Clearly you've never been to the
Barney's warehouse sale.

september 9th – 11 p.m.

I told Stephen all about Anita's decision to become a mother with the help of some sperm-for-hire. I was shocked by his reaction.

Generally speaking, Stephen's a thoughtful, nonjudgmental person. His computer-programming mind enables him to examine situations from all points of view, with logic guiding the way.[45] Plus, he really likes Anita. So I was stunned that he had nothing nice to say about her decision.

At first I thought he was still in a bad mood because I made him go to the grocery store at ten o'clock to buy more American cheese. But what could I do? The slices he'd bought on his way home from work weren't individually wrapped. And that makes a HUGE difference in the way they taste. Trust me.

But it wasn't that. After listening to his thoughts, it was clear that he's truly upset by Anita's decision. He thinks it's ignorant – she doesn't have the vaguest sense of what it takes to be a single mother. Selfish – the child will be without a father. And self-defeating – how's she going to maintain her joie-de-vivre lifestyle with a baby?

And although I defended Anita because she's my friend and I felt a certain sense of obligation, secretly I couldn't help but wonder if Stephen was right.

september 10th

I told Lucy about my pregnancy. She was thrilled. She yelled

---

[45] Notable exception – his initial reaction to the idea of our having children.

so loudly that the on-duty nurse at the senior center burst into her room with a first-aid kit. As it turned out the nurse was a man, a cute one, too, so she capitalized on the situation and feigned heart palpitations.

september 11th

Nicole stopped by the apartment last night to borrow my black leather miniskirt. It took me half an hour of searching through our storage closet to find it. In fact, it'd been so long since I'd worn the skirt that it actually crackled when I opened it up. Not wanting to waste time, Nicole slipped the skirt on in the middle of the living room and frowned. "Darn, it's too big."

A total lie. It's *designed* to hang low on the hips.

"Maybe if I wear your pink tank top no one will see the waist."

And off she went, into the storage closet, to borrow yet another article of my clothing – which at this point should really be called stealing since half the time she doesn't return things. Case in point: my dark blue skirt with the side slit.

"It's hard to believe this is going to be a baby's room. It's such a mess."

From where I stood in the kitchen eating my fifteenth slice of American cheese, I could hear her opening boxes and tearing apart dry cleaning bags. "In fact, it's hard to believe that you guys are going to have a baby. Which doesn't mean that I'm not happy. I think it's great, and certainly Dad needs the good news."

She emerged from the storage closet wearing my hot-pink

tank top, my black leather miniskirt, and a push-up bra I used to wear on first dates. On her feet, a pair of three-inch "Fuck Me" pumps – her own. "I just can't believe *you're* going to be someone's mother."

That's the second person in four days who can't believe I'm going to be someone's mother. Are they *trying* to freak me out? Uncertain how to respond, I said the first thing that came to mind:

"You look like a hooker."

Nicole was not pleased.

september 12th

I was racked with guilt about my mixed, mostly negative, feelings about Anita becoming a single mom. Of course, I haven't expressed any of these negative feelings, but I haven't expressed any enthusiasm, either.

And in this case omission is equivalent to disapproval.

Which stinks, because Anita's been very supportive of my pregnancy, and because it makes me her "Mandy" – a dark cloud turning what should be a joyful decision into a topic of dissension. And if I dislike when Mandy does that to me, how can I turn around and do that to Anita?

So I decided to call Anita and discuss it with her. After all, maybe if I understood her reasons for choosing single motherhood I'd be more comfortable with her decision.

Her answer was simple and straightforward: "I have no interest in being monogamous. Or in waking up every morning to do wifely things. I know for a fact that I would not be a good wife. But all the things I have no interest in doing for a companion, I can't wait to do for a child. As bad a wife as I'd be, I know I'll be a wonderful mom. So does that mean I shouldn't have kids? Or that I should hook up with some guy, have kids, put us all through a horrible relationship, and end up a single mother anyway? Because let's face it, a divorced dad could be a great contributor to a child's life, or he could simply vanish."

In short, she wants a baby, has lots of love to give, and enough money to do it alone. So what is she waiting for?

Nothing. She's considered it for several months, done research, even met with single moms. As for her joie-de-vivre lifestyle? She's fully prepared to tone it down. In her words, it's worth the trade.

Shame on me for not giving her the benefit of the doubt. I'm her best friend. I should know better. After all, it's unfair and overly simplistic to reduce Anita to a vigilantly independent woman whose pursuit of pleasure, be it carnal or alcoholic, defines her existence. Because Anita, like the rest of us, is far more complex than that. She's an extremely intelligent, sensitive, caring person. And just because I don't understand her choice, and would never make it myself, doesn't make it wrong.

The bottom line? It's her life. And as her friend it's my job to be supportive.

So I wished her a speedy conception and offered the only advice that sprang to mind: Don't buy a single-test pregnancy kit.

september 13th

I'm almost at the end of my third month which, according to *BH, BN,* is the ideal time to start thinking of a name.

116

One problem. Since Stephen and I have decided not to learn the sex of the baby we'll need to choose two names – one for a girl and one for a boy. Twice the work? Sure. But with the whole Dagmar experience fresh in my mind I know it's worth the effort. In fact, I put the highest premium on naming our child. And while Stephen thinks I'm nuts, I still contend that next to conceiving, naming this child may be the most important task we have.

But which name? I've always had names I liked and names that I wished I'd been born with. But those change every few years, and I'd hate to saddle a kid with a name I thought was fabulous one day and years later think is the stupidest thing ever. After all, if you'd asked me my favorite girl name twenty years ago I would have said Ludmilla, after a transfer student from Russia who was the most popular girl in our junior high because she had enormous breasts. And while there's nothing wrong with the name Ludmilla, *Ludmilla Stewart* has a rather odd ring to it.

september 14th

I had the strangest revelation today in the produce section of the grocery store. Somewhere between a stack of moldy endive and a pile of grapefruit I looked at my shopping cart and realized that in six and a half months, instead of my handbag, I'll be putting a *baby* in that folding child seat.

What a rush!

Only, where does my handbag go?

Stephen and I were reading in bed before going to sleep. He was reading some computer manual that looked more convoluted than pregnancy math, and I was reading *BH, BN*. I'd had a pain in my lower abdomen, sort of a cramp, for several days, and I was hoping that *BH, BN* might help me figure out what it was. So I skimmed the book's index, cross-referencing *pain* with *cramping*, to find out what it might be, and that was when I stumbled onto *ectopic pregnancy*.

Not uncommon, ectopic pregnancy is where the fertilized egg completely misses the uterus and rolls into any number of areas, including the fallopian tubes. Suffice to say, it's BAD. In the worst-case scenario it can lead to infertility. The list of symptoms seems positively innocuous: lower abdomen cramping – generally on one side (got that), nausea (got that in spades), weakness (I did feel sort of tired this morning), and shoulder pain (my shoulders have been aching for DAYS).

I was four for four. And completely petrified. I'd only just become pregnant. It was far, far too soon not to be pregnant anymore. The book advised an immediate trip to the emergency room. Instead I rolled over and started frantically babbling at my husband.

Unable to make sense of a word I said, Stephen grabbed the book and began to read, his eyes growing wider with each word. "You've got these symptoms?"

"*All* of them!"

Stephen's face went white. I could tell he was trying to remain calm. To keep his cool. But he's a really bad poker player. He looked like he was shitting his pants.

Not wanting to ignore it but also not wanting to run to

the hospital emergency room and seem alarmist – although we were both alarmed – we compromised by staying up all night worrying.

september 16th

First thing in the morning I called the Crotch Whisperer. I told him all my symptoms and, in case he couldn't put two and two together, I explained that I had an ectopic pregnancy.

There was a pause at the other end of the phone. I freaked. Was he gathering his strength before delivering bad news? Or was he simply gathering strength to project into the phone? Maybe he was *already* talking and I simply couldn't hear him.

Damn his dainty vocal cords!

Unwilling to take any chances, I put him on speaker phone and cranked up the volume as far as it would go. This brought the man's speaking voice to a very low hiss. But just loud enough for me to understand his response: I was okay. Stephen immediately resumed breathing. Something he'd stopped doing around five A.M.

The Crotch Whisperer went on to explain that his office tests would have shown an ectopic pregnancy before my eighth week. I'd just finished my twelfth. He also said, I think, that I would have had to pass blood. Which I haven't. Thank God. His assessment? I probably had gas. Delighted, I thanked him for his time and hung up the phone.

As Stephen and I hugged, relieved and exhausted, all I could think about was how incredibly lucky we were to have *Baby How, Baby Now*. Before reading about it in *BH, BN*, I'd never even heard of an ectopic pregnancy. But if in fact I'd had one, *BH, BN* might have saved my fertility.

Now that's a good book!

september 17th

I spent a long time looking in the mirror last night. I'm already in my thirteenth week and you still can't tell I'm pregnant. I look exactly like I did in college.[46] No one would ever guess I'm pregnant. It's my little secret. Like walking around without underwear.

No one knows but you!

september 18th

I arrived home this evening to find Mr. Elbin waiting for the elevator.

Mr. Elbin is my pompous next-door neighbor who likes to throw cocktail parties for other pompous people. About fifty years old, I think he's an architectural photographer, but I'll never know for sure because he hasn't said a word to me since the Sanitation Saga.

Last year I spearheaded an effort to get my fellow tenants to recycle, finally persuading our landlord to enforce what the city already requires us to do – separate our trash.

You see, while being neighbors affords Mr. Elbin the luxury of hearing me and Stephen quarrel, laugh, and have sex, it affords me the knowledge of knowing that he doesn't

---

[46] OK, fine. My butt's bigger, but my hair's a lot better and my use of eye shadow is significantly more judicious.

separate his trash. And trust me, those cocktail parties result in plenty of empty bottles.

Why people have such a difficult time putting glass in one bag and paper in another I'll never know. But apparently it's more than Mr. Elbin can bear. As a result of my actions he avoids eye contact and refuses to exchange pleasantries with me. So waiting for the elevator together is never a comfortable situation. But again silence, like patience, is not a virtue that I possess.

> ME
> Good evening, Mr. Elbin.

Nothing.

> ME
> Hey, guess what? I'm pregnant.

> MR. ELBIN
> Oh, really?

This finally broke the ice . . .

> MR. ELBIN
> I thought your ankles looked fatter.

Into shards.

september 19th

We went upstate this evening to have dinner with Stephen's father. Mr. Stewart lives across town from Mrs. Stewart, in a fancy apartment complex. Predominantly occupied by divorcées, it's like a five-star refugee camp for middle-aged men. Instead of seeking therapy, they all subscribe to *Esquire*. And on any warm summer day the pool is filled with kids on visitation and young girlfriends in bikinis.

Not to be outdone, Mr. Stewart also lives with a young woman – Misty. Although Misty went to high school with Stephen and his older brother, Tom, she didn't actually meet Mr. Stewart until after his divorce. And while it would be easy to assume that Misty's winter-spring romance with my father-in-law is the familiar social climbing, financially motivated stereotype, it's not. She and Mr. Stewart actually love each other. A fact that still boggles Stephen's mind, but which he's tried hard to accept.

As long as he doesn't have to call her "Mom."

Luckily, Misty makes things as easy as possible. A dead ringer for Marcia Brady, she's an intelligent, straightforward woman who works part-time in a medical clinic while pursing a degree in veterinary medicine. I used to think she'd make a nice friend for Nicole. But that was before Nicole metamorphosed into Cher.

Since coming to understand that she's not with Stephen's dad because of some creepy unresolved daddy complex – Mr. Stewart's sixty-two and Misty's just a few years older than me – I've developed a good deal of respect for her. Although I'll *never* understand her taste in men.

Over a hearty meal of steak, string beans, and rice, Mr. Stewart freely volunteered an unsolicited list of baby names. Stephen and I just smiled. We were wholly unprepared at that exact moment to select a baby name. Especially since most of the suggestions were profoundly Waspy, wildly outdated, or names of gay movie icons. And oddly, all boys –

Rock, Troy, Wesley, Wendell . . .

Hearing the list, Misty shook her head. "Those will never do. They're having a girl."

I thought back to the Crotch Whisperer's receptionist and wondered if Misty was also getting some kind of *sense*. So I decided to ask how she could tell.

Misty, the future veterinarian, excitedly replied, "From the look in your eyes. Bright and alert. It's the same way with hamsters!"

Nice.

september 20th

Stephen surprised me today by coming home with a huge grin on his face and an industrial-size package of individually wrapped slices of American cheese in his arms – 550 slices, to be exact. The thing weighed a ton.

And it was beautiful.

It was the kind of mass-produced food product that's sold to large organizations like hospitals and summer camps. He'd gotten a friend whose husband works at a food warehouse in Yonkers to buy it for us. God bless his dear heart!

september 21st

Despite the fact that #43 on my Things to Do list is choose a hospital, it seems there isn't much choice. The Crotch Whisperer has privileges at Memorial Hospital on the Upper East Side, so come March 29th, that's where we'll be. End of story.

If only everything were so easy.

Things to Do

1. ~~Find ob/gyn~~
2. ~~Get prenatal checkup~~
3. ~~Get prenatal vitamins~~
4. Find physical exercise
5. Decide childbirth method
6. Join childbirth class
7. Buy crib
8. Buy bassinet
9. Buy crib mattress (doesn't come with!)
10. Buy crib bedding
11. Buy changing table
12. Decide cloth or disposable diapers
13. Buy diapers
14. Buy diaper bag
15. Buy diaper pail
16. Buy crib mobile
17. Buy layette
18. Buy stroller
19. Buy infant bathtub
20. Buy baby monitor
21. Buy infant swing
22. Buy night-light for baby's room
23. Choose color for baby's room
24. Paint baby's room
25. Buy pacifiers
26. Buy dresser for baby's clothes
27. Buy infant-size hangers
28. Create medical emergency kit
29. Prepare emergency phone lists
30. Decide nursing or formula
31. Buy nursing supplies or formula supplies

32. If nursing, decide to rent or buy breast pump
33. If nursing, buy nursing bras
34. If nursing, buy nipple cream
35. Decide on legal guardian
36. Prepare wills
37. Plan estate
38. Create college fund
39. Begin Kegel exercises
40. Buy first-year memorabilia scrapbook
41. ~~Decide whether to learn gender~~
42. Choose name(s)
43. ~~Choose hospital~~
44. Take tour of hospital maternity ward
45. Find pediatrician
46. Appoint someone to organize baby shower
47. Make invite list for baby shower
48. Register for baby shower
49. Buy thank-you notes for baby shower
50. Select birth music
51. ~~Prepare for appropriate religious ceremony~~
52. ~~Book venue for religious ceremony~~
53. ~~Arrange for priest, rabbi, or *mohel*, etc.~~
54. ~~Buy baby's outfit for religious ceremony~~
55. Buy maternity clothes
56. ~~Decide who will be in delivery room with you~~
57. Prepare baby announcements
58. Prepare overnight bag for hospital
59. Make birth plan

60. Schedule maternity leave
61. Make phone list for announcing baby's birth
62. Buy baby's take-home-from-hospital outfit
63. Decide on postbirth child care

september 24th – 3 a.m.

What have I done?!

I'm not ready to have a baby. I haven't sailed up the Nile. Gone skydiving in Africa. Had group sex![47] There are so many things I want to do in life, and now I'll have to wait until my kid's in college!

Oh, my God! "My kid." That just sounds too weird. I need ice cream.

Ice cream!

I'm already craving ice cream??? Next thing you know I'll be reaching for the pickle jar, and pickles give me gas!

september 27th

I don't know what happened.

This morning I opened the refrigerator to find that huge hunk of American cheese just sitting on the shelf like a brick of yellow latex, and I practically vomited.

Stinky and rubbery, it was the most disgusting thing I'd ever seen. So I slammed the refrigerator shut and demanded that Stephen throw it into the trash. All remaining five hun-

---

[47] OK, theoretically marriage precluded that last one.

dred slices. Because if there's one thing I NEVER, EVER want to see again, it's American cheese.

Confused and more than a bit distraught, Stephen – dressed only in his bathrobe – dutifully lugged the brick out to the garbage. Far too wise to argue with his pregnant wife.

october 3rd

I went to the Crotch Whisperer today for a checkup. In addition to the routine examination he did another ultrasound. I assume everything looked good because the Whisperer smiled, and no one smiles when they're telling you you're having serious health complications.

Right?

october 5th

With Eddie's help I surreptitiously investigated the Brinkman/Baines maternity leave policy and discovered that they offer eight weeks of paid leave with the option to take an additional month without pay. Sounds reasonable. Although Eddie tells me that some Scandinavian countries give women as much as six months off.

I wonder if I could find work in Norway.

october 7th

My father called this evening with a grand announcement. Having been unshackled from his desk job, he's discovered a passion for physical labor and is going to MAKE us a crib.

And no, he didn't mean assemble one from Baby Land or build one from a kit. He meant go to the lumberyard, buy the wood, and work his way up from there.

And as my father rhapsodized about the pleasure of connecting with nature and creating something special for his grandson, my mind raced from splinters, to toxic lacquers, to the hundreds of safety regulations regarding cribs, about which my father would have absolutely no knowledge.

So with fear in my heart, and the image of my child's head wedged between the ill-distanced bars of his/her crib, I thanked him for his extraordinary offer and began to hyperventilate.

october 8th

Today's my thirty-second birthday. Hard to believe.

But not nearly as shocking as the fact that next October 8th I'll have a baby!

october 10th

Brinkman/Baines's parent company has run into financial difficulty. The CFO has been indicted on suspicion of fraud, and the entire corporation is feeling the fallout. According to Anita's mole over at *Focus,* the job I applied for has temporarily been put on hold. And here at Brinkman/Baines, we too are feeling the effects. Our supply closet is now locked and you can only procure important items such as staples and paper clips by submitting a request form to our receptionist – who is NOT pleased with her increased responsibility. We've also laid off one Junior Account Manager and our college intern. Which is pathetic, because the poor kid wasn't getting paid anyway. Only travel money.

october 13th

As I finish my fourth month I'm determined to keep my pregnancy a secret from Mr. Nealy for as long as possible. I want to continue to prove myself in the workplace before giving him a reason to strategize my removal. Who knows, now that the company's having financial difficulties he may decide that one Senior Account Manager is all they need.

Luckily I'm still able to disguise my pregnant body. In fact, I look fairly similar to the way I did last month, with the notable exceptions of a fuller set of boobs and a more bulbous belly. The first I've chosen to highlight – let 'em think it's a Wonderbra. The latter is easily concealed with baggy clothing and elastic waistbands.

Although it's hard for me to believe that people can't guess. After all, why else would I be so happy all the time?! It's certainly not because Abe Hamen's offered me a twenty-percent discount on his newest massage video, "Tantalizing Touchpoints." Total crap.

But thus far only Eddie has guessed or even commented. Which is why I acted like I did when I literally ran into Mr. Nealy while making my daily sprint to the ladies' room. Sheet-white, trembling, and starting to perspire, I made an off-the-cuff remark about having had too many gin-and-tonics last night at a hot new club in Tribeca.

Patting me on the back, Mr. Nealy complimented my

"strong grip on the cultural pulse." Little does he know the only thing I'm gripping is the porcelain goddess.

october 14th

Larry and Mitch came over to watch a football game last night.

In addition to his horrible plaid sofa, by marrying Stephen, I also become part owner of an enormous entertainment center with remote control doors. Just a push of a button and the doors open wide to reveal a large-screen TV. It's the ultimate male fantasy – after the Reese twins – and, needless to say, far too attractive for Larry and Mitch to resist. So it's inevitable that at least once every few weeks I come home to find the gruesome twosome in my living room.

Never in my wildest dreams did I imagine that marrying Stephen meant formalizing a relationship with these guys. But that just brings me back to marriage, and the art – or rather the challenge – of compromise.

But tonight Larry and Mitch must have told me ten times how good I look. And even though I know Stephen *told* them to say that, it was still nice to hear. Of course, it leaves me horribly conflicted – torn between loathing them because they're vile and inevitably leave their warm butt imprints on our sofa, and enjoying their company because they're so good at kissing up.

Either way, it's all about asses.

october 15th

I called my friend Margo tonight, and much to my surprise

she actually answered the phone. With three kids ranging in age from eighteen months to five years old, it seems answering the phone is alternately an infrequent luxury and just another chore. Hence my repeated attempts to contact her.

But tonight we connected long enough for me to tell her about my pregnancy and to suggest that we get together to catch up. After all, as one of my only friends with kids, I had hundreds of child-related questions for her – cribs, diapers, stores, doctors . . .

Thrilled to hear I was pregnant, Margo eagerly agreed to meet, and, consulting her date book, suggested we do it as soon as possible – how was *November 20th* for me?

Apparently Mommy Time is even slower than pregnancy.

october 16th

You'd think my newfound party image would earn me some brownie points with the junior staff. No such luck. Although polite and respectful, they reek of disdain – the type of disdain I used to feel when older people tried, unsuccessfully, to be cool.

Well, screw 'em. I've got my own cubicle.

Losers.

Of course, having Mandy pick me up at the office for lunch did little to raise my cool factor. As she strutted through the door in her Calvin Klein suit with her Coach purse dangling from her elbow I could just feel my colleagues roll their eyes. But the final nail in the coffin of my coolness came when she got a call on her cell phone regarding an apartment she'd just shown. "I know a million three seems steep for a two-bedroom, but it's *Madison Avenue.*

You're walking distance to the Met and Armani."

Seconds later, I was hustling toward the elevators with my shoulder bag and Mandy in tow. And just as we were halfway out the door, Eddie handed me a fax regarding a talk show booking for our new client, chef Roy "Sizzle" Perkins – The Grill Guy. It was official. Come next Tuesday morning, Roy would show all of America how to fry bacon with a minimum of effort and mess. This was a huge coup – national exposure during peak viewing hours. And he'd only been our client for two weeks! Eddie and I hugged in delight. Mandy was only vaguely impressed, "Oh, I love that show. But bacon's so high in cholesterol. You know, the *bad* cholesterol."

I quickly introduced them. After all, Eddie was entitled to know who was raining on his parade. "Eddie, this is my friend Mandy. She's got a problem with fats."

Mandy shook her head. "Does the term 'heart disease' mean nothing to you people?"

Not a bit bothered, Eddie reassuringly patted Mandy on the shoulder and said, "Stop worrying. It encourages wrinkles." Mandy self-consciously touched her face. Then, leaning close, he whispered in my ear, "There's a great bassinet sale over at Baby Land. The ones with the vibrating feature." Then off he went to call chef Roy "Sizzle" Perkins about his date with America.

Mandy was not pleased. The minute we stepped into the elevator it started.

MANDY
So who's Mary Poppins?

ME
That's Eddie. He's the other Senior

Account Manager. He's been incredibly
supportive about my pregnancy.

MANDY
I bet he has.

ME
What's that supposed to mean?

MANDY
Really, Amy. Has your heightened estrogen
level weakened your powers of deduction?
Mary Poppins is "supporting" you out of
your job.

ME
That's what I used to think. Except he's
not. He's just a genuinely nice person.

MANDY
Fine, turn a blind eye. But remember, Jon
worked very hard to get you this job.

Hold on. Jon may have TOLD me about this job but he
certainly didn't get it for me. I seem to remember the submission of a résumé, a rather extensive interview, and numerous hours spent praying for the position while watching
daytime TV from the comfort of my ugly plaid sofa. In fact,
the only thing Jon's ever gotten me is annoyed. But the day
was young, so I decided to end the discussion on a peaceful
note.

ME
I'll bear that in mind.

It was still early when we arrived at Frutto di Sole, so when Rocco led us to our favorite table in the back, claiming to have saved it especially for us, I took it with a grain of salt. The place was only half full. But it didn't matter. We still love being treated like queens even if the house is made of cards.

MANDY
Are you having wine?

ME
Hardly the beverage of choice for pregnant women. But don't let that stop you.

MANDY
Don't be ridiculous. I can't drink alone. Especially at lunch. It sends the wrong message.

What? That she's thirsty? And who exactly was she sending messages to? Was the Etiquette Mothership hovering over the West Village?

MANDY
You know the Europeans drink throughout their pregnancy.

ME
Which explains their fascination with Jerry Lewis.

Putting down her menu, Mandy sighed dramatically.

> MANDY
> You're turning into such a drag. First you
> stop drinking, next you'll be wearing those
> horrible muumuus that look like draperies
> from a dental office.

> ME
> Is this your idea of being supportive?

> MANDY
> Supportive? Have you any idea how
> difficult your pregnancy will be for me?

Really, I shouldn't be surprised. Mandy made her wedding my nightmare. That she should make my pregnancy about her shouldn't be such a shock. But how the hell do you respond to something like that?

> ME
> Why? Are you bearing my child?

> MANDY
> No, just the onus of your act. You're setting
> a dreadful example. Now my mother and
> Jon will never stop nagging me to breed.

She daintily dabbed the corners of her mouth with a napkin.

> MANDY
> If you ask me, everyone's gone barking
> mad. Especially you.

And she was right. I must be mad. Because this pregnancy is ruining my career. When I returned to the office I found a brochure for Alcoholics Anonymous in my mailbox. Seems I've been playing the part of a late-night partyer a little too well.

I'd like to the thank the Academy . . .

october 17th

I was so disturbed by my lunch with Mandy and my anonymous referral to a twelve-step program for alcoholism that I finally made my way to Balanced Breathing – the prenatal yoga center that Eddie told me about.

I went in search of balance, but also for a sense of community. After sixteen and a half weeks of being pregnant, I'm beginning to feel very lonely. Sure, it's fun to talk about the pregnancy with Stephen, or my mom, and sometimes even with Anita – when I'm able to get past the fact that she's going to be a single mother with the help of a pricey tube of toss – but the reality remains that I have very few friends with children and absolutely no girlfriends who are currently pregnant. Hell, half my girlfriends aren't even married, let alone mothers. I need to speak with people who are going through this experience *now*. To compare notes. To share thoughts. And no matter how often I stare at Lily, I simply cannot read her mind. I have no idea if she's nervous about her delivery. If she's feeling pressures at work. Or even where she got that groovy peasant blouse. Simply put, I need a friend who can talk.

Which leads me to another point. Granted, I have very few friends who are mothers so my observation is hardly scientific, but it's clear to me that women with children are IM-POSSIBLE to socialize with. The last time I actually saw Margo was a chance meeting in the lingerie section of Macy's. Still employed at *Round-Up,* I'd just finished editing a piece about the hygiene habits of deli workers. That was over a year ago. I was buying a kimono-style robe with lace details, and she was picking up a three-pack of Hanes for Her – the kind that reach up to your bra line. After a hug and a harried hello, she was throwing some cash at the sales-woman and racing for the exit to pick up her daughter from tap class, a tattered Barbie doll dangling from her shoulder bag and a can of Slim-Fast in her hand.

This will *never* happen to me. I vow to keep my social life active, my underwear attractive, and my attitude positive long after I give birth.

All the more incentive to try Balanced Breathing.

Balanced Breathing is on the second floor of an old mat-zoh factory in the East Village. A brick building with huge industrial windows, it's completely unassuming except for the large BALANCED BREATHING banner dangling from the roof – the "A"s containing tiny babies sitting cross-legged with amused smiles on their little faces. And though the matzoh may be long gone, my dog nose immediately de-tected lavender oil wafting from the open windows like a silent olfactory call beckoning pregnant women to come.

And come they did. Through the crowds of fashionistas, geriatrics, Hispanic schoolchildren, and Asian delivery men, came pregnant women in droves. And as I looked at these women I immediately understood why I'd never heard of Balanced Breathing: The circles I travel in don't dabble in homemade saris, underarm hair, or lambskin mats. Wearing pressed pants and last season's leather jacket from Banana

Republic, I felt distinctly out of place.

Yes, despite the fact that these women were all in some stage of pregnancy, I was fairly certain that this was not the community I'd been hoping for. But despite my hesitation I forged on. After all, xenophobia is not my style. Not to mention that I hadn't traveled forty minutes in rush-hour traffic only to turn around and go home.

After climbing two flights of rickety stairs I entered the yoga studio. Large, airy, and covered with wall hangings from the Far East, it had a warm and inviting feel – despite the heavy hand with the lavender oil. Making my way to the minuscule dressing room, I slipped into a pair of sweatpants and an old college T-shirt of Stephen's.

Minutes later I was one of about thirty pregnant women sitting on yoga mats facing yoga guru Pippa Ploos – a strange mix of Norwegian and New Age dressed in flowing purple gauze. As I would soon learn – by reading the back of her yoga video box, which is available for sale at the front desk – Pippa is pregnancy yogi to the stars. Sure she teaches slobs like me, but she also gives private instruction to the majority of pregnant celebrities living in this city. During the casual conversation that starts each class, she drops names of Tony Award winners and trust-fund socialites. And yet, as she is quick to point out, pregnancy is a universal experience no matter who you are.

In short, even Uma Thurman gets morning sickness. Except she can probably afford to pay someone to hold her hair back while she pukes.

Though I've never done yoga before, let alone pregnancy yoga, I was pleased to discover that I like it. It's soothing and relaxing even if it was delivered in a nutty-crunchy environment. We stretch, we bend, we even dance a bit. Who knows, perhaps a respite in the land of nutty-crunchy is exactly what I need. The perfect antidote to my hectic days spent promoting the Grill Guy and two gals with beef on their minds and silicone in their breasts.[48]

There was also something to be said for being with other pregnant women. Even if we aren't all cut from the same cloth, we're all sharing a common experience. We're all adjusting to the idea of becoming mothers, we're all struggling to choose names, and we're all dealing with physical changes. Some more than others.

WAY more than others.

Good lord, even if the yoga had been dreadful and the place had been a pit, it would have been worth the trip just to see the other women in their various spherical stages. That's right, I was shocked and relieved by the realization that, just as so many people have already told me, I'm looking damn good. At least by comparative terms. Because some of these women look like they've been through hell. Fat and waddling, they're like the Oompa-Loompas from *Willy Wonka,* only they're not blue.

I, on the other hand, am already four months pregnant and can still wear my jeans. Sure, I can't zip them. But who cares? That's nothing an oversized shirt won't take care of. In fact, unless I tell them, people don't even know I'm pregnant. They just think I'm retaining water. Or have been doing taste tests on high-fat pastries. A little pudgy? Yes. But definitely not pregnant.

During the portion of the class where we work with partners, I found myself holding a woman's ankles as she stuck

---

[48] Note to self: Investigate cross-promotional ops with Roy "Sizzling" Perkins and the Reese twins.

her butt in my face and attempted to touch her hands to the floor.[49] Turns out she's also four months pregnant. Except, while she's built like Lily – a slender, sticklike frame – she's got a belly the size of a beach ball. Happy to actually meet someone at my stage, I casually said, "What a coincidence. I'm four months pregnant, too. Although you'd probably never know it."

And without missing a beat this stick woman with her ass in my face reassuringly replied, "Don't worry. They say people who start off heavy take longer to show. You know, all that extra space."

Bitch.

Had she not been four months pregnant I might have let go of her ankles and sent her head tumbling up her own butt. But of course I couldn't. So instead I smiled a big smile at her tiny little ass and made a mental note never to partner with her again.

The class ended with a five-minute chant, during which time I sat cross-legged repeating the words *"Sat Nam,"* although I had no idea what the hell they meant. All I knew was that it was supposed to calm me and balance the vibes in the room.

Whatever.

It made me forget the stick woman's fat comment. Good enough. And by the end of the class I was relaxed, invigorated, and only somewhat nauseous from the scent of lavender oil and the sight of underarm hair.

So I bought a ten-class series and vowed NEVER to mention any of this to Anita or Mandy – both of whom would mock me mercilessly if they knew what I'd just done.

---

[49] A position called something like "Open Flower," though it looks closer to "Ass Wiper."

Perhaps it was all the relaxation from Balanced Breathing. Or maybe I got confused with a last-minute time change. But in either event, I forgot to tell Glyniss O'Maley's manager about a phone interview that I'd arranged with *Teen Flair*. At three-thirty P.M. I got a call from Anita saying that her writer had been trying to reach Glyniss for over an hour without any luck. What was going on?

I couldn't believe it. I never forget details like that. I'm always careful to write them down and triple-check that everyone's been notified of their appointments. But this time I'd somehow managed to tell everyone except Glyniss. It was horribly unprofessional, and had I not been dealing with one of my closest friends it could have been a mini-disaster. Luckily Anita covered for me at her end, and we rescheduled for the following week. And though it ended up being a nonevent, I spent the afternoon kicking myself for being so forgetful.

When I got home that evening I recounted the story to Stephen, who chuckled. Not a sympathetic chuckle, but an annoying self-satisfied chuckle that had more to do with being amused than being understanding. Irritated, I asked what was so damn funny. At which point he told me that Martin, his procreation-junkie coworker, had warned him *this* would happen. Martin claims that his wife, the former television chef turned stressed-out mother, completely lost her ironclad memory and superior organization skills when she was pregnant.[50] It was an anecdotal account that Martin

---

[50] If you ask me, she's yet to regain them, but perhaps I'm being uncharitable.

says is supported by scientific research – the female brain shrinks during pregnancy.

How convenient. Sounds like a male plot designed to keep women barefoot, pregnant, and without power of attorney. Needless to say, I was unconvinced. It's going to take a whole lot more than the testimony of some freak with superstitious beliefs about a fertility chair to make me believe my brain is shrinking.[51]

october 18th – 10:30 p.m.

As a result of pregnancy, I'm now an ideal contestant for *Let's Make A Deal*. Remember that game show? People from the audience were randomly asked if they had any of a bizarre array of items in their purse. If they did, they were given the chance to win big prizes like a washer/dryer or a trip to Scranton, Pennsylvania. Well, a quick glimpse into my handbag now reveals what a complex – if not strange – woman I've become.

Ginger tea, a plastic barf bag, and a pamphlet for AA.

Things to Do
1. Find ob/gyn
2. Get prenatal checkup
3. Get prenatal vitamins
4. Find physical exercise
5. Decide childbirth method
6. Join childbirth class
7. Buy crib

---

[51] Note to self: Research that claim on the Internet.

142

8. Buy bassinet
9. Buy crib mattress (doesn't come with!)
10. Buy crib bedding
11. Buy changing table
12. Decide cloth or disposable diapers
13. Buy diapers
14. Buy diaper bag
15. Buy diaper pail
16. Buy crib mobile
17. Buy layette
18. Buy stroller
19. Buy infant bathtub
20. Buy baby monitor
21. Buy infant swing
22. Buy night-light for baby's room
23. Choose color for baby's room
24. Paint baby's room
25. Buy pacifiers
26. Buy dresser for baby's clothes
27. Buy infant-size hangers
28. Create medical emergency kit
29. Prepare emergency phone lists
30. Decide nursing or formula
31. Buy nursing supplies or formula supplies
32. If nursing, decide to rent or buy breast pump
33. If nursing, buy nursing bras
34. If nursing, buy nipple cream
35. Decide on legal guardian
36. Prepare wills
37. Plan estate
38. Create college fund

39. Begin Kegel exercises

40. Buy first-year memorabilia scrapbook

41. ~~Decide whether to learn gender~~

42. Choose name(s)

43. ~~Choose hospital~~

44. Take tour of hospital maternity ward

45. Find pediatrician

46. Appoint someone to organize baby shower

47. Make invite list for baby shower

48. Register for baby shower

49. Buy thank-you notes for baby shower

50. Select birth music

51. ~~Prepare for appropriate religious ceremony~~

52. ~~Book venue for religious ceremony~~

53. ~~Arrange for priest, rabbi, or *mohel,* etc.~~

54. ~~Buy baby's outfit for religious ceremony~~

55. Buy maternity clothes

56. ~~Decide who will be in delivery room with you~~

57. Prepare baby announcements

58. Prepare overnight bag for hospital

59. Make birth plan

60. Schedule maternity leave

61. Make phone list for announcing baby's birth

62. Buy baby's take-home-from-hospital outfit

63. Decide on postbirth child care

Worried about the number of things yet to do on our Things to Do list, I decided to accomplish almost half of them by going to the Baby Bargains discount store in Brooklyn. After all, the word "buy" appears numerous times on that list, and I figured a productive hour or two would yield a solid registry and a few well-chosen purchases.

How wrong I was.

The size of the average Olympic stadium, Baby Bargains is lined with rows of shelves stacked twenty feet high and jammed with boxes. Cribs, strollers, high chairs, tubes of this, and jars of that. It's like a U.N. storage facility for third-world nations. Bad lighting, stale air, dust from the last regime . . . And forget about finding a salesperson. Apparently it's called a discount store because they save money by not hiring staff. If you want it, you find it. And God help you if you've got a question.

Unfortunately, I had tons. For instance, what's the difference between a color mobile versus a black-and-white mobile? And why would I want the infant tub with the detachable sling instead of the molded plastic version from Europe? And what exactly is a wipes warmer? And where does that nursing pillow go?

Woefully uninformed and completely overwhelmed, I clearly hadn't done my homework before making this pilgrimage. As I looked at the countless rows of mystery items, it was as if every label were written in a language that I had yet to learn. The language of parenthood. And suddenly I felt completely unprepared to be a mother – still scrambling at the base of the learning curve wondering when an infant became a toddler and if a rubber ducky was considered a choking hazard.

So I left. Annoyed that I'd wasted my time but amazed by the thought that someday I'd walk into Baby Bargains and know what every one of those products is used for.

october 20th

Eager for a sense of accomplishment, I spent the afternoon timing the ride from my apartment to Memorial Hospital. Without traffic, it's a five-minute taxi ride. With traffic, it's ten. Which is great. Because although I may not be a lady, even *I* can keep my legs together for ten minutes.

october 21st

This morning I ran into Mr. Elbin in the bodega across the street from our apartment building. He came in for a copy of the *Times* just as I was ordering a cup of coffee. Scoffing with aloof disdain, he snorted, "Well, well. I thought even *semi*-intelligent women avoided caffeine during pregnancy."

"Rest assured, Mr. Elbin, it's decaffeinated." Now bite me.

"Doesn't mean caffeine-free, you know. Might as well give the kid a jolt of a/c current." And out the door he went. Big mouth and all. Leaving me to seethe, swear, and sheepishly change my order to a cup of herbal tea.

october 22nd

I arrived home this evening to find a package in the mail

from Gram. It was a little photo album filled with pictures of her when she was an infant. It was accompanied by a note –

Darling Amy,
So that your baby will know that even Great-Grandma was once a baby, too.
All my love, Gram

It was a lovely gift. But even if Gram hadn't sent this gift, she's already been more supportive of my pregnancy than I ever thought possible. Every week she calls to see how I feel and how our doctor appointments are going. She asks if we've chosen a color for the baby's room.[52] And if Stephen's got a box of cigars ready to go.[53]

Her excitement over this baby is the last thing I would have expected, but a wonderful surprise.

Even Lucy is surprised by Gram's behavior. She's spent decades watching Gram clamor for attention – first as a 1956 contestant on the *Queen for a Day* show,[54] then in her cantankerous marriage to my late grandfather,[55] and now as an octogenarian whose vitality carries her through bingo championships and family celebrations.[56] And yet even Lucy admits that this pregnancy seems to have done for Gram what age failed to do – it's mellowed her.

Yes, folks, it's the MIRACLE of birth.

---

[52] No, but it's #23 on my list of Things to Do.
[53] Guess she hasn't heard about that cancer research.
[54] Think Marie Antoinette.
[55] Their favorite spats revolved around who would outlive whom in order to collect the life insurance. Gram won.
[56] Remember my wedding?

Eager to resolve this name issue – and to cross it off my Things to Do list – I asked Stephen to make a list of names he likes. One for girls and one for boys. I did the same.

He hated all of mine. I hated all of his. Naturally. After an hour of bartering we agreed on two names: Nicholas for a boy. Madison for a girl.

What a relief. Now we can actually have this baby.

Of course, first we have to get Nicole off our sofa.

So Sunday morning I finally told her that it was time to cut the cord and find another couch to sleep on. Eventually the baby would start to wonder why the sofa was stained with Auntie Nicole's pressed powder and drool. Not to mention the fact that four people in 650 square feet with one bathroom was starting to feel a bit too Ellis Island for my tastes.

Sitting on the sofa with her feet on the coffee table and a bowl of cornflakes in her hands, Nicole shook her head dismissively and spoke with her mouth full.

> NICOLE
> Don't be so pushy. You're only four
> months pregnant.

> ME
> Four and a half.

> NICOLE
> Well, unless there have been new
> developments since my sex talk with Mom, it
> takes *nine* months for a baby to arrive.[57]

---

[57] *What* sex talk? I never got a sex talk. Just a bunch of wildly inaccurate facts from Betsy Emmerson during third grade recess!

ME
First off, Smarty Pants, it takes ten months.
That nine-month thing is total bullshit.
Secondly, Stephen and I have decided not
to start the baby's room until you move out.
Which means the longer you're here, the
longer it is before I can get things done.

A big, satisfied grin spread across her face.

NICOLE
Oh, I know what this is about. This is
about one of your crazy Things to Do
lists, isn't it? You're just itching to cross
more stuff out.

ME
I don't know what you're talking about.

Damn her!

NICOLE
Yeah, right.

She padded over to the kitchen.

NICOLE
Do you guys have any eggs?

ME
No, and I'm not asking you to disappear
tomorrow – just sometime before my third
trimester, okay?

NICOLE

No problem. Besides, in all fairness I
should be thanking you.

Huh? After all this time she was FINALLY going to thank us
for housing her, feeding her, and enduring her string of
poorly chosen perfumes? Amazing.

NICOLE

Now that you're pregnant, Mom and Dad
will get off my back and let me do my
own thing.

Wait a minute . . . Isn't that what *I* used to say about *her*
when she and Chet were the happy homemakers and I was
single?

october 24th – 3 a.m.

I awoke in a cold sweat. And this time it wasn't a wave of
nausea or a whiff of broccoli. It was the chilling reality that
I'm going to be someone's mother!

I can't be a mother. I don't know if it's starve a cold or
feed a fever. If the chicken was first or the egg. And God only
knows why the sky is blue!

And what about food? I can't even cook meat loaf. Sure,
Stephen's a great cook, but he cooks less than once a month,
so unless this kid likes order-in Chinese food we're screwed.

What was I thinking?!

Stephen called from the office to say he'd be working late. All jazzed up, he explained that the company may have finally figured out the basis for a computer program that could translate medical information from things like X rays into computer data, which would facilitate its dissemination among doctors and hospitals via the Internet. Yes, the project was at its nascent stages, but if successful it would be a huge break for the company – and in turn for us. We're talking braces, summer camp, *and* college fund.

Needless to say, I was thrilled – despite the fact that success was not guaranteed, the work would consume an overwhelming amount of Stephen's energy, and his ability to participate in baby preparations would significantly decrease.

Hmm . . . Funny how after months of trying to crack this computer program they have a breakthrough *now*.

On the upside, my "morning" sickness seems to have gone away. It's been three days since I sprinted for the bathroom, and I'm starting to expand my menus beyond bananas and rice. And yet my reputation as a major partyer lives on. Despite putting an immediate end to discussions of clubs and hangovers – thank you, AA brochure – Stella just asked me if I knew where to buy speed.

Great.

Now not only will I never work at *Focus*, but as the resident "hookup" for illegal narcotics I'm certain to be fired from Brinkman/Baines.

october 25th

Stephen's grandparents came in from New Jersey to have dinner with us this evening.

The Brocktons have been married since the dawn of time, proudly finish each other's sentences, and still go out for Valentine's Day. After sixty years of marriage they remain completely in love.

In addition to being fabulous role models, the Brocktons have always been very kind to me. After all, they gave me my heirloom emerald engagement ring – much to Kimberly's horror – and this evening they mentioned at least five times how fabulous I looked.

Yeah. They're good people.

In fact, they're such good people that they went out of their way to order a special nonalcoholic wine so we could all toast the baby. And after we clinked our glasses, Mrs. Brockton dabbed her napkin against her teary eyes and said, "I'm just so happy you're finally pregnant. We were beginning to think something was wrong."

Finally pregnant?

We've barely been married two years, and they thought something was *wrong*?

Who knew that such sweet and loving people could belong to the same cult as Mandy's mom.

october 26th

Stephen and I love the names Nicholas and Madison.

Unfortunately the rest of the country does, too. According to Internet census records and my mother, the fourth grade schoolteacher, Nicholas and Madison are all the rage. This year alone my mother has one Madison and two Nicholases – neither of whom likes making macaroni art, in case you were wondering.

It's not as if I want my kid to have some crazy made-up name like Shanella, or some insane spelling that insults both common sense and the English language like Monikka or Phrank. But after going through life with the name *Amy*, I insist my kid's name is at least vaguely unique.

october 27th

I went back to Balanced Breathing after work. This time Pippa had us on our hands and knees wagging our butts in the air. Apparently we weren't doing it right because in her effort to correct our positioning, Pippa, with her flowing purple gown of gauze and her Norwegian accent, instructed us to "Imagine a paintbrush is stuck in your anus and you're making circles in the sky."

Excuse me?

Call me crazy, but the idea of having a paintbrush jammed up my butt doesn't seem particularly appealing. Or artistic. So I glanced around the room for support from my fellow yogis. And got none. No one even flinched.

They just rotated their asses like good little Chagalls.

october 28th

I saw a couple on Columbus Avenue this evening walking arm in arm while pushing their infant daughter in a carriage.

They looked so happy and filled with joy. I couldn't help but cry. In almost five months this is going to be me and Stephen.

I am the luckiest person on Earth.

october 29th

Misty came into the city today to visit an animal shelter as part of her veterinary studies. We decided to meet for lunch at an upscale burger place near my office. While I was happy to hear from Misty, I have to admit I was surprised. We've never hung out alone. Our socializing has been limited to strained family affairs that include Stephen and his father. But I like Misty, so I looked forward to her visit. Besides, I was really craving a burger.

Over cheeseburgers and fries we discussed her school-work, my job, and of course the pregnancy. Commenting on how good I looked, she kept marveling about how pregnant women all seem to glow.

I didn't have the heart to tell her that the "glow" she was so enamored of was nothing more than a thick coating of clammy perspiration – the result of a wildly fluctuating body temperature, and the newest addition to my physical journey. Far from romantic, it was unpredictable and often embarrassing. One minute I'm shivering from a chill, the next my scalp's so hot I'm wishing I had a crew cut.

No doubt it's the body's little preview of menopause.

> Things No One Tells You About Pregnancy
> 1. No sushi
> 2. Twenty-four-hour morning sickness

3. Forty weeks (ten months) of pregnancy
4. No aspirin
5. Dog nose
6. "Glow" is sweat

october 30th

Anita called to ask if I wanted to join her at the bank.

> **ME**
> What? The line's so long you need
> companionship? Try an A.T.M.

Turns out she meant the sperm bank.

> **ANITA**
> It'll be exciting. I get to choose a donor.
> The perfect father – on paper. My Sperm
> Daddy.

Ick. But how could I say no?

> **ME**
> Sounds great.

october 31st

It's official. I am a New Woman. That's right. Comfortably in my second trimester, with morning sickness just an ugly memory staining some of my best shoes, I am exactly what

Chapter Five of *BH, BN* said I would be: energetic, happy, renewed. I feel like my old self again, only without a waist.

In fact, I feel so fabulous that I even agreed to join Stephen at Mitch and Larry's Halloween party – an annual event that brings out the worst in both of them. To prove this point, Larry and Mitch went as the Reese twins. They spent the entire evening inviting people to touch their boobs. I declined the offer.

Stephen showed his true computer-geek colors by dressing up like Bill Gates. It was that or Steve Jobs, and *nobody*'s nerdy enough to get that one. Capitalizing on my newfound curves, I went as a belly dancer.

If you've got it, flaunt it.

november 1st

Upon my insistence, Stephen ducked out of work to join me at my Crotch Whisperer appointment. Today was the structural ultrasound – a test designed to check the baby's head, heart, and spine. And as the baby's father, wouldn't he want to verify that his kid's got a head?

Turns out it wasn't the head he was interested in. Halfway through the ultrasound we caught sight of a huge sticklike object. Stephen went wild. "That's my boy!"

The Whisperer shook his head and apologetically held up his arm. Stephen sheepishly shrugged, realizing that instead of a penis the size of a garden hose he'd merely glimpsed a limb.

I was furious. Hadn't Stephen said he didn't care about the sex as long as the baby was healthy? Well, maybe guys consider a penis the size of a garden hose to be the ultimate sign of well-being, but I don't. As far as I was concerned Stephen's true desires had finally been exposed:

No matter how much he claims otherwise, he clearly wants a *boy*.

Fine. Well, guess what? I want a *girl*, but that doesn't mean I'm gonna act like a lottery winner if I spot a vagina floating around on the next ultrasound. And I'm certainly NOT going to admit it to anyone.

On the way out of the office, the nurse held up our chart and grinned. "Sure you don't want to know the sex?" Before he could open his mouth I grabbed Stephen's jacket and yanked him into the hallway.

Don't even *think* about it.

november 2nd

Chapter Five of *BH, BN*, and #35 on my Things to Do list, suggests that parents-to-be decide upon a legal guardian for their yet-to-be-born child. Someone to care for our child in the event that we're killed, incapacitated, or imprisoned for some unforeseen reason. A quick assessment of our choices – my parents, Stephen's parents, our siblings – prompted us to decide unanimously to talk about it some other time.

november 3rd

Anita's mole over at *Focus* has confirmed that despite recent financial difficulties the company has reopened its search for a new writer, and that among the front-runners is a Brinkman/Baines employee!

I spoke with Lucy last night. And although I completely forgot to tell her about Stephen's mystical sighting of the ten-foot penis, I did remember to tell her about Gram's latest act of goodwill – the harassing of Nicole to hurry up and vacate our apartment.

Once again, Lucy was stunned by Gram's behavior. After musing that perhaps it's because she'll now officially have the title "great" in front of her name, we decided to accept Gram's actions at face value.

Although it was the face of a woman we'd never seen before.

Meanwhile, Lucy has finally moved and is really enjoying her new home. In addition to having better food, nicer grounds, and TiVo, the Society of Advanced Living has a diverse and interesting group of residents. Everyone from a onetime football star to a retired Rockette. In fact, Lucy's even found a beau: Emmet. A widower from Maine, Emmet's a former fisherman who shares Lucy's love for the arts and fried clams. Who could ask for more?

Seconds after hanging up with Lucy the phone rang again. It was Mandy wondering if I wanted to join her tomorrow at Saks for a designer shoe sale.

> ME
> Can't. I'm going to the sperm bank with
> Anita.

> MANDY
> This is criminal. That woman shouldn't
> be a mother. Isn't there a screening process
> to become a parent?

ME
Only if you want someone else's child.

MANDY
That's insane. It's easier than getting a handgun.

ME
Personally, I find that comforting. Now, do you honestly think Anita's unfit to be a parent?

MANDY
Honestly? I think that parents should be two mature and well-grounded people. Of which she's not even one.

I was suddenly overwhelmed with anxiety. Forget Anita. I'm not sure Stephen and I fit that bill, either.

november 6th

Today was our trip to the sperm bank – an experience which I was completely unprepared for. Trust me, there is not a single reference to sperm banks in *BH, BN*.

On the way there, I was so uncomfortable that I didn't know what to say. I had absolutely nothing intelligent to share about the purchase of bodily fluids. So I shared what I did know. "Do yourself a favor. Once you're pregnant, find a gynecologist who speaks really loudly."

Anita laughed. "Sounds like the setup for a good dirty joke."

Yeah. Too bad the joke's on me.

Destiny Labs was not at all what I expected. For some reason I assumed we'd end up in a dingy room, in the back of a crumbling midtown office building, rummaging through a collection of sealed test tubes while wearing double-thick rubber gloves and face masks. An hour later we'd emerge onto the street with a brown paper bag, a wet-nap, and an instruction sheet.

Luckily, despite my faltering grip on rational thought, Anita exhibited nothing but grace and nerves of steel.

Of course, she's already been involved in this process for several months. She's chosen Destiny Labs and has had her initial interview, physical examination, and financial review. So when we arrived in the lobby she felt right at home. Which is amazing, considering how very clinical the atmosphere was. White granite tables, taut leather sofas, and a selection of magazines covering everything from race cars to spa vacations.[58] But the worst part was the air-conditioning. It was so damn cold *I* felt like a sample being chilled.

But I said nothing and kept smiling. Because this was not about me. No. This was about Anita, and as her best friend I was there to support her choices and to offer encouragement. No matter how freaked out I was.

After a frosty ten-minute wait, an attractive lab assistant in her mid-twenties wearing a tidy pantsuit and a big smile led us to a private room filled with "donor binders." Each donor binder contained an anonymous information sheet describing a donor and his vital stats – coloring, education, hobbies, etc. Encouraging us to sit and relax, the lab assistant quietly left the room.

---

[58] Who exactly is their clientele?

160

And for the next hour Anita and I searched for the father of her child. The donors were endless, and some of their descriptions were hysterical: Tall Jewish man with hearty appetite and degree in nuclear physics. Accomplished cellist with red hair and large member. Yeah, right. I immediately questioned the accuracy of these profiles. Did the guys fill them out themselves? Was there any fact-checking involved? Had anyone actually seen that man's member?

Because really, what would motivate an accomplished cellist with a huge schlong to donate sperm? A desire to populate the world? Doubtful. Try a couple thousand dollars a shot. True, they could be using the money to pay for graduate school. Or they could be using it to finance a drug cartel. Who the hell knew?

Yet Anita seemed unconcerned. The lab did medical screening on every donor, so they were guaranteed to be healthy and free from disease. Beyond that she wanted good-looking and tall. Everything else she figured she could supply either genetically or environmentally. But how to ensure the donor was good-looking?

Luckily Anita hit upon the perfect way – ask the lab's female employees. After all, those gals personally met everyone who came into the office. Donors *and* clients. So we immediately summoned our lab assistant and three of her colleagues into our room and posed the big question: Who's the hottest guy they'd ever seen walk through their doors?

The women dissolved into giggles. The vote was split – #68 and #119, depending if you preferred blonds or brunettes. Clearly they'd had this discussion before. A fan of blonds *and* brunettes, Anita took copies of both profiles and decided to think it over for a while.

A decision I support wholeheartedly.

As we were leaving the lab, one of the assistants pointed to my stomach and said, "You're gonna have a girl." I was shocked. Not only could she tell I was pregnant but she could predict the sex? I quickly asked if it was a *sense* she got.

"Oh, no. I can tell by the way you're carrying. High and narrow. Classic girl."

november 7th

Clearly I've begun to show, because a complete stranger stopped me in the grocery store this afternoon to say I'm going to have a boy. How could he tell?

"It's the way you're carrying. High and narrow. Very boy."

I might as well get a Ouija board.

november 7th – 9:30 p.m.

Stephen swears I barely look pregnant. And yet I've come to realize that every time he discusses my appearance he sweetly pats my belly and peppers his sentences with heavy doses of "fabulous" and "beautiful."

Coward.

Eager for an honest assessment of my appearance, I called the one person who would be candid without a hint of fear or a streak of sarcasm. Nicole.

"Well, I suppose the totally ignorant might think you've gotten really fat, but you've been looking preggers to the rest of us for at least a month."

What?
"Maybe longer."
Shit!

november 8th

With a more realistic understanding of my appearance, I've stepped up my efforts to conceal my pregnancy with outfits featuring large prints and multiple layers. And yet no matter how hard I work to hide this baby I can't hide from the fact that I still haven't chosen its name. It seems the larger my stomach gets, the smaller our name pool becomes.

The latest to go the way of the dodo was my suggestion of Sebastian. Stephen says it sounds like a bisexual male prostitute. Eager to help, Eddie has given me a name book – *9,999 Names for Your Baby*.

Apparently my search has only just begun.

november 9th

I felt gassy all day long. But a strange gas. The kind that circles your intestines but never comes out. Instead it was *flutter-flutter-flutter* every few hours. That's when I realized it wasn't gas, or the burrito I ventured to have last night.

It was the baby. *Moving.*

Something was roaming around my belly, maybe even tapping its foot or snapping its fingers.

I was fascinated. And a little freaked out.

Mr. Nealy's secretary called to schedule an appointment for first thing tomorrow morning. A sudden, early-morning meeting without an apparent agenda.

I AM GOING TO BE FIRED.

They're firing the alcoholic party animal who they've finally noticed is pregnant!

Only I *can't* be fired now. I need the salary. The health insurance. The paid leave. Not to mention the fact that I just spent two hundred dollars on a collection of loose-fitting clothing with garishly large prints to mask my bulging stomach!

Panic-stricken, I left work early and went to Stephen's office. After ten minutes of listening to me rant hysterically, Stephen handed me a box of tissues and told me to sit down. He said I was overreacting. Mr. Nealy probably wanted to discuss some urgent Reese twins business – maybe there'd been a recall on silicone implants?

In any event I was being irrational, no doubt ruled by my overactive pregnancy hormones. After all, doesn't *BH, BN* mention that hormonal changes during pregnancy can lead to unexplained emotional outbursts?

Well, yes, *BH, BN* does say that.[59] But how would *he* know? Had he secretly been reading the very book at which he was so quick to scoff?

But before I could confront him, I noticed something awful: Although he kept insisting that I was overreacting, and that Mr. Nealy was not going to fire me, Stephen was *doggedly* picking at an ingrown hair on his cheek. It was not

---

[59] Chapter Three.

a dermatologically approved action or an O.C.D.-related gesture. Oh, no. These were the rabid strokes of a man anxiously calculating how to support a family on one middling salary. It was a physical gesture that belied a psychological state – TERROR.

At this rate he'd hit bone within the hour.

So I began to wail because if Stephen, the infinitely more clearheaded of us, was worried, then we were definitely SCREWED.

november 10th – 11:50 p.m.

I've been up all night wondering how we're going to pay the rent, the doctor, and the hospital all on one salary.

And adding insult to injury . . .

I think my low-rise stretch jeans have finally hit maximum capacity.

november 11th

Brinkman/Baines's biggest client, sitcom star Tangy Blair – a multiple Golden Globe nominee whose P.R. needs Mr. Nealy personally handles himself – has just finished writing a book and is about to embark on a promotional tour. Brinkman/Baines needs someone who can keep up with a wild television star to ensure that the book promotion is a grand success. In short, they need a major swinger.

And who better than the bloated alcoholic writer with a penchant to party?

Yeee-haa!!!!

It's like a promotion, only without the raise. The title. Or the fourth wall to my cubicle! And sure, the fact that Mr. Nealy still hasn't noticed my pregnancy proves his complete disinterest in me as a human being. But it doesn't matter. This is my opportunity to shine. If I can make a high-profile assignment like this book promotion a success, then I'll be a shoo-in for that job at *Focus*.

After sharing the good news with Stephen, I immediately convened a meeting of the minds at Frutto di Sole. Both Anita and Mandy were tickled by my assignment, a mix of amusement and curiosity spurring their delight. And together we spent the next hour theorizing about what an airhead like Tangy Blair could possibly write.

Mandy's convinced it's a tell-all book about her sex-capades with other good-looking sitcom stars, while Anita senses it's a stab at fiction. Perhaps the fictional account of a popular sitcom star who writes a book. Either way, it's a huge opportunity for me that deserved to be celebrated in style. So we did.

With two pieces of ricotta cheesecake and a dish of tiramisu.

Buoyed by a new lease on my professional life, and a serious sugar-induced high, I reviewed Eddie's name book on the way home. With almost ten thousand names, it's got to have something Stephen and I both like. Unfortunately, in addition to offering names the book also offers definitions for those names.

And now that I know Cameron means "crooked nose," it seems a lot less attractive.

november 12th

Tangy Blair is flying in from Los Angeles a few days after Thanksgiving to discuss the promotion of her book. I can't wait. I'll definitely have to buy some cool clothes. After all, I want to seem hip and NOT pregnant. At least until she gets to know and trust me professionally. And while I'd *never* admit it, there's something a bit thrilling about working with a big TV star. Hanging out together. Hearing tales from the velveteen trenches. Even if she is outrageously insipid. Which she is. But it doesn't matter. Because unlike the lame Gen-Y lusting for celebrities that goes on among the Junior Account Managers, mine is a more refined, *sophisticated* fascination with the "power" of celebrity.

After all, Tangy's made the cover of *People* magazine FOUR times.

november 15th

I was in the theater district early this evening to check out a small mom-and-pop baby store that Eddie told me about. Unfortunately, they were closed for inventory. As I made my way back to the subway, cursing myself for not calling ahead, I ran into Mandy and her mother on their way to a pre-theater dinner.

Mandy's mother, Mrs. Irene Alexander of Westchester County, is charming yet tough as perfectly lacquered nails. Set in her ways – which include a pearl choker and an Hermès handbag – she's always been very polite to me. Although I know for a fact that she thinks I'm a bad influence on Mandy. But for the record, Mandy was a total nympho long before she met me at college.

Mrs. Alexander was mid-sentence, something about the renaissance of Broadway theater, when her laser vision caught sight of my slightly bulbous belly. She immediately stiffened. "Amy, dear, you're pregnant."

I looked at Mandy. She was sheet white. A chill went up my spine. "Um, yes. Actually, I am."

Mrs. Alexander glared at Mandy. "I had no idea." Then, gently kissing my check, she said, "Your *mother* must be thrilled." It was so pointed a comment that it could have drawn blood.

The phrase "Like mother, like daughter" was never more appropriate than with Mrs. Alexander and Mandy. Except when it comes to the issue of children. With this in mind I began my good-byes, eager not to become collateral damage in the duel that was bound to ensue. Unfortunately, not even the shock of my pregnancy could shake Mrs. Alexander from her adherence to etiquette, and seconds later she was graciously inviting me to join them for dinner at Joe Allen's.

I was all set to decline until I saw the pleading look in Mandy's eyes. Clearly this bad situation was destined to get worse the minute she and her mother were alone. So I accepted Mrs. Alexander's offer, knowing full well that I would be the evening's human buffer.

Foolish me. I'd forgotten that people like the Alexanders – well-heeled, old money, with conservative values and repressed feelings – never actually fight. Especially in public. They merely spar while passing the pâté with a smile.

During the appetizer course, Mrs. Alexander visited the topic of Jon's infertility. She was so pleased that her ten thousand dollars had enabled him to resolve his problem with a specialist. My mind flashed back to Mandy's trip to

Canyon Ranch and the five pounds she had lost on their spa meals.

Then Mrs. Alexander mentioned how lovely it would be if Mandy and I had children the same age. They could have play dates at the Central Park Zoo. To that end she suggested that Mandy look into her own ability to conceive. After all, there must be some explanation for why she had yet to have a child. "Perhaps it was all that cheap hair dye you used – against my wishes – in college. Maybe it had a negative effect on your reproductive organs."

Mandy tossed back her Pinot Noir. "It wasn't hair dye, Mother. It was lemon juice."

"Then perhaps you've soured your ovaries."

Yikes! I closed my eyes, clicked my heels three times, and wished I weren't there. Too bad I was. Desperate to help Mandy, I tried to change the subject.

"This blackened salmon is delicious, Mrs. Alexander. May I offer you a taste?"

A strained smile spread across her face. "No, dear. The sodium causes me to flush, and by the way, Mandy, your cousin Whitney just had twins, and she's only twenty-three."

"She's also completely without ambition."

"In my day we applauded that."

And so it was, until the moment I left them outside the theater. The production they were about to see? *'Night, Mother.*

Good luck.

november 16th

After yet another humiliating moment in a quiet public

venue, I'm forced to make a new addition to my ever-growing list.

Things No One Tells You About Pregnancy
1. No sushi
2. Twenty-four-hour morning sickness
3. Forty weeks (ten months) of pregnancy
4. No aspirin
5. Dog nose
6. "Glow" is sweat
7. Excessive flatulence

That's right, slap a propeller on my ass and I can fly myself to work.

november 17th

I opened the day's mail to find a large manila envelope from my father. Inside, carefully protected by thick sheets of cardboard, was an illustration of the infamous crib that he's decided to build for our baby. It was accompanied by a note that read, "Suitable for framing." Subtle. But how can I complain? I can't. Because in addition to being part of his healing process, this is clearly an act of love. Every man should welcome the arrival of his first grandchild with such enthusiasm.

If only his enthusiasm were childproof. Because this crib is NOT. First off, it looks closer to a cage for a wildebeest than a sanctuary for peaceful slumber. It's got tons of bars at various distances and heights, simultaneously creating a sense of whimsy and multiple opportunities for strangulation.

Secondly, it's *triangular*. Both an attempt at originality and a space-saving solution for a small bedroom. Which is a nice thought, but highly impractical. After all, how many stores do you know that sell *triangular mattresses*? Or sheets? Or blankets?

None. Which means for all the money we'll be saving on the crib, we'll be spending twice as much on custom bedding. How grand.

november 18th

We've got less than five months to our birth date but over fifty outstanding items on our Things to Do list. At this rate we'll be having our nameless baby on the living room floor, alongside our deathtrap of a triangular crib.

But what can I do? Sure, I've decided to breast-feed, which knocks another item off the list, but there are plenty more to go. And now, more than ever, I'll be unable to research the various baby products because I'll be swamped with work as I struggle to solidify my professional future by dedicating my life to kissing Tangy Blair's perfectly buff-puffed ass. So where does this leave me? I'll tell you where:

In need of a husband who participates.

What a sucker I was to make that pact with him about not starting the baby's room until Nicole finds an apartment. This is Manhattan, for Christ's sake. Our kid could be in *college* before Nicole finds something she can afford.

And don't get me started on Stephen's "exciting" new computer project. He's averaging sixty-hour workweeks on that crazy program, which will enable medical institutions to better communicate with each other. Well, how about communicating with your wife? Sure, this computer program could be a huge boon to our lives *if* it's successful. But that could take *eons*!

Things to Do
1. Find ob/gyn
2. Get prenatal checkup
3. Get prenatal vitamins
4. Find physical exercise
5. Decide childbirth method
6. Join childbirth class
7. Buy crib
8. Buy bassinet
9. Buy crib mattress (doesn't come with!)
10. Buy crib bedding
11. Buy changing table
12. Decide cloth or disposable diapers
13. Buy diapers
14. Buy diaper bag
15. Buy diaper pail
16. Buy crib mobile
17. Buy layette
18. Buy stroller
19. Buy infant bathtub
20. Buy baby monitor
21. Buy infant swing
22. Buy night-light for baby's room
23. Choose color for baby's room
24. Paint baby's room
25. Buy pacifiers
26. Buy dresser for baby's clothes
27. Buy infant-size hangers

28. Create medical emergency kit

29. Prepare emergency phone lists

30. ~~Decide nursing or formula~~

31. Buy nursing supplies or formula supplies

32. If nursing, decide to rent or buy breast pump

33. If nursing, buy nursing bras

34. If nursing, buy nipple cream

35. Decide on legal guardian

36. Prepare wills

37. Plan estate

38. Create college fund

39. Begin Kegel exercises

40. Buy first-year memorabilia scrapbook

41. ~~Decide whether to learn gender~~

42. Choose name(s)

43. ~~Choose hospital~~

44. Take tour of hospital maternity ward

45. Find pediatrician

46. Appoint someone to organize baby shower

47. Make invite list for baby shower

48. Register for baby shower

49. Buy thank-you notes for baby shower

50. Select birth music

51. ~~Prepare for appropriate religious ceremony~~

52. ~~Book venue for religious ceremony~~

53. ~~Arrange for priest, rabbi, or *mohel*, etc.~~

54. ~~Buy baby's outfit for religious ceremony~~

55. Buy maternity clothes
56. ~~Decide who will be in delivery room with you~~
57. Prepare baby announcements
58. Prepare overnight bag for hospital
59. Make birth plan
60. Schedule maternity leave
61. Make phone list for announcing baby's birth
62. Buy baby's take-home-from-hospital outfit
63. Decide on postbirth child care

november 19th

Margo called this evening to cancel our date tomorrow, a date I've been counting on for over a month. Seems she forgot about her second son's preschool presentation of *A Pilgrim's Story*. He's the turkey. The fact that he's destined to be slaughtered didn't seem to bother her. Vowing to reschedule as soon as possible, she raced off the phone to stop her daughter from sticking a fork into the toaster oven.

november 20th

Never having been a smoker, beer guzzler, or consumer of mass quantities of microwave burritos, I had no idea what that burning sensation was in the back of my throat. But when night after night of waking up with it evolved into day after day, I turned to *BH, BN* and made the shocking discovery.

> Things No One Tells You About Pregnancy
> 1. No sushi
> 2. Twenty-four-hour morning sickness
> 3. Forty weeks (ten months) of pregnancy
> 4. No aspirin
> 5. Dog nose
> 6. "Glow" is sweat
> 7. Excessive flatulence
> 8. Heartburn

Seems heartburn doesn't actually come from your heart. It comes from your gastrointestinal juices being forced up your esophagus. Yum. And it's a common phenomenon during pregnancy, when a growing baby starts pushing upward.

While pleased to have a medical explanation, it still feels like I'm breathing fire. *BH, BN* suggests eating ice cream or Tums to coat your throat. Naturally I chose ice cream. Unfortunately the dairy content pushed my excessive flatulence to its limits, so I've settled on a jumbo bottle of Tums.

november 21st

Today at Balanced Breathing, Pippa spent forty minutes discussing natural childbirth.

My first reaction was that Pippa had been sniffing way too much lavender oil. After all, natural childbirth is basically labor without pain medication. That means you feel *everything*. And while I've never been through labor, I do have vivid memories of those grisly childbirth films from health class. I swear those movies are made by sadists. The woman, spread-eagled on a bed, screaming her lungs out for *hours and hours* until finally some doctor fully covered in protective surgical garb pulls a slimy screaming newborn from her crotch. Watching those was worse than dissecting frogs in biology class.[60]

But after listening to Pippa extol the virtues of a medication-free birth – both for the baby and the mother – I decided to seriously consider it. It sounded so . . . responsible. A more cognizant experience for the mother, a less drowsy newborn. Sure, it wasn't the most common method of childbirth in this country, but that doesn't make it inferior. In fact, if you keep your ear to the ground and listen to Pippa and her band of navel-ring beauties, you'll hear that natural childbirth is actually superior – having been the method of choice for thousands of years until multinational drug companies made prostitutes of the medical industry and the whole bunch decided to make a few bucks at the expense of women and their children.

Curious, I turned to *BH, BN*, which offered only a few paragraphs on the topic, basically stating what I already knew – that natural childbirth was a viable option, yet not the one promoted by *BH, BN*. But a review of my Things to Do list reminded me that deciding my type of childbirth was, in fact, #5. So I decided to discuss it with Stephen, who was working late at the office.

I could hear his concern loud and clear over the phone. "I

---

[60] In fact, if we're really serious about curtailing teen pregnancy in this country, all we need to do is show a few of these birth videos to our girls. Trust me, no pickup line is smooth enough to wipe THOSE images from your mind.

have to admit you've never struck me as the natural child-birth type."

"What's that supposed to mean?"

"Just that I have this image of you being wheeled down a hospital corridor threatening orderlies for more pain medication."

"Based on what?"

"Based on the time you threatened to poke my eye out with a butter knife if I didn't let you have the last Alka-Seltzer."

Shoot, I'd forgotten about that.

But never mind. Determined not to be shamed by personal history, or to be manipulated by big business and cultural "norms," I vowed to consider the topic further.

november 22nd

Margo called to reschedule our date.

To *January 24th*.

november 23rd

With the long Thanksgiving weekend upon us, I assumed that Stephen and I would finally get around to tackling our Things to Do list. Unfortunately, Stephen had other plans.

Citing nostalgia, general interest, and his long hours spent in a cramped office, he decided that this year he'd spend the evening before Thanksgiving watching the parade balloons being inflated outside the Museum of Natural History.

Sounds like a nice, wholesome event, doesn't it? Guess again.

It's an activity predominantly pursued by college students. Which makes Stephen more than a decade too old. Hordes of college kids on school break meet up at the floats and drink beer after beer from brown paper bags, then barf in the gutter while Kermit the Frog gets hot air pumped up his butt.

Making the scene even more unattractive is the fact that Larry and Mitch will be there. Larry because beer's involved. And Mitch because he'll be trolling for drunken college girls who have lower mating standards than those who have already earned their degrees. He hopes.

Which means that I definitely won't be in attendance. And when I told Stephen that I thought our time would be better spent deciding on a childbirth plan, researching the benefits of cloth diapers, or perhaps choosing a *name* for our future child, he gave me a quick hug and told me not to stress. That we had plenty of time, and besides, once the baby was here, we wouldn't have the option to do things like this.

Yeah, I'll really miss stepping in other people's puke.

But what could I say? He really wanted to go and I really didn't want to be a nag. So I waved him good-bye and told him to enjoy himself. But he clearly felt guilty.[61] So as he put on his coat he attempted to appease me by offering the "perfect" baby name: Taylor.

> ME
> Why is that perfect?

---

[61] As well he should.

STEPHEN
Because it works for a boy *and* a girl.

Talk about lazy! It'd be different if he really liked the name Taylor. If he showed some real passion for it. But all he showed was the relief that comes with convenience. It's one thing not to assist in selecting your child's layette, but to cut corners on selecting the kid's name? That's the depth of bad parenting. Besides, life's hard enough without having to navigate it with a sexually ambiguous name. Not to mention the fact that Taylor sounds like a job description. So I decided right then and there to take matters into my own hands.

ME
No.

november 24th

Today was Thanksgiving. We spent it with Stephen's family, since they'll be scattered across the country for Christmas.

Following the routine we've established over the past few years, we had dinner with Mrs. Stewart because she's an amazing cook, then we went across town to have dessert with Mr. Stewart because even a man can go to the store and buy a pie. Except this year the routine had a new twist – Mrs. Stewart invited her latest paramour, Roger.

Apparently, this one is serious. So much so that Mrs. Stewart has stopped "playing the field." Reason enough for Stephen to like him. But there are more reasons. Not the least of which is that Roger's a charming and friendly man who is unlike Mr. Stewart in every possible way.

While Mr. Stewart is an armchair golfer who likes to overeat and owns an extremely successful electrical repair company, Roger is a skinny fabric importer specializing in Asian silks. He's trilingual (English, French, and a pinch of Hindi). And he's not part of the country club set. Which is ironic, since Mrs. Stewart seemed determined to work her way through the membership roster. Preferring long walks to golf, Roger met Mrs. Stewart through a mutual business acquaintance. And judging by the way they interact, it's clear that the two are deeply enamored.

There's only one problem. He's *not* a dog person.

Something which was immediately evident from the way he cringed when learning that the fifth table setting was not for Stephen's sister Kim or his brother Tom – both of whom were spending the holiday with their father – but instead was for Chuffy.

After all this time Stephen and I have grown accustomed to Mrs. Stewart's odd relationship with Chuffy. At times we don't even flinch when she hot-oils Chuffy's coat or flosses Chuffy's teeth. So we forget that to most normal, two-legged creatures, Mrs. Stewart's affection for Chuffy borders on the *unnatural*.

But to his credit, Roger chose to hold his tongue, and look away, as Chuffy ate off Mrs. Stewart's plate and drank from a crystal water glass. He even went so far as to offer Chuffy seconds on stuffing.

Chuffy declined.

And yet despite this uneasy interspecies gathering, the evening was very enjoyable. Mrs. Stewart had outdone herself with the food, and Roger is an excellent conversationalist, able to recount his numerous trips to the Far East with fascinating detail and humor. But the good times came to a screeching halt when Roger offered me some wine.

Reminding him that I was pregnant, I politely declined. At which point Mrs. Stewart sprang up from her chair, babbling about the double-boiler full of gravy that was sitting on the stovetop and wouldn't I be a doll and go get it? Confused, but unwilling to appear ungracious, I readily agreed. But not before Roger congratulated me on the pregnancy and announced that this was the first he'd heard about it. A comment that caused Mrs. Stewart to release a strange, almost hysterical laugh before launching into a story about how when Chuffy was a puppy she ate nothing but pudding.

Roger seemed amused. "A puppy eating pudding." However, Stephen and I weren't falling for the pudding ploy. Looking at Stephen, I could tell he was equally horrified that his mother would go to such lengths to conceal the fact that we were going to have a child. Sure, she'd asked us not to mention it to anyone. But that was months ago. Since then we'd hoped that she'd made peace with the idea of becoming a grandmother. Apparently not. If anything, her resolve to keep our pregnancy a secret appeared to have grown stronger. Her desire to appear "hot" clearly outweighed her joy at having a grandchild.

But what could we say? Nothing. So we quietly ate our meal, then begged off as soon as possible to visit Stephen's father – leaving Mrs. Stewart, Roger, and Chuffy to enjoy their dessert in front of the fireplace.

Thirty minutes later we were sitting at Mr. Stewart's fold-out dining table with him, Misty, Tom, and Kimberly. A motley crew at best.

Over pecan pie and whipped cream, Tom told tales of his latest job promotion at Xerox, which included a hefty pay raise and a "foxy" new secretary. Which caused me to wonder two things: First, what could Tom possibly do so well to deserve a paycheck, not to mention a promotion? And second, how stupid were the folks at Xerox to give a lech like Tom a female secretary? The guy is a sexual harassment suit just waiting to happen. It was with this in mind that I repeatedly dodged his attempts to rub my belly. In addition to crossing all sorts of personal boundaries, there were sanitary issues to consider –

Lord knows where that hand's been. *Ick*.

When the pecan pie was done and Tom had sucked the last bit of whipped cream out of the can, I helped Misty clear the dishes into the kitchen. Anything to get away from Tom's tales and Kim's pouty expressions – she'd been hoping for pumpkin pie instead of pecan.

While loading the dishwasher, Misty asked me the usual questions about the pregnancy: How was it going? How was I feeling? But this time there was something sad about her inquiries. A sense of longing in her voice. So as nonchalantly as possible, I asked if she ever thought about having kids. She smiled and shook her head, explaining that while she and Mr. Stewart might someday decide to marry, three was more than enough children for him. At sixty-two, his daddy days were over. Chuckling, she said that Stephen, Tom, and Kimberly would be her only kids. It was an attempt at levity but it felt incredibly sad. Like saying you'd always wanted to be a dancer but instead you fix toe shoes.

It's amazing what people will give up for love.

Afterward, when the dishes were cleared and we were all in food comas, we sank like lead weights onto the overstuffed furniture to watch a movie. Tonight's video? *Rosemary's Baby*. Courtesy of my sweet sister-in-law Kimberly.

Trust me, it's the last movie a pregnant woman should see. Unless, of course, you'd enjoy giving birth to the spawn of Satan.

On an up-note, I did spark to Mia Farrow's cool hairdo. Short, sassy, and extremely easy to manage. Hmmm . . .

november 25th

Anita called to tell me that she's going brunette, and has chosen donor #119 to father her child. As a Christmas present to herself she's going for the implantation next week.

I quickly thought back to how important Anita's support for my pregnancy has been, and how disappointing Mandy's lack of support continues to be. And not wanting to be Anita's Mandy, I did what I thought was right.

No, I didn't scream "gross!" Or mention that for all she knew #119 was in fact #68, and who the hell knew who that was, anyway? And hadn't she heard of the sperm clinic where the guy running it had donated ALL of the samples. Sure, he must have had a lot of time and energy, and probably a few calluses after the ordeal was through. . . .

But no, I couldn't say any of this. So I simply volunteered to go with her. And prayed she'd decline the offer.

Unfortunately, she accepted.

november 26th

I finally found out what a Kegel exercise is: It's basically squeezing the muscle that stops your pee. Which is great, because aside from its being easy, you can do it anywhere.

How funny. I've spent months avoiding #39 on my Things to Do list because I thought it involved going to the gym. Turns out I can do it anywhere. On the bus, during staff meetings, even at the bank!

november 27th

This afternoon, Tangy Blair's publishers are messengering me an advance copy of her book. That gives me twenty-four hours to read it and prepare a basic promotion strategy before our lunch meeting tomorrow. No problem. Tangy's famous. Little girls want to be her and big boys want to do her. This book is going to fly off the shelves of every bookstore in the country, thus ensuring that Tangy is delighted and that I look like a superstar. Trust me, after finding steady employment for the Reese twins, positioning Abe Hamen's citrus-scented massage oils as a "must-have" for the holistic set, and helping Representative Blanca Fernandez to keep her job despite a tendency toward ugly public outbursts,[62] selling Tangy's book will be a breeze.

That's right, this vapid starlet is going to put my career back on track.

After all, how hard can it be to promote a crappy star book?

november 28th – 12:30 a.m.

VERY HARD.

No wonder Mr. Nealy passed this assignment on to me.

---

[62] Remember the excrement-tossing gorilla?

It's a professional Waterloo, and I'm its knocked-up Napoleon!

Turns out that Tangy Blair is an articulate, passionate woman – albeit horribly misguided. Far from a crummy novel, *The Damned* is part political treatise, part personal rant about how society scorns people who choose not to procreate and then burdens them with other people's children via social pressures, workplace disparities, and taxation. In short, the only thing Tangy dislikes more than kids is the people who have them.

Trust me, she makes Mandy look like Mother Goose.

Sure, at a mere 120 pages it might aptly – on every level – be retitled *An* Incredibly *Modest Proposal*, but it doesn't matter. Regardless of how I approach this situation it's BAD. First off, forget Mr. Nealy. There's no way *Tangy* can know I'm pregnant. That would be the most expedient way for me to lose this assignment. That means I'll have to hide my pregnancy until I'm indispensable to the job.

Given my bulbous profile, I'll have to work quickly.

Second, there is no way a nonfiction treatise on the suffering of childless people at the hands of "spawners" will ever hit the best-seller list. Especially since the closest the author's gotten to being an academician or social scientist is playing one on TV. And honestly I don't think Tangy's even done that. Her current sitcom role is that of a fashion designer whose roommate is a monkey. Literally. Which means that we'll be lucky to get a handful of reviews and a smattering of interviews on the less popular news shows. Because no matter how famous Tangy Blair is, there's nothing the public likes less than an overindulged sitcom star acting like she knows something. Show us how to style our hair or where to get a cute handbag, but don't tell us how to lead our lives or cast our votes.

Save *that* for the dramatic actors.

november 28th

Getting dressed this morning was like preparing for a covert military operation. Tossing aside all the trendy clothes that I'd purchased for my meeting with Tangy, I went in search of the baggiest sweater in my closet. I then tossed an oversized, "decorative" scarf around my neck in hopes of drawing attention from my midsection to my face. To cap off the ensemble, I dug out the chunkiest earrings I could find from my collection of 1980s jewelry. It was the Go-Go's all over again. But I was desperate. The best chance I had of making my belly appear smaller was to increase the scale of the surrounding items. It was all about relativity. And if I hadn't been so vain, I would have teased my hair.

The bottom line: If I was lucky, Tangy would assume that far from being pregnant I'm simply a fat chick without a shred of fashion sense.

Unfortunately, my choice of clothing had little impact on the rest of my day.

I immediately got off to a bad start by showing up ten minutes early to our lunch date. Too bad I was at the wrong restaurant. Mona Lisa didn't have a reservation for Blair, despite the fact that I was certain I'd made one.

I quickly called Eddie at the office and asked him to look on my computer calendar. And yes, there was my one P.M. lunch meeting with Tangy Blair – all the way across town at a lovely Greek restaurant called Paros. Desperate, I ran into midday traffic knowing full well that I'd never find a taxi and wishing for the first time that I actually looked pregnant so that someone, *anyone,* might take pity on me and offer up their cab. No such luck. As it turns out, fat, desperate, and tacky do little to attract goodwill.

So I began to run – bogged down by a winter coat, a baggy sweater, an enormous "decorative" scarf, and earrings the size of tambourines – across five avenues and up ten blocks. I haven't run so much since taking the Presidential Fitness Challenge in junior high.

How I could have been so absentminded as to show up at the wrong restaurant I'll never know. I briefly flashed back to Stephen's story of the shrinking brain. But there was no time to mull. By the time I arrived at Paros, Tangy Blair was seated at the bar impatiently tapping her stiletto heel and glancing at her Gucci watch. Introducing myself, I apologized profusely and suggested we take our table. Not so easy. After rejecting our original table, Tangy demanded a window seat and had the waiter adjust the overhead light to give her a more flattering shadow.

Minutes later she was chastising "spawners" for egocentrism while blowing air-kisses to all the businessmen[63] who ogled her from the sidewalk. Thus ensuring that any chance I might have to disclose my pregnancy and chuckle with Tangy over the irony of the situation disappeared before we even saw menus.

When the menus did arrive, Tangy ordered a Greek salad with extra cucumber, no olives, and a low-fat dressing on the side. Unfortunately for me she kept the feta cheese, which was so pungent and stinky that my dog nose could

---

[63] Delivery men, garbage men . . . even men who love men.

smell it before it ever left the kitchen. But unable to complain, I kept smiling and nodding my head as she spewed her antichild rhetoric. Desperate to fend off dog nose and avoid puking over her delightful entrée, I spent the entire meal with my left hand draped across the lower part of my face. She probably thought I had a tick or was hiding a zit, but anything was better than revealing myself as one of *them*.

The closest we got to the topic of me and *them* was when Tangy asked if I had kids. I immediately said no. And technically, I was telling the truth. I don't have a child. Just something that according to the Crotch Whisperer's measurements is currently half an inch long and necessitates an increased intake of folic acid. God bless semantics.

In an effort to familiarize me with her beliefs, as if reading her stupid dopus-opus hadn't already done that, Tangy took it upon herself to explain why she's so disgusted with parents. "I'm tired of having baby strollers run over my toes at Bergdorf's. Of paying thirty percent of my salary in taxes to fund a public school system that is of no use to me. And of paying a small fortune for a duplex apartment in Soho only to listen to the hyperactive brat in the co-op upstairs jumping on his parents' bed thirty thousand times a day. And it's not just New York. Even in L.A. it's near impossible to find a decent estate that doesn't have a bunch of Barney-obsessed cretins living next door. And *that's* the parents."

Trying to appear sympathetic, I listened intently to everything Tangy said. But it was no use. No matter how hard I tried to sympathize, or how valid I felt some of her points may be, I couldn't help but feel she was a total moron. Perhaps if she were better educated or more contemplative, her arguments would be more persuasive. But as it was, her complaints were ultimately narrow-minded and shortsighted.

Sure, being run over by a stroller is no fun. And certainly no one enjoys a noisy kid. But one of those hyperactive brats whose public school education her taxes are helping to fund may someday be her cardiologist, or, more likely in Tangy's case, her plastic surgeon, called upon to help lift her eyes or prop up her saggy boobs when gravity comes a-calling.

You have to take the good with the bad in this life. And perhaps that was more than a pampered sitcom star could comprehend. After all, the woman actually looks better in real life than she does on TV. Her skin is brighter, her hair is shinier, her butt's even smaller! Of course, her jeans are actually tighter, but that's neither here nor there. . . .

The fact remains that I have a job to do which includes, above all else, keeping Tangy Blair happy. So I nodded my head in agreement all the way through her Greek salad to her baklava – of which, ironically, she ordered the child-size portion.

When I returned to the office I told Eddie all about Tangy Blair's "masterwork." Even more horrified than I am by her antichild stance, he's decided that she's the Devil and has vowed to stop watching her sitcom. And while I appreciate his protest vote, it does little to help me. Because for the next two months I have to write press releases, secure key interviews, organize a book release party, and, most important, keep Tangy Blair happy – all the while being the human embodiment of everything she hates:

A "spawner."

november 29th

For all the anxiety that accompanied my getting pregnant it

was NOTHING compared to the experience that Anita just went through. Oh, my God.

Having informed Destiny Labs of her decision, #119's good-and-plenty was transferred from cold storage at the sperm bank to a fertility clinic, where a doctor whom Anita had met only once before was ready to inseminate her – not once but twice. That's right; in an effort to increase her chances of conception, she was scheduled to be inseminated today *and* tomorrow, her peak ovulation days. And while Anita has decided to go alone tomorrow, she was certain that she wanted me there today.

Mercifully, I was not allowed to accompany her into the examination room. I say mercifully because, according to the literature in the waiting room, a rather large hypodermic needle is employed in the process.

Yikes.

Afterward, buoyed by her potential pregnancy, Anita and I discussed childbirth methods over cups of hot chocolate. Unfortunately, not even the euphoria of possible mother-hood could erase my past behavior from her memory. "*You* want natural childbirth?" She broke into hysterics. "You won't even wax your bikini line because it hurts too much! Everyone knows that."

Great. My low threshold for pain is famous.

As if to underscore this low threshold for pain, I was im-mediately overwhelmed with irritation by the sight of Larry and Mitch sprawled out on my sofa when I returned home. If the horrible plaid fabric and Nicole's drool weren't enough reasons to dump this sofa, then Larry and Mitch's collective scent was. Not to mention those indelible butt prints.

On an even more disturbing note, both Larry and Mitch requested personal introductions to Tangy Blair. The very mention of her name gives them erections, and the possibility of meeting her has sent them to dizzying heights of ecstasy. Yet another reason to get them off our sofa. Well, they can forget it. There's no way I'm jeopardizing my job by introducing Beavis and Butt-head to my star client.

Besides, if ever there was an anti-children argument, it's Larry and Mitch.

november 30th

Stepping out of the shower this morning I caught a glimpse of myself in the mirror – and screamed. At first I thought it was one of those bumps in the glass that warp reflections. In fact, if I were a pinch more paranoid or a drop more delusional I'd say that someone had secretly filled my apartment with a bunch of fun-house mirrors. Unfortunately, I'm not *that* out of touch with reality.

Thus I'm left with only one plausible explanation: In protest to Tangy Blair, and everything she believes in, I "popped" overnight. As vulgar a term as that may be, it accurately describes my new look – that of a woman who's storing the Great Pumpkin under her shirt.[64]

Eager for some hand-holding to cushion the shock, I turned to *BH, BN*, where Chapter Six discusses the emotional implications of weight gain. It says that women often feel lost. Like a shadow of their former self.

Who are they kidding? A *shadow* of my former self? Ha! I'm a MULTIPLE of my former self. It's me to the *nth* degree!

---

[64] Note to self: Double-check that I'm not having twins.

Which means that there is absolutely no way I can continue to hide this pregnancy. It would be like going to work bald and yet continuing to wear a headband. People would sense something was wrong. Especially since, unlike the bulk of the truly obese, my weight is fairly well confined to my abdomen. And a little around my butt. My ankles. My face. Whatever. The point is that it's time to *tell*.

So tell I will. Risking dismissal, destitution, and derision. After all, mine is a natural and glorious condition – even if Tangy Blair will hate me.

november 31st

Well, I outed myself today.

Yes, people, I'm pregnant! If you don't believe me, then read my gynecologist's lips.

On a certain level, my disclosure was a wonderful relief. I no longer had to worry about being discovered or revealed. But first there was the anxiety surrounding my announcement.

After discussing it with Eddie, I decided to start at the top of the food chain and work my way down. This meant that Mr. Nealy was first. After all, he's my boss and it's only his opinion that matters. Luckily he took it in stride. Or at least appeared to do so. Pacing around his office in his customary jumpy manner, Mr. Nealy repeatedly offered his congratulations and okayed my maternity leave. Then, careful not to open himself to any ugly sexual discrimination suits, he indirectly inquired about my ability to continue working given my "delicate" condition.

Delicate condition? Who is he kidding? No one who farts

as much as I do could possibly be described as delicate.

I immediately assured him that I'm completely able to handle my professional duties. At which point he brought up Tangy Blair and the touchy situation we faced given the subject of her book. Then, as casually as a man who can't stop moving could, he suggested that Eddie assume responsibility for Tangy's book promotion. My heart skipped a beat. As much as I loathe Tangy and her dopus-opus, and as difficult as the promotion of her book will be, it was still the best opportunity I had to strut my stuff for the people at *Focus*. Sure, it's not going to be a best-seller or a media frenzy, but it's as high a profile as I'm going to get in this job.

Besides, when else would I get a chance to hear firsthand accounts of the Emmy Awards ceremony?

So I adamantly implored Mr. Nealy to allow me to stay on the project. I assured him that despite my pregnancy I could strike a positive working relationship with Tangy and successfully promote her book. Although not wholly convinced, Mr. Nealy reluctantly agreed to let me stay on the assignment. His one bit of advice? Perhaps I shouldn't mention my pregnancy to Tangy.

Well, unless Tangy's gone *blind* since our lunch meeting, I'm pretty sure she's going to notice whether I tell her or not. I mean, really, had it not occurred to Mr. Nealy that I'm beginning to look like the Michelin Man? Then it struck me: No, it hasn't occurred to him, because he doesn't pay any attention to me or anyone else at Brinkman/Baines. As long as the coffee's brewing and the work is good, he's satisfied to hole up in his office and bounce around. I may be a lofty Senior Account Manager to my subordinates, but to Mr. Nealy I'm just another warm body in a yellowed cubicle. How humbling. So despite being dumbfounded by his ridiculous suggestion, I nodded my head in a noncommittal "whatever you say" way and exited his office.

I told the rest of my coworkers – all three Junior Account Managers and our receptionist – during an informal coffee klatch in the office kitchen. And while I expected the responses to range from complete disinterest to "No wonder you got so fat," I got none of that. Instead my disclosure was met with an icy silence. Maybe a few gasps. Until finally Josh, the pasty Junior Manager from Des Moines, shrieked, "You're six months pregnant and you've been *drinking* all this time?!"

Hmmm . . . I hadn't anticipated this. But it made perfect sense that my carefully crafted identity as a party animal with a lust for liquor would cast a cloud of criminality over my pregnancy announcement. But what was a girl to do? To admit that I'd been lying to them, especially out of fear, would undermine my position of authority. And really, why bring it up if Mr. Nealy hadn't bothered to put the two together? So I did the only thing I could think of. I held my ground.

And pretended to be European.

"Oh, please. We do it all the time in *France*."

december 1st

Wanting to spend quality time with Mandy, but respecting her disinterest in anything baby-related, I called to propose an activity that I knew she'd appreciate – shopping.

· She was delighted. "I'm glad to hear you're still interested in fashion. There's nothing worse than those women who use childbearing as an excuse to let themselves go." If only she knew I was sitting at the other end of the phone in a stained T-shirt, a pair of sweatpants, and a cotton scarf wrapped around my head to keep my greasy hair from touching my already broken-out face.

Luckily there was plenty of time to shower before meeting her.

In an effort to earn brownie points, I agreed to start our adventure at Bloomingdale's, then make our way over to Madison Avenue, hitting all the stores that Mandy loves and I can't afford to shop at. I figured, if nothing else, the walk would be good exercise.

Although Mandy's affluent, she's no spendthrift. For her, shopping isn't just about the purchase. It's about the art of the acquisition – getting the best deal for the best quality for the best label. She tirelessly paws through sales racks and shamelessly browbeats clerks into giving her an additional fifteen percent discount for a missing button or a torn hem. An hour into our spree she'd purchased two suits, a cocktail dress, and a robe. I had three pairs of socks and a winter hat.

But it didn't matter, because we were having fun. Shopping, gossiping, splitting a hot pretzel from a street vendor – arguing over whether or not to put mustard on it. It was just like old times. No tension or anxiety. Just old friends doing their thing.

Right up to the moment we passed a fancy Madison Avenue maternity store called Bountiful Mother. Normally I wouldn't have thought twice about it, except today there was a huge sign in the window advertising a fifty percent sale. Sensing a break in my gait and noticing my wandering eye, Mandy sighed and said, "Oh, for God's sake, just go in."

"Are you sure you don't mind? I promise I won't be more

than a minute."

"Make it ten. I'm going across the street to look at body creams at Le Corps de Beauté."

Ten minutes later I was giddy from my purchase of a stunning holiday dress for a sensationally reasonable price. And Mandy was the proud owner of some outrageously expensive décolletage cream from Switzerland.

Our next stop was Barney's, which is where I officially stopped shopping and became Mandy's valet. In addition to my own shopping bags, I lugged hers so she would be free to scour the ready-to-wear sales racks with two hands. Feeling a bit overwhelmed, and loaded down with packages from Bloomingdale's, Le Corps de Beauté, and Bountiful Mother, I turned to sit in a nearby chair – which is when I ran directly into Tangy Blair. It took her a second, but she finally recognized me.

> TANGY
> Ann, right?

> ME
> Amy.

You bitch.

> TANGY
> Sure. Are you here to see the new
> Blahniks, too?

> ME
> *Of course.* That and a few other items.

I absently lifted my packages to punctuate my point. And that's when Tangy's eyes fell on my Bountiful Mother bag. Sure it was a faint sound, but I was certain that I could hear the synapses firing in her head. Desperate and without any options, I did the unthinkable: Holding the Le Corps de Beauté and Bloomingdale's packages in front of my belly, I hurled the Bountiful Mother bag at Mandy.

> ME
> I don't care how pregnant you are, you'll
> have to hold your own bag. I'm too tired
> to be your Sherpa.

Mandy just stood there, stunned, as the bag smacked her in the head and tumbled to the floor. I quickly turned back to Tangy.

> ME
> So selfish. You'd think she invented giving
> birth. *Please,* it's been happening for
> thousands of years!

Tangy threw her hand up in disgust.

> TANGY
> Don't get me started.

And with a flick of her wrist she was off to the shoe department – leaving me to grovel for Mandy's forgiveness.

> ME
> I'm soooo sorry. But that was Tangy Blair,

and there's no way she can know I'm
pregnant, and –

Mandy grabbed her shopping bags from my arms, purposely stepping on my Bountiful Mother bag in the process.

> MANDY
> I do NOT appreciate being dragged into
> your pregnancy hysteria.

And that was the end of our quality time.

december 1st – 10:30 p.m.

Thank goodness for *BH, BN*. It's like having a best girlfriend who's already been through the experience of pregnancy and is willing to help you without passing judgment
or relating terrifying labor tales. Yes, despite her
reserved manner, I'm certain that Lily is rooting for me.

Unlike my two best girlfriends – one who keeps reminding me that my body will never be the same, and the other
who's impregnated herself with semen donor #119.

december 2nd

Sensing my need to meet other pregnant women, Eddie took
me to a café in the East Village to meet his friend Jillian.
She's one week away from her due date and HUGE. And
while I detailed the joys and tribulations of my own pregnancy, turns out she's exclusively experienced joy. No morn-

ing sickness, no fatigue, no emotional roller coasters, and no work hassles. Nothing. While my journey's had shades of a slow boat to Hell, she's been on the all-expense paid luxury liner. While I was happy for her, I was also envious. How do *I* get on that ship?

To that end, Jillian stressed the importance of being with other pregnant women, and asked if I was part of a prenatal group. For a moment I panicked. Prenatal group? That wasn't on my Things to Do list. Was there an association to join? A secret handshake to learn? Were there twelve steps to motherhood and was it too late to start taking them?

Turns out she was talking about exercise classes, not Preggers Anonymous.

I told her that I was going to Balanced Breathing but that while I enjoyed the yoga I wasn't sure the other women were "my people." Having been to Balanced Breathing herself – also upon Eddie's suggestion – she knew exactly what I was talking about. Eager to help me out, she told me about another prenatal yoga class at a place called the Garden of Lauren. Although she'd never made it there herself, she'd heard through the grapevine that it was good. I immediately wrote down the name.

I really liked Jillian, and thought we'd clicked until I asked what she was going to name her child. Unlike us, she knew what she was having – a boy – and with her being a mere week from delivery, I just assumed she'd chosen a name. She had. But she was completely unwilling to share it. Instead she acted like she hadn't heard me and changed the topic. "Have you ever seen a placenta?"

Freak.

Afterward, Eddie explained to me that in a society that values the unique and noteworthy, favorite baby names are highly proprietary information. Like classified documents or a celebrity's real hair color. Theft, it seems, is rampant. The smart parents-to-be keep their lips sealed and their choices close to the cuff.

Good to know.

december 3rd

I may not know much about this baby stuff, but one thing I know for sure – there's nothing like the grateful expression of a pregnant woman who's just taken a shit.

> Things No One Tells You About Pregnancy
> 1. No sushi
> 2. Twenty-four-hour morning sickness
> 3. Forty weeks (ten months) of pregnancy
> 4. No aspirin
> 5. Dog nose
> 6. "Glow" is sweat
> 7. Excessive flatulence
> 8. Heartburn
> 9. Ungodly constipation

Trust me on this one.

december 4th – 9:30 p.m.

Somewhere between pondering my father's triangular crib and reviewing my Things to Do list, I freaked out about having a child in such a small apartment. We're talking 650 square feet. It's like a modern-day nativity tale set against the backdrop of Manhattan real estate!

Frantic, I called Mandy to ask what people with our budget could afford in this market. Her response?

"Nothing."

Unwilling to accept her answer, I explained that I didn't think two adults and a baby could exist in our space, and that even Nicole thought it was a stretch, and –

And that was as far as I got before Mandy blew her stack. "I'm sorry, Amy, I've tried to be supportive, but I just can't listen to you anymore. You're boring me. You and all the other financially overextended parents who whine constantly that they need an apartment with three bedrooms for less than the cost of a bus ride, and why don't I have any hot tips for them. Well, here's a hot tip: the suburbs. Now if you'll excuse me, Jon and I are in the middle of a game of bridge." Two seconds later I heard a dial tone.

I was floored. In the entire history of our friendship Mandy has NEVER hung up on me. And since when does she play *bridge*?

Clearly my pregnancy and Mandy's strong disinterest in all things baby are putting a strain on our friendship. Which is crazy because we've been best friends since freshman year of college. Our relationship has survived hundreds of obstacles, including her disgust with my tendency to swear, my amusement with her selective adherence to social traditions, and the mother lode of all albatrosses – her marriage to Jon.

And yet it's this baby which is slowly creating a major divide between us. I know we've always been different people, but my pregnancy is an unsettling reminder of exactly how different we are.

Will this be the straw that breaks the camel's back?

december 5th

I've spent the last two weeks using every available resource to craft an impressive and successful promotional platform for Tangy Blair's dopus-opus.

But is she happy? No. Is she vaguely appreciative? No. Instead she's mad that I'm not booking her on the morning talk show circuit. "Martha Stewart and Henry Kissinger are on all the time."

Yes, because people are interested in *their* books.

But it's no use. No matter how hard I try to explain things, she simply can't understand why the American people, especially American mothers, don't want to sip their morning coffee while Tangy Blair tells them they're the Devil.

And for the record, I did try. I called seven different show bookers, all of whom laughed at me, then asked if we still represent Doug Tucker.

Meanwhile, Councilman Hastings has asked me to help promote his campaign to *lower* the drinking age. Now, there's a crowd-pleasing issue, especially in a year when drunk-driving fatalities are up by five percent.

december 6th – 3 a.m.

Why is it that the woman has to carry the child? Is it because men can't be trusted to take their prenatal vitamins?

This is what consumes me as I sit on the toilet for hours, constipated.

december 6th

I was supposed to be pursuing print interviews for Tangy, but I was tired. Tired of people being excited about interviewing sitcom star Tangy Blair, but refusing to discuss anything related to her book. So I turned my attentions to #45 on my Things to Do list: Find a pediatrician.

It took me twenty minutes to identify New York's top ten pediatricians from an article on the Internet. It took me another twenty minutes to call them all – only to learn that none of them accept Brinkman/Baines's insurance plan. Nor, for the record, do any of the top one hundred doctors in N.Y.C. That bit of information took an additional three hours to unearth.

So it looks like I'll have to do my research the old-fashioned way – by word of mouth. Which won't be easy since I don't know very many people with kids, and the ones that I do know are so busy they're barely able to answer the phone, let alone have a conversation. But it can't be *that* hard to find a referral. After all, I'm not asking for much. Really. Just a doctor who's patient, speaks English, and has been educated at a fully accredited medical institution.

On an up note, Stephen and I decided on a boy's name: Lucas.

december 7th

While my bus ground to a complete halt during rush-hour traffic I had entirely too much time to think – we simply HAD to start getting ready for this baby! It's already the end of December, and by the time the holidays are over and the dust settles it'll be mid-January, and then it's basketball season and lord knows that between that and his new computer program Stephen won't be able to do anything productive.

So I exited the bus and ran into the first children's store I could find, determined to buy items #11, 17, and 20 on our list and register for everything else.

One problem. It was one of those outdoorsy places for active parents who like to hike, and bike, and wear special clothing that "wicks" away moisture and doesn't chafe your privates. There were packs for carrying babies on your back, on your front, over mountains, and through the air. And then there were special crib tents with mosquito netting and strollers that transform into backpacks and a bed and a dining table with seating for three.

It was ridiculous. Because, aside from the occasional winter sled ride or sex on the beach,[65] we don't embrace the outdoors. Hell, the only way I've ever crossed Central Park is on the bus.

But I had to buy. To nest. To control!

So in between my head spinning and my heart pounding, I bought a car seat.

I thought Stephen was going to shit when I walked through the door. Up till now this whole baby thing's been nothing more than an exciting concept accompanied by a significant weight gain. Now it needs safety devices.

Too bad we don't own a car.

december 8th

Now that I've outed myself at work, I can't resist telling

---

[65] And even that I'm more likely to drink than do.

anyone who will listen that I'm pregnant. I don't even have to know them.[66] It's one of the few times that people get excited and fuss over you. It must be what Tangy Blair experiences every day. All the fawning. The deferential treatment. No wonder she doesn't want kids. Being treated like a princess is a way of life for her.

Bitch.

Well, it's new to me, and I can't tell you how much I love it. Appreciate it. And won't ever grow tired of it. And while it may seem a bit self-serving, is it really so wrong of me to enjoy all this attention? I don't think so. Let's face it, once this kid is born, no one's gonna remember my name, let alone care how I feel. So bring it on!

It was in this spirit that I called Suzy Parks. Suzy was my first boss out of college. That was back when I thought it'd be great to work in book publishing. Fool. After a few months it became readily apparent that, being neither masochistic nor independently wealthy, I wasn't publishing material. Fourteen-hour workdays for 20K a year was simply *not* a viable life choice. So my foray into publishing was brief, but my friendship with Suzy endured.

Ours was the perfect relationship. Brilliant, ambitious, and stylish, she was my professional role model. And I was her favorite assistant. Able to answer phones with grace and take messages with letter-perfect accuracy.[67] Since then she's scaled the corporate ladder at South Publishing to become its first female president, and we're old friends who dine together a couple times a year – generally at fancy restaurants

---

[66] In fact, in some cases not knowing them is better – witness the reactions of my mother-in-law and Mr. Nealy.

[67] These particular praises seemed a lot more flattering when I was twenty-two.

where she picks up the tab.

But it's no longer the fading memory of my exceptional clerical skills that bonds Suzy and me together. Oh, no. Ever since my wedding it's been much more. Because it was at my wedding that Suzy, the successful executive without a love life to speak of, met Hans Lindstrom, my mother-in-law's optometrist and favorite design client. And three months after that fateful day, they eloped. They've been happily married ever since.

So I gave Suzy a call. We hadn't seen each other in almost a year, so we were due for a visit. Besides, I knew she'd be ecstatic about my pregnancy. And ecstatic she was. Because her life is perfect. Something you could tell the minute she entered the restaurant: She was attractive, successful, married – and oh, yeah – *eight months pregnant.*

So much for my feeling special.

I spent the entire evening listening to her talk about how she's having a boy, how *my mother-in-law* decorated her nursery in a nautical theme, and how she's chosen the absolute best name for her baby: Lucas.

december 9th

Stephen is completely unable to understand why we can't use the name Lucas. "You barely see Suzy Parks. The kids will never even meet."

"Doesn't matter. It's too close a circle for a duplicate name. It will seem odd. Not to mention the fact that she'll think we stole it from her."

"Stole it? People don't own baby names. There's no stealing."

He is *so* naive.

Meanwhile, I had the misfortune of finding my first stretch mark this morning. Totally depressing. It's like finding your first gray hair – it's all downhill from there. And according to Chapter Seven of *BH, BN,* there's nothing you can do to stop them. It's all about genetics. Well, judging from the line across my abdomen, my gene pool was clearly fetid. No wonder my mother hates swimming.

Sensing I was bummed about something, Eddie removed his teeth-whitening strip and asked what was wrong. I told him about my stretch marks and how it signaled the official demise of my once-youthful body. I was falling apart without ever having been "built." Eddie laughed and said that I should have tons of kids because I'm so beautiful. Then, patting my belly, he told me not to worry about the stretch marks. He'd read somewhere that Jerry Hall had used kitchen grease to get rid of hers. Vowing to look into it for me, he went off to search the Internet.

Now *that's* a pal.

december 10th

Late this afternoon I happened to notice the note that I'd put on my computer specifically to remind myself to send out a press release regarding Councilman Hastings's proposal to lower the drinking age in New York State. Seems I should have made a second note to remind me to look at the first, because I was supposed to send the release out by noon. It was now four-thirty P.M. Tomorrow's papers were already being laid out and in some cases had been sent to press. Shit!

It was a total disaster, because not only had I neglected to send the press release, but I'd also forgotten to *write* it! In short, I'd screwed up big. The kind of screwup where you lose accounts, get dumped by clients, and are fired by your high-strung boss who drinks too much coffee and never seems to comb his hair.

Eddie must have sensed my panic because he sent me an instant message asking if something was wrong. Was the baby kicking? Did I need some ginger tea? I explained the situation. And Eddie, the world's most supportive male, told me to breathe deeply – that the baby could sense my anxiety – then volunteered to write the release and personally fax it to all the papers by the end of business. If we made a few calls to the editors, we could probably get into eighty percent of our venues. I was eternally grateful.[68]

december 11th

While I'm not ready to concede that my brain is shrinking, something is definitely afoot. Given my huge screwup with Councilman Hastings's press release, my appearance at the wrong restaurant for the Tangy Blair meeting, my failure to alert Glyniss O'Maley's manager about her interview with *Teen Flair,* and this morning's hour-long search for my house keys, I realize it's time to add another pregnancy phenomenon to the list.

> Things No One Tells You About Pregnancy
> 1. No sushi
> 2. Twenty-four-hour morning sickness

---

[68] Note to self: Get Eddie a really nice Christmas present.

3. Forty weeks (ten months) of pregnancy
4. No aspirin
5. Dog nose
6. "Glow" is sweat
7. Excessive flatulence
8. Heartburn
9. Ungodly constipation
10. CRC (Can't Remember Crap)

It's like walking through life with early-onset Alzheimer's. Or a two-day-old hangover. Either way, it sucks.

december 11th – 7:30 p.m.

Further illustrating the CRC syndrome, it seems I forgot to add yet another fun fact about being pregnant.

Things No One Tells You About Pregnancy
1. No sushi
2. Twenty-four-hour morning sickness
3. Forty weeks (ten months) of pregnancy
4. No aspirin
5. Dog nose
6. "Glow" is sweat
7. Excessive flatulence
8. Heartburn
9. Ungodly constipation
10. CRC (Can't Remember Crap)
11. Public petting

That's right. Now that I'm showing, an ugly phenomenon has begun: people rubbing my stomach without asking. And I'm not just talking about Stephen's lecherous brother Tom. Oh, no. I've found myself dodging the infiltrating hands of everyone from Mitch to the elderly cashier at my video store.

It's like I've got a RUB ME sign taped to my abdomen.

december 12th

Tangy called me this afternoon to say that she didn't like the publicity photos we're planning to use for the book promotion. Despite the fact that we'd gotten them directly from her manager and she'd already approved them. Twice. Seems she's changed her mind about her eye shadow. Too taupe. Not enough "pop."

I'll give her a pop. Doesn't this woman know when to stop?

Apparently not, because she's insisting that we pay to have the photos digitally altered to render her eye shadow a more flattering shade – preferably that of Chanel's "Rose Allure."

In order to fulfill Tangy's request, I would have to go out and buy Chanel's "Rose Allure" eye shadow, then locate a lab that can color-match it digitally on the original photo – all within the next few days, because with the holidays just around the corner we've got no time to spare, since our pre-arranged schedule with the printer is already very tight.

I was beside myself. And completely annoyed. So annoyed that I suddenly wanted to make this obtuse, pampered starlet just as annoyed as I was. So I took my best shot – and told her I was pregnant.

There was a very long silence. I eagerly hoped that I'd

shocked her into a coma. No such luck.

"That explains why you're being so difficult about my request. It's just like I say in my book: Pregnant people think they should be given slack at the expense of others."

Great. Now she was *shaming* me into doing her bidding.

"Trust me. My pregnancy does not in any way compromise my desire or my ability to do my job. I'm just not convinced that you have an accurate understanding of the situation."

To which she quipped, "What is that? Your hormones talking?"

The only thing worse than not expressing your thoughts is expressing your thoughts and having them dismissed. The wench! If it weren't for maternity leave, health insurance, and possible imprisonment, I would have gone to her apartment and wrapped my hands around her swanlike neck until it snapped.

"Have a nice day, Tangy. I'll get back to you tomorrow."

Hanging up the phone, I was at my wit's end and ready to storm Mr. Nealy's office to suggest that we drop her as a client. After all, what can you do with a client as antagonistic as Tangy? But of course I couldn't say anything, because only days earlier I'd assured Mr. Nealy that nothing, including my pregnancy, would impede my ability to promote Tangy's book.

Damn my big mouth!

december 13th

Anita called, depressed. Seems #119 didn't have what it takes, because she's not pregnant. She sounded sad and exhausted. I was afraid to even ask if she was going to try again after what she's gone through.

I almost felt guilty for being pregnant myself.

december 14th

I had an appointment with the Crotch Whisperer today, where everything from the baby's heartbeat to my blood work got a thumbs-up. Literally. And thank goodness, because without physical gestures I wouldn't have a clue what the man is saying.

Like when I started to talk about natural childbirth. Although I couldn't hear him, I definitely *saw* him roll his eyes. It was the physical equivalent of being patronized.

And I hate being patronized.

So I vowed then and there to have natural childbirth.

december 15th

Something magical happened last night – we saw the baby kick.

I was sitting on the sofa watching a decorating show on TV when I felt a flutter. Nothing unusual. After all, the baby's been moving around for over a month. But tonight I saw something *poking out*. Like an elbow, a heel, or a really big nose. I immediately called to Stephen, who was in the bedroom alphabetizing our CD collection.[69]

And for the next two hours we just sat there, holding each

---

[69] And people say *I'm* a control freak.

other, mesmerized by what would someday be our child taking her/his first steps inside my belly.

But the best part? It didn't freak me out. On the contrary, I felt peaceful. And natural. And that's when it hit me. This whole childbearing thing? It really is a miracle.

Later that evening I lay in bed unable to sleep. As difficult as pregnancy can be on the body, the mind, and the career, it's also infinitely wonderful. And being able to share it with someone makes it all the more meaningful.

I'm eternally grateful to have Stephen by my side. Despite his increased work hours he helps with the household chores, lifts my spirits when I'm down, gets excited about ultrasounds, and helps find my keys when I misplace them for the hundredth time. In short, I don't know what I'd do without him.

And it's precisely this that makes me worry about Anita.

I know I swore to support her decision to become a single mother, but that was before I understood how completely overwhelming this process is. It's going to be extremely difficult for her. And not just because she basically lives on sushi, Diet Coke, and Chardonnay. But because she's without a partner.

It'd be different if she had family close by. But she doesn't. Anita's from Chicago and her closest relative is a sister in Queens who's totally consumed with the responsibility of raising her own child. And no matter how many good friends you have to hold your hand and help you decide between donors #119 and #68, they can't possibly supplant that person who's equally invested in the process with you.

But how can I tell that to Anita?

december 16th

I took Jillian's suggestion and went to the Garden of Lauren yoga studio after work today. I'd foolishly assumed that Lauren was the owner. Judging from the clientele, it's Lauren as in *Ralph* Lauren . . . Donna Karan, Calvin Klein, and a smattering of Tommy Hilfiger.

That's right, Toto, we're not at Balanced Breathing anymore.

First off, you have to be buzzed into this place, which is on the ground floor of a converted brownstone on East Eighty-second near Fifth Avenue. It's got floor-to-ceiling windows that open onto a garden whose focal point is a fountain featuring a nymphet whose breasts, for reasons that totally confound me, spew sparkling water.

Second, the women here aren't dragging around scraps of lambskin and they certainly aren't wearing homemade saris. The Garden of Lauren dress code is strictly designer. And preferably this year's. Complete with diamond jewelry, coiffed hair, and full makeup – and that includes base. I suspect that just uttering the words "underarm hair" will get you escorted out by the receptionist.

And you won't have to worry about any paintbrushes up your anus. It's far more likely you'll be asked to squeeze your buns like you're clenching a platinum Visa card.

Which isn't to say that the experience was a total waste. Because it wasn't. As I sheepishly huddled in the back of our class of fifteen – me the only one not in a designer exercise ensemble – I learned a lot. You see, the class may be called prenatal yoga, but after twenty minutes of light, don't-worry-you-won't-sweat-off-your-makeup stretching, we all sat down to talk. Evelyn, our thirtyish instructor in a forest green Ralph Lauren track suit complete with modest-sized breast implants and tastefully highlighted hair, led us through a lively discussion that included child development, nannies, and strollers.

Strollers?!

I won't even address the issue of nannies since just saying the word makes me feel poor, but *strollers*? None of these women could have been farther than five months along, and they were already comparing notes on strollers – Italian, French, leather, titanium . . .

That's right. *Titanium*. Clearly the pocketbook wars of Prada versus Bottega Veneta were giving way to the stroller wars of titanium versus collapsible leather. Personally, I'm just hoping for one that meets safety standards with a budget-conscious price. Preferably in a pleasant navy blue.

How do they have time for this? And the money? But before I could wonder further, I was being asked whether I was having a boy or a girl.

"I don't know. We've decided not to find out."

This caused instant panic. "How will you know what color to paint the baby's room?"

Hello! This is the twenty-first century. Days of girls-must-have-pink and boys-gotta-have-blue have gone the way of the manual typewriter and homemade bread. Besides, I've got bigger fish to fry, like how to GET a baby's room. And while I considered telling these poor, myopic women that I'd decided to paint the baby's room jet black, one of them – whose nail polish matched the racing stripe on her Prada exercise pants – devised a way to save my poor child-to-be from a life of gender confusion. "I suppose you could do yellow."

The group let out a collective sigh of relief. Crisis averted.

Clearly these were not my people. So where *are* my people? Probably at home eating Chinese food on their sofa.

december 17th

I went to Saks today to finish[70] my Christmas shopping. Sweaters, socks, CDs. While I was there I couldn't resist popping into the baby department. Unfortunately, it still felt like another planet. A secret world filled with all sorts of mystery products that vibrated, warmed, and sterilized. Yes, folks, I'm still as ill-prepared to be a mother as I was last month. Just look at my Things to Do list.

To ease my pain, I decided to browse through the children's clothing, because even I know what a pair of booties is for. And good lord, are those things cute! I'd love to think that I'll be a practical mother who doesn't go nuts buying all sorts of expensive clothes and fashion accessories – a little hat here, a teddy bear sweatshirt there. But seriously, have you *seen* some of this stuff?

For reasons beyond my comprehension, there's an undeniable physiological attraction between mothers and cute baby clothes. Perhaps it's the scale, the color palette, the decorative trim. In any event, who am I to defy biology? Especially if I have a girl.

Next Christmas I'll be here shopping with my *child*!

While I was leaving the store, I happened to pass the sunglasses counter, where I found the most beautiful pair of Ray-Bans for Eddie. I don't usually buy stuff like this, but I

[70] OK, start.

knew that Eddie would love them. They're very trendy and fashionable. The kind of thing a rock star would wear while vacationing on the Riviera. Perfect for a guy who routinely exfoliates.

Unfortunately, Stephen found the sunglasses on the kitchen counter and assumed they were for him. Like he would ever wear *those*. Stephen's more the drugstore sunglasses guy. Casual plastic frames without much fuss. So I was surprised by his mistake. And even more surprised by how annoyed he got when I told him they were for Eddie.

"You bought that guy high-end Ray-Bans? How much did those things cost?"

"Around a hundred dollars."[71]

"Since when do you spend a hundred dollars on a coworker?"

"He's not just a coworker. This guy's been killing himself to help me out at work. He's covered for me, he's worked overtime for me, and he brings me ginger tea. The least I can do is buy him a nice gift to say thank you."

"Fine, but it's not like he's going to use them. It's the middle of friggin' winter."

I was about to remind him that there was plenty of glare in winter, especially if you go skiing, which I know for a fact Eddie enjoys doing and for which these glasses have a special headstrap included in the box. But I decided to drop the subject altogether. First, because Stephen was being irrational and I was too tired to fight. Second, because his breath was killing me. My dog nose could smell his gyro lunch a mile away, and to continue arguing would have made me physically ill.

---

[71] It was actually closer to two hundred, but really, why go there?

So I made a mental note: Renewing Stephen's subscription to *Sports Illustrated* would NOT be enough of a Christmas gift.

december 18th

Anita and I met for lunch today. I purposely avoided the topic of babies, but she brought it up almost immediately. She's debating whether to try another implantation next month or to wait a while longer.

"Look, I've been thinking about you doing this alone, and I'm not sure it's the best idea."

"I thought you supported my decision."

"I did. I do. I support *you*. But you're my best friend and I have to be honest with you. It's not easy being pregnant. And being a mother's going to be a thousand times more challenging. Especially alone."

"So you think it's wrong to do this without a man?"

"No. I just think being a good mother's hard enough without the pressure of doing it all alone."

"So you don't think I'll be a good mother?"

"I didn't say that. Hell, I haven't got the faintest idea what it means to be a good mother."

"No kidding." And with that she stood up and exited the coffee shop, leaving me completely uncertain – What *did* being a good mother really mean? And was being honest with Anita the right thing to do?

The only thing I knew for certain was that she's definitely not speaking to me.

december 19th

After investigating some on-line sites I've come to realize how incredibly *expensive* this baby stuff is. Diapers alone will send you to the welfare office. How the hell do people afford this? And forget about the birth process. Sure, we have insurance, but we've also got a deductible to meet, and according to the fine print on our insurance contract, there could potentially be people or procedures involved in this birth that are NOT covered by our plan. Which means more bills. More out-of-pocket expenses . . .

And while we're on the topic of cost, would someone please tell me why electric breast pumps are so damn expensive? For that kind of money I could hire a *human being* to nurse my child. Maybe even my husband. The whole thing is ridiculous.

Which is probably why #46–49 on my Things to Do list relate to having a baby shower. Showers and registries and all the other thinly veiled ways that people extort gifts from friends and loved ones have always made me uncomfortable. And yet I know how valuable they can be, especially when you consider the cost of being a parent. So I've decided to bite the bullet and hop on the bandwagon.

There's only one problem: Mandy bristles just talking about babies, and Anita's not talking to me about *anything* right now. So my chances of getting a baby shower? Slim to none.

december 20th – 4 a.m.

I couldn't sleep. My heart was racing and I had a slight fever.

I just didn't feel right. So I turned to *BH, BN* wondering if there was anything I could take for a fever, since aspirin is discouraged during pregnancy. What I found was horrifying. After looking up *fever* in the index I came upon chorioamnionitis – a pregnancy infection. Symptoms can include fever and rapid heartbeat. Or there may be no symptoms at all, which means that I may have had it for months and never even known!

I quickly woke Stephen and told him the situation. After reading through *BH, BN,* he was equally horrified. Uncertain what to do, we finally decided to go to the emergency room.

By the time we arrived at the emergency room my heart was beating so fast I was sure people across the waiting room could hear it. Accosting an E.R. resident who was just starting his rounds, Stephen demanded that I be seen right away. After being escorted to a bed, we waited an hour and a half for a doctor. Apparently people with severed limbs and no pulse take priority over women with jeopardized pregnancies.

When the doctor finally appeared I became hysterical. All the waiting had only increased my anxiety. I explained that I had a disease so scary that I couldn't even pronounce it. So I spelled it for her. Over the next forty minutes she took my temperature, listened to my heartbeat, and asked a variety of medical questions. "When's the last time you saw your obstetrician?"

"A week ago."

"Have any of your blood tests come back abnormal? Or with an elevated white blood cell count?"

"No. Nothing. Never." What was this woman getting at? *BH, BN* hadn't said anything about a white blood cell count!

She scratched her head and closed her folder. "You're fine."

Excuse me?

"Your temperature's ninety-nine point two. Chorio-amnionitis generates a higher fever. Your heartbeat is steady. The discomfort you felt was probably gas. And if you don't have an elevated white blood cell count, then you definitely do not have chorioamnionitis."

It could have been horrible. But thanks to *BH, BN* I got examined and was declared healthy. I was elated and relieved. Stephen was exhausted and irritated and fell asleep during the cab ride home.

december 21st

Recognizing that the Garden of Lauren is not my speed, I went back to Balanced Breathing after work. Unfortunately, even that place is getting hard to deal with.

Today Pippa had us chant *Sat Nam* for a whopping twenty minutes. I still don't know what it means. She says it's supposed to center us and to focus our anxieties – especially during natural childbirth. Almost a narcotic mantra. Which is probably why they do it for so long, since according to *BH, BN* labor can last for *days*. And while I don't know if it actually relaxes you or makes you one with the greater cosmos, I *do* know that if you do it long enough you're certain to become catatonic. Maybe that's the point.

But let's face it. I'm the last person to sit still and chant endlessly. Especially with my eyes closed. Which is why I peeked today – hoping to see other restless women looking around, checking their watches, wondering when all this was going to be over. But no. All I saw was row after row of chanting drones sitting motionless.

Sat Nam . . . Sat Nam . . .

And the really disturbing thing? I'm now bigger than almost all of them.

december 22nd

This evening was both the Brinkman/Baines and Stephen's company parties. Since Stephen's a principal in his company we *had* to go there, so we made only a brief, perfunctory stop to share good cheer with my coworkers.

That was more than enough.

Due to the company's financial woes, the party was held in our office. The receptionist had been given a hundred bucks and told to make it festive. "Festive" to a twenty-two-year-old minimum-wage employee is a relative term. As a result, we had a case of Brooklyn Lager, a few bags of tortilla chips, some salsa, and the pleasure of listening to Beck's new CD playing on a portable radio. Oh, yes, and let's not forget the visual delight of some white Christmas lights draped across the cubicle walls.

My guess? The girl spent $44.50 on the party, then stepped into Bebe and used the remaining $55.50 to buy the trendy new fringe skirt she was wearing. But who could blame her? She looked really good.

All my coworkers were there except Mr. Nealy, who left this afternoon for a trip to the Caribbean. Hence a sense of the lunatics running the asylum permeated the atmosphere. The three Junior Account Managers all brought dates, most of whom seemed to be platonic friends looking for free booze. And while our more successful entertainment clients didn't show up, almost all of our spokesmodels and game show regulars made an appearance. As for the political clients, only Councilman Hastings came. And by the time I left he was making out with Stella on my cubicle floor.

Ick.

Stephen and I were just about to leave when Eddie arrived. This was the first time that Stephen had met Eddie. Unfortunately, Eddie was wearing the new Ray-Ban sunglasses I'd given him for Christmas, and Stephen would NOT shut up about it. "He's wearing sunglasses indoors? What is he? A moron?"

And while I was fairly certain that Stephen was most bothered by the fact that Eddie looked so good in the glasses, it was clear that something about Eddie rubbed him the wrong way. After an uncomfortable introduction, where Stephen was borderline rude and Eddie was as nice as could be, we were on our way out the door. Which was too bad. Because I was really hoping that Stephen and Eddie would hit it off. After all, they're both great guys who have been crucial to my pregnancy. But it wasn't to be. Stephen groused about Eddie's sunglasses, feathered hair, and chartreuse silk shirt all the way to his company party.

Which, thankfully, was significantly more impressive than the one thrown by Brinkman/Baines.

I'm always amazed how a bunch of computer nerds who are constantly teetering on the edge of bankruptcy manage to throw such fabulous holiday shindigs. This year's was held at a famous Russian dive down on the Bowery. Between all the frozen vodka, the live Russian music, the endless dancing, and the vats of beet borscht, no one noticed that the blinis were rubbery and the bowls of sour pickles had flies floating in them.

Except me, because I was stone sober.

Not so for Mrs. Martin, who was so delighted to be out for a night of pleasure that she was hammered out of her mind. Asking for her pediatrician's name was like asking for the combination to her first school locker. Forget it.

Later, watching her struggling to stand, certain that she'd wind up headfirst in a vat of borscht before the night was through, I began to wonder if motherhood was so demanding that extreme intoxication was your only means of relaxation.

Who knows? In any event, it's better than insanity.

december 23rd

Pregnancy's a funny thing. You mark your weeks and months so closely. And you subject the minutiae of your days to such intense scrutiny – Is the baby kicking? How much do you weigh? Are you showing?

And yet as slowly as time seems to pass, it also flies by. Because suddenly it's the end of December, and I've almost completed my seventh month.

december 24th

Tonight was Christmas Eve. Having survived the crunch of holiday masses on the train ride upstate, we arrived at my parents' house just as the sun was setting. Although it had yet to snow, there was a nice chill in the air, and every house from the train station to my childhood home was decorated with twinkling lights and wreathes. As much as I loathed growing up here, I have to admit that my hometown's old-fashioned charm and simple ways make it an idyllic place to spend Christmas.

As long as you're not with the Thomas family.

After sitting around the same plastic tree that my parents bought in 1978,[72] we exchanged the usual gifts of CDs, sweaters, and socks. Seconds later Nicole, who had shown up looking like Erin Brockovich,[73] was stuffing her loot into her shoulder bag and racing to make the seven o'clock train back to the city in order to meet Pablo.

While my mom put the finishing touches on our dinner, my dad took the opportunity to give us a tour of his "workshop" – a metal shed from the home improvement store that he's erected behind the garage over what had previously been a bed of my mother's favorite pansies.

It's here that he's crafting the infamous death crib. And to be honest, it looks even scarier in real life. Sharp edges, unsanded surfaces, and only three legs to stand on. Great.

The pervasive sense of danger was even more heightened by my father's heavily bandaged hand. After a fleeting reference to having skinned it on the lathe and taken a trip to the emergency room, I chose not to pursue it further. Focusing on the fact that although ill-conceived and infinitely perilous, my father's efforts are based on love, I kissed him on the cheek and told him the crib looked great. Ever the dutiful son-in-law, Stephen readily agreed.

After the grand tour we went back into the house, where

---

[72] After my mother continued to step on dried pine needles throughout the month of January, thus ending her love affair with live foliage.

[73] Where she shops these days is a mystery. But between the low-cut dresses and the fuck-me heels, I'd say they only accept cash.

Gram complimented my outfit, then insisted I sit down and re-lax. Minutes later she sat down alongside me and announced that her Christmas gift to the baby was that of her name.

Stephen looked at me. I looked at Gram. Gram beamed. I turned back to Stephen. Stephen turned around and walked into the kitchen. Chicken.

I didn't know what to say. It'd be one thing if she *asked* me to name the baby after her, but here she was *gifting* me with her name. Well, gift or no gift, there's no way I'm nam-ing my child Esther. Especially if it's a boy.

As I scrambled to think of polite ways to return her gift, I remembered back to when I was preparing to marry in a Presbyterian church and Gram suddenly announced that we were Jewish. A fact which we chose to ignore, since for as long as any of us could remember we'd been drinking eggnog and watching Christmas specials on TV. But now seemed like a good time to bring it up.

> ME
> Thank you, Gram. But as a Jewish
> woman, isn't it bad luck to name a baby
> after a living relative?

Gram didn't flinch.

> GRAM
> It would be wrong of me, but not of you,
> since you don't consider yourself to be
> Jewish. Remember your wedding?

It was like arguing with Mandy about socially acceptable ways to wear "winter" white. I tried again.

ME
But, Gram, I'm worried that naming the baby Esther, and that's assuming that it's a girl, will make the child feel awkward. After all, while Esther is a lovely name, it is fairly old-fashioned.

Gram laughed.

GRAM
Oh, I don't expect you to name the baby Esther.

Thank goodness.

GRAM
I expect you to name the baby Sessy.

ME
Who's Sessy?

GRAM
I'm Sessy.

I gasped. At eighty-one, the poor woman had finally begun to lose her mind. Leaning in close, I spoke slowly and deliberately.

ME
No. Your. Name. Is. *Esther.*

Gram rolled her eyes, exasperated.

GRAM
Thank you, Amy, I'm well aware of that.

So much for senility.

GRAM
Sessy is my nickname.

ME
Since when?

GRAM
Since childhood. It was my name around
the old neighborhood. And it's very
distinctive. Just like you wanted.

Well, that's dandy, but there's no way I'm naming my kid
Sessy. It's stupid and ridiculous and sounds like a slang
word for urination. But before I could say anything, Gram
was shoving a platter of mixed nuts and candied fruits at me
with a smile.

GRAM
Snack for the mother-to-be?

And that's when I realized that Gram couldn't care less
about me or my pregnancy. On the contrary, her kind words,
thoughtful phone calls, and deferential treatment had all
been part of a well-crafted campaign to sweet-talk me into
naming the baby *Sessy*.

Yes, folks, the old broad was up to her old tricks!

In an effort to minimize potential damage, and to avoid

the unpleasant behavior that she displayed regarding my wedding, I effusively thanked Gram for her generous offer, then politely declined her name. Without saying a word, Gram pursed her lips together and forced a smile.

At which point I knew I was in trouble.

Turns out I was right. Seconds after sitting down to dinner, Gram repeatedly passed me the dish of steamed broccoli despite the fact that she knows it aggravates my dog nose. Then she yanked the basket of warm rolls out of my hand, warning that carbohydrates would cause me to *further* bulk up. And finally, when I declined a second serving of pie on the basis that the pregnancy had made my complexion sensitive to sugar, Gram just smirked.

> GRAM
> Go ahead. Enjoy. It's not like your skin
> was so great before you were pregnant.

Ho-ho-ho? Try ha-ha-ha. Merry Christmas.

december 25th

This morning Stephen and I slept late, then stayed in bed kissing, cuddling, and watching the baby move. Sometime around noon, we ventured into the kitchen to make breakfast.

Over eggs, toast, and a slice of cold pepperoni pizza[74] we exchanged gifts. In addition to renewing his subscription to *Sports Illustrated,* I gave Stephen a beautiful cash-

---

[74] What can I say? I'm pregnant.

mere sweater. Warm, soft, and *almost* as expensive as Eddie's sunglasses.

As for my gift, Stephen did what he's done for the past two years: He added another sterling silver charm to the charm bracelet he gave me the year we became engaged. The first charm he gave me was a heart and key. Last year, in honor of my work as a writer, it was a tiny typewriter whose keys actually moved. This year it was a miniature baby rattle. But, mindful of respecting me as an individual while celebrating our child-to-be, he thoughtfully wrapped the charm in a *gorgeous* silk robe.

I was stunned. As the queen of frayed terry-cloth robes covered with coffee stains I couldn't imagine wearing such a stunning thing. Five minutes later you couldn't pry it off me if you tried.

Later in the afternoon I called Lucy to wish her a happy holiday and to thank her for the pregnancy pillow she sent me. It's as long as my own body, and unlike Stephen it doesn't complain when I prop my stomach on it for some nighttime comfort. Turns out Lucy was equally pleased with the collection of Woody Allen videos we sent her. She and Emmet are already on their third. So far *Zelig* is their favorite.

But nothing gave her as much pleasure as the heartwarming story of *Sessy*.

After laughing for five minutes straight Lucy managed to regain her breath long enough to express her relief that Gram's unusual show of support for my pregnancy had ultimately been self-serving. After all, had it been sincere, we would have had to consult a priest for an exorcism because, really, the woman was simply *not* herself.

Yes, it was a wonderful day – except for the unguarded moment when Stephen caught sight of my profile and gasped,

"Wow, you're huge!"

But he's right. I am tipping the scale in a direction I've never seen it go before. And yet that's natural. I'm supposed to be big. Big is beautiful where pregnancy is concerned.

Isn't it?

december 26th

I've left three messages for Anita and haven't heard a thing. I'm guessing she's still mad at me.

december 27th

Unwilling to start the new year on bad terms with both my best friends, I called Mandy to say hello and to mend fences. She readily accepted my apology and offered her own: "Every day I get baby pressure from Jon, or my mother, or my gay dentist.[75] So I count on my friends to provide a sane environment that doesn't revolve around having children. But I promise, I'll be really nice to yours. I just don't want my own."

Okay, she's back as honorary aunt.

"After all, I've got a wonderful life. Why ruin it with kids?"

Alrighty. In addition to taking my kids shopping and to the museum, *she* can give them the birth control lecture.

---

[75] We go to the same guy.

december 28th

It was like receiving a beautiful Christmas gift – then getting a paper cut while unwrapping it.

Nicole has finally found a place of her own! A share with a coworker from her new, Manhattan-based paralegal job. Why anyone would ever live with a coworker is beyond me. But whatever. All I know is that she was finally at our apartment packing up her stuff. Unfortunately, the slippery minx was trying to pack some of my stuff, too. My leather miniskirt, my sequin halter top, some satin capris, and a studded bustier from my college days that I once got stuck in and from which Nicole had to come to my apartment to free me. They were my party clothes from before Stephen and I were married. The good stuff.

Furious, I reached into her suitcase to retrieve my belongings.

> NICOLE
> Come on, don't be so stingy.

She whisked them out of my hands.

> ME
> Stingy? They're *mine*.

I snatched them back.

> NICOLE
> Yes, but they look better on *me*.

> ME
> Bullshit!

Moments later we were bitch-slapping each other like two bargain hunters at a sample sale. Then, with my sequin halter top clenched between her teeth, Nicole laid it on the line.

> NICOLE
> Who are you kidding? You never go out
> anyway.

> ME
> What do you mean? I go out all the time!

> NICOLE
> Face it, Amy. The last club you went to
> said *Health & Racquet* on the front door.

And suddenly it hit me – I'm a married woman with a baby on the way and no interest in staying out past eleven. As I stood there wondering if Duran Duran was still a popular dance band, I was forced to accept reality. Nicole, my vaguely younger sister, who'd spent the better part of her twenties anesthetized by the hegemony of married suburban life is now COOLER THAN ME.

It was the cruelest cut.

So I gave her all the clothes. Except the bustier, which I kept for myself to ease my pain – and to punish Nicole for bringing the topic up in the first place.

december 28th – 10:47 p.m.

I've made a shocking discovery: back fat!

december 29th

As I was leaving the apartment to meet Stephen and some of his buddies at a restaurant down the block, Mr. Elbin's holiday party was in full swing. The hallway was teeming with middle-aged design types with expensive black sweaters and fancy eyeglasses from Japan.

And as I waited for the elevator, Mr. Elbin himself emerged from his apartment with two trash bags – teeming with empty, unrecycled liquor bottles. Choosing to indulge in the holiday spirit and not crucify him for destroying our planet, I wished him a Happy New Year. To which he flatly returned the good wishes, then added, "Although, judging by your size, it must be difficult to feel any joy."

december 30th

Stephen's grandparents, the incredibly thoughtful Brocktons, have sent me a Christmas gift. A charming little throw pillow embroidered with the word MOTHER.

After calling to thank them, I stuffed the pillow in the back of our linen closet alongside the pillow they sent when I got married. That pillow said MRS. STEPHEN STEWART.

Who knew it could get worse?

> Things No One Tells You About Pregnancy
> 1. No sushi
> 2. Twenty-four-hour morning sickness
> 3. Forty weeks (ten months) of pregnancy
> 4. No aspirin
> 5. Dog nose

6. "Glow" is sweat
7. Excessive flatulence
8. Heartburn
9. Ungodly constipation
10. CRC (Can't Remember Crap)
11. Public petting
12. Final erosion of personal identity

december 31st

One of the few physical traits left untouched by pregnancy is the sense of hearing. Something that was readily evident as I stepped out of the shower in time to hear Stephen talking on the bedroom phone with his coworker Martin.

At first the conversation centered around their plans to seek additional development funds from major medical institutions. After all, if their new program could ultimately translate X rays and other patient data into computer code, it would be tremendously beneficial for the entire medical community.

As I stood in the bathroom towel-drying my hair, I smiled. Proud of my brilliant and ambitious husband, who works so hard, even on New Year's Eve day.

Then my smile faded. Because as Stephen's voice dropped, I began to catch phrases like "big as a house," "defies the imagination," and "huge bubble butt." This was no computer program they were talking about. This was ME! After all these months of his saying how fabulous and beautiful I look, the truth was finally out. Furious, I stormed into the bedroom. "Bubble butt! You think I have a friggin' *bubble butt*?!"

Stephen slammed down the phone. His eyes grew wide with fear. "I was speaking figuratively."

Like *that* makes it any better.

"Listen up! I'm carrying our *child*. Which means that in addition to worshipping this bubble butt you ought to be *kissing it*!"

Stephen pulled me down alongside him on the bed. "Amy, I love you. It's just that sometimes, and I really only mean *sometimes,* I get a little spooked by your new shape. Which isn't to say that you're not fabulous and beautiful. Because you are. Really. I've just never seen the human body expand this way before."

Whether he was immensely sorry for hurting my feelings or for being busted I'll never know. But I had to give Stephen credit. He was trying hard to be both apologetic and honest. And if there's one thing we've always strived for in our relationship, it's honesty. OK, that and good sex. But these days sex was getting more and more difficult to manage, so I settled for honesty. Even if it did leave me feeling like a sideshow attraction.

january 1st

Stephen and I went to Larry's New Year's Eve party last night.

The good news was that Mitch wasn't there, because he's feuding with Larry. Seems that Larry, the sleazy lawyer, has scored himself a steady girlfriend, and Mitch, the perennially single dog-walker, is bitter about sharing Larry's time with "some woman." If I didn't know them, I'd say there was latent homosexuality at work here. But I do know them. So I can say without hesitation it's outright childishness.

And who, you may wonder, would date Larry? You'd be surprised. Valerie's smart, attractive, and has citizenship. She's also a successful tax specialist – which is probably another reason Mitch is avoiding her. Seems Valerie saw Larry's ad for legal services at a bus stop and thought he was cute.[76] And after six weeks of dating she shows no signs of irritation or disgust. Astonishing.

But perhaps the biggest surprise in this equation is that Valerie's got a kid from a previous marriage – a five-year-old son named Kevin, whom Larry adores. Despite the fact that Kevin was spending the holiday with his father, and that Larry was supposed to be mingling with his guests, he spent most of the evening telling me and Stephen how fabulous Valerie is and how much he enjoys being with Kevin.

And when the clock struck midnight, and Larry and Valerie hugged each other tight, I toasted the New Year with a glass of sparkling water and the sneaking suspicion that we were all growing up.

january 2nd

Apparently people needed the holidays to recover from the stunning news of Tangy Blair's book, because I had a whopping ten e-mails in response to my publicity inquiries when I arrived at work this morning.

---

[76] Which proves that there's no accounting for taste.

From: MPARKER@NYChronicle.com

To: ATHOMAS@BBPR.com

Subject: Tangy Blair

This is Mark Parker from *The New York Chronicle*. After reviewing the press packet I can safely say we have no interest in reviewing Ms. Blair's forthcoming publication.

From: HDENNIS@MetMag.com

To: ATHOMAS@BBPR.com

Subject: Tangy Blair

Hi, I'm writing on behalf of Dana Angelinas of *Metropolitan* magazine. Ms. Angelinas is currently on maternity leave, but she wanted me to express her complete disgust over Tangy Blair's new book. Thank you.

From: JVOILE@CourierMail.com

To: ATHOMAS@BBPR.com

Subject: Tangy Blair

Ms. Thomas, this is Jason Voile from the book review department of *The Courier*. Unfortunately we've decided not to review Ms. Blair's new book. Trust me. We're doing you a favor.

From: DMURPHY@EastcoasterNews.com

To: ATHOMAS@BBPR.com

Subject: Tangy Blair

Is this some type of joke?

From: WHASSAN@NYLR.com

To: ATHOMAS@BBPR.com

Subject: Tangy Blair

This is Wanda Hassan from *The New York Literary Reader*. Due to our strict adherence to quality work the *Reader* officially declines the offer to interview Ms. Blair.

From: RUSTY@PEYE.com

To: ATHOMAS@BBPR.com

Subject: Tangy Blair

Hey, there. Rusty Miller here from *Public Eye* magazine. Just got your press release about Tangy Blair. We don't care about her book, but if she's interested in posing in a swimsuit for us we'd love to talk.

From: EFLOUGART@CultureMag.com

To: ATHOMAS@BBPR.com

Subject: Tangy Blair

This is Emilio Flougart of *Culture* magazine. I suggest you take a good look at our publication before sending any more press releases to our office. And, please note, our name is *Culture*.

From: EFLOUGART@CultureMag.com

To: ATHOMAS@BBPR.com

Subject: Tangy Blair

On second thought, don't *ever* send us another press release.

From: ECOHENDE@PlannedParenthoodNY.org

To: ATHOMAS@BBPR.com

Subject: Tangy Blair

Ms. Thomas, while we here at Planned Parenthood appreciate your interest, our newsletter is not an appropriate venue in which to profile Ms. Blair's new book. Sincerely, Edna J. Cohende

---

From: EADLER@HumanitasWeekly.com

To: ATHOMAS@BBPR.com

Subject: Tangy Blair

You ought to be ashamed of yourself.

january 3rd

My newest hobby seems to be urinating. I do it morning, noon, and night. Constantly. In fact, last night I set my own personal best with six trips to the bathroom.

As annoying as this is, it's no surprise. The fact that pregnant women constantly need to pee is fairly well known, unlike all the dirty little secrets I've learned during this journey. But interestingly, I never knew *why* pregnant women pee so much. Turns out it's related to the size of the baby. As the baby grows, it starts to push against the bladder, making it harder for it to fill to maximum capacity comfortably.

Now there's some chitchat for my next cocktail party.

january 4th

I was reviewing the print and television appearances I've been able to secure for Tangy Blair, when Eddie offered to throw me a baby shower. He was so sweet about it. He kept encouraging me to invite all my girlfriends, including my new pregnant friends from Balanced Breathing. To which I just smiled, too embarrassed to admit that I haven't made a single gal pal among the ranks of the *Sat Nam*-ers.

But the best part? He insists that I do nothing. All he needs is a guest list. He's sending the invitations, choosing the venue, and buying the food. How strange that in barely nine months a guy I originally thought was out to ruin my career would become one of my closest confidants and the host of my baby shower. Maybe I should make *him* an honorary aunt.

Yeah, right.

Stephen would love that plan. Especially since he spent more than an hour mocking Eddie for even knowing what a baby shower is. The word "freak" was bandied about more often than I care to recall.

Without fail, every time I talk about Eddie, my open-minded, highly evolved husband regresses on the evolutionary scale. Well, screw him. Thus far Eddie's been the only person other than me to lift a finger to welcome this child's arrival.[77]

As excited as Stephen is about this baby, he has yet to participate in any tangible way beyond his original sperm donation and a few visits to the Crotch Whisperer. And while I understand that he's working extremely hard on his computer program, I *don't* understand why he thinks getting ready for this child can be accomplished at the last minute.

This isn't like preparing for a Super Bowl party or organizing a poker game. This is a baby we're talking about. You need more than a six-pack and a pizza.

ME
You're like an absentee father.

STEPHEN
I can't be a father, absentee or otherwise,
without a baby. And the baby isn't here yet.

ME
Tell that to Eddie. He's already put tons of

---

[77] Yes, my father's also working toward that end, but I'm not sure how welcoming a death-crib will be.

effort into this child. You, on the other hand, haven't prepared the room, researched strollers, or given a single thought to the baby's layette.

STEPHEN
What are you talking about? I don't even know what a layette is.

ME
That's my point![78]

STEPHEN
There's plenty of time before the baby comes. Now, don't worry. I promise the room and everything else will get done.

Suddenly I flashed to *Terminator 2,* one of Stephen's all-time favorite movies. Halfway through the film, while simultaneously mothering her teenage son and kicking some serious butt, Linda Hamilton decides that the Terminator, a *machine,* would be a perfect father because he's more reliable than human men.

I think she was on to something.

Things to Do
1. Find ob/gyn
2. Get prenatal checkup
3. Get prenatal vitamins
4. Find physical exercise

---

[78] Note to self: Figure out what a layette is before Stephen asks me.

~~5. Decide childbirth method~~
6. Join childbirth class
7. Buy crib
8. Buy bassinet
9. Buy crib mattress
10. Buy crib bedding
11. Buy changing table
12. Decide cloth or disposable diapers
13. Buy diapers
14. Buy diaper bag
15. Buy diaper pail
16. Buy crib mobile
17. Buy layette
18. Buy stroller
19. Buy infant bathtub
20. Buy baby monitor
21. Buy infant swing
22. Buy night-light for baby's room
23. Choose color for baby's room
24. Paint baby's room
25. Buy pacifiers
26. Buy dresser for baby's clothes
27. Buy infant-size hangers
28. Create medical emergency kit
29. Prepare emergency phone lists
~~30. Decide nursing or formula~~
31. Buy nursing supplies or formula supplies
32. If nursing, decide to rent or buy breast pump
33. If nursing, buy nursing bras
34. If nursing, buy nipple cream

35. Decide on legal guardian

36. Prepare wills

37. Plan estate

38. Create college fund

39. ~~Begin Kegel exercises~~

40. Buy first-year memorabilia scrapbook

41. ~~Decide whether to learn gender~~

42. Choose name(s)

43. ~~Choose hospital~~

44. Take tour of hospital maternity ward

45. Find pediatrician

46. ~~Appoint someone to organize baby shower~~

47. ~~Make invite list for baby shower~~

48. Register for baby shower

49. Buy thank-you notes for baby shower

50. Select birth music

51. ~~Prepare for appropriate religious ceremony~~

52. ~~Book venue for religious ceremony~~

53. ~~Arrange for priest, rabbi, or *mohel*, etc.~~

54. ~~Buy baby's outfit for religious ceremony~~

55. Buy maternity clothes

56. ~~Decide who will be in delivery room with you~~

57. Prepare baby announcements

58. Prepare overnight bag for hospital

59. Make birth plan

60. ~~Schedule maternity leave~~

61. Make phone list for announcing baby's birth

62. Buy baby's take-home-from-hospital outfit

63. Decide on postbirth child care

january 5th

Nicole came over to borrow my studded bustier.[79] While she was here I told her all about the Gram situation. "It's just like when I got married. She's trying to be the center of attention. To make my pregnancy all about her."

"What's the big deal? So she asked you to name the kid after her. You said no. End of story."

Ha!

"You don't get it. Everything changed the minute I said no. I'm telling you the woman can't stand to be near a major life event that doesn't focus on her."

Nicole shrugged. "She didn't want in on my divorce."

Who would? "I'm talking about joyous life events. I bet she wouldn't want in on a funeral, either."

"Are you equating my divorce with a funeral?"

"No. I'm just saying she's on the warpath again."

"Amy, she's eighty-one years old and borderline incontinent. The only path she's on leads to the toilet."

Yeah, right. Despite Nicole's Pollyanna view of the situation, I'm savvy enough to see that Gram's attempting another attention-stealing coup. Well, it's time she faced facts and reviewed the pecking order. It's the baby first, and me second.

Gram can duke it out with Stephen for a distant third.

---

[79] *Where* is she going?!

january 6th

I couldn't stop thinking about Anita. We haven't spoken since I decided to speak too much, and it just doesn't feel right. Anita's my best friend. Not talking to her is like losing part of myself. The fun, exciting part that does as she pleases and won't take crap from anyone.

And maybe that's part of the problem. Maybe in addition to worrying that being a single mother is an overwhelming prospect – even for someone like Anita – I'm also worried that with both of us having children there'll be no one left to be fun and exciting. Could I possibly be so selfish?

I'll take the Fifth.

Unable to stand it any longer, I went to Anita's apartment armed with trashy magazines and a video copy of *Top Gun* – hell-bent on making amends. I started to apologize before she even opened her door: "I'm an idiot. You make your decision, and I'll be there for you. I'll be your husband. We'll argue about whose fault it is that the kid's spoiled and whose turn it is to change the crappy diaper. In the meantime I thought we could hang out for a while."

Anita laughed, hugged me, then, looking at *Top Gun*, scolded me for not renting the version with the extended shower scene.

january 7th

Surprise!

    Things No One Tells You About Pregnancy
     1. No sushi

2. Twenty-four-hour morning sickness
3. Forty weeks (ten months) of pregnancy
4. No aspirin
5. Dog nose
6. "Glow" is sweat
7. Excessive flatulence
8. Heartburn
9. Ungodly constipation
10. CRC (Can't Remember Crap)
11. Public petting
12. Final erosion of personal identity
13. Incontinence

Now that the baby's grown big enough to rest on my bladder it seems my margin of error has greatly diminished. That's right, a little sneeze, a heavy cough, or an innocent laugh can make me piss myself just the teeniest bit.

Unfortunately, in the world of public urination even the teeniest bit is far too much.

january 8th

Stephen managed to leave work early enough to join me, Mandy, and Jon down at Frutto di Sole for dinner. Of course, Jon started the evening on the wrong foot.

> JON
> So what are you naming the baby?

It was the last thing I wanted to discuss, since we still haven't made a decision. And it didn't help that Jon used the opportunity to tell us the incredibly boring origins of his own name. As soon as I realized that he intended to drag us all the way back to the *Mayflower,* I decided to silence him immediately.

> **ME**
> I was thinking if we have a girl we'd name her Mandy. And if we have a boy we'd name him Jon. I hope that doesn't make you uncomfortable.

Instead of freaking out, the moron actually thought I was serious. Is there no justice in this world? Turning to Mandy, he winked.

> **JON**
> Wouldn't it be nice to have a little Jon or Mandy scampering around our apartment?

Mandy frowned.

> **MANDY**
> I didn't baby-sit for five dollars an hour as a kid. There's no way I'm doing it for free as an adult.

Jon looked at Stephen and shrugged.

> **JON**
> At least I won't have to deal with saggy breasts.

What an asshole. Thank God Mandy doesn't want kids, because Jon couldn't fuck his way out of a paper bag. In fact, I'm really beginning to appreciate Mandy's refusal to have children. It's not antichild or antimother. It's self-defense. After all, the kids could end up like Jon.

january 9th

Things No One Tells You About Pregnancy
1. No sushi
2. Twenty-four-hour morning sickness
3. Forty weeks (ten months) of pregnancy
4. No aspirin
5. Dog nose
6. "Glow" is sweat
7. Excessive flatulence
8. Heartburn
9. Ungodly constipation
10. CRC (Can't Remember Crap)
11. Public petting
12. Final erosion of personal identity
13. Incontinence
14. Broken capillaries

Considering how big I am these days, I can't say exactly when they first appeared. For all I know, they may have been there for weeks. But today I clearly caught sight of thin red lines spreading across my thighs. Like train tracks. Or the blueprint for a new ant colony, only in red.

Either way, it's incredibly distressing. According to Chapter Eight of *BH, BN,* they're broken capillaries caused by my elevated level of estrogen. A woman can have as much as a thousand times the normal amount of estrogen in her system by the end of her pregnancy. But the worst part is that the broken capillaries won't necessarily go away after you deliver. They could still be there when your kid's in college!

While still coming to grips with this information, Nicole called. She sounded cold and distant. At first I was ticked off. Sure, they weren't *her* legs but would it kill her to show a little compassion? Turns out she was the one who needed compassion. After nearly three years of having sex on the sly, dancing till dawn, and being wildly happy, she and Pablo are calling it quits.

He wants to share an apartment. To take their relationship to the next level. To make a commitment. In short, Nicole's boy-toy was growing up. And she wanted nothing to do with it.

> NICOLE
> I still feel like my divorce was yesterday.
> And that I've just started to breathe again.
> For the first time in years I can paint the
> walls purple and make pancakes for
> dinner – without having to ask for anyone
> else's opinion. I love Pablo. But I also love
> this process of figuring out who I am. I
> guess I'm not ready to give that up.

So Pablo ended it, leaving Nicole shaken and sad. I offered to come over and keep her company but she wasn't interested. She preferred to be alone.

january 10th

Long ago I vowed to go through this pregnancy wearing normal, nonmaternity clothes in very large sizes. But while a large size may accommodate my heavier butt and thighs, it does *not* make room for my forty-inch waist. Only Santa Claus and pregnant women ever attain this particular shape. So after wearing the same pants six days in a row, I finally bit the bullet and ventured into the world of maternity clothing.

Sensing my fear, Eddie volunteered to come along. Which was a good thing, because in addition to offering moral support he knew exactly where to go: Fashionable Mom, a huge discount center in the garment district.

Nowhere is the confluence of human ingenuity and modern technology more perfect than in the world of maternity clothes. Yes, folks, thanks to cutting-edge plastics and a dream, even pregnant ladies can wear pantyhose.[80]

And then there are all the other items such as dresses, exercise clothes, pantsuits, and blouses, which have been specially crafted to take a woman through nine months of pregnancy. That's right, they grow with you. Like sea monkeys and Chia Pets.

And to help you see how you'll look when your ninth month rolls around, maternity stores provide a special tummy pillow that straps to your body with Velcro. This way you can simulate your future figure as you try on that tailored blazer with those hidden buttons. Or those capri pants with the expandable pleats.

Unfortunately, for all the advanced science involved with

---

[80] Although the very thought of stuffing myself into a pair of pantyhose makes me hyperventilate.

maternity wear, there's a painful dearth of taste. It's as if they think you're so high on estrogen that your fashion IQ's been completely decimated. As if yellow-and-orange checks suddenly seem like a good idea. Or like tying some little strings behind your back will make that muumuu look any less like a garbage bag. Ha! It just looks more like a muumuu!

And yet, if you're willing to fork out some extra bucks and spend some extra time, there are nice clothes to be found. That's right. You needn't look like a hausfrau, or Farmer John in "fashionable" overalls. You simply need to accept the idea of costly disposable clothing. Because, even if you have three kids, you'll still be wearing the stuff for less than three years.

As much as this idea upsets me, the idea of looking like a parade float upsets me even more. So two hours later I emerged from Fashionable Mom with a smile on my face and three pairs of pants in my shopping bag.

january 10th – 10:46 p.m.

Stephen's come up with a boy's name: Zeus.

Considering how cruel children can be, he figures that no one's going to mess with a kid named Zeus.

That's right. Zeus Stewart. Like *that*'s not gonna be a source of pain.

january 11th

Frustrated by Stephen's pathetic name suggestions, I called Anita to vent. If nothing else, as a single mother she won't have to contend with some fool suggesting names like Zeus.

Anita immediately agreed. "That is ridiculous."

"Isn't it, though? Imagine, naming a child Zeus!"

"No. It's ridiculous that you think school kids are smart enough to know who Zeus is. You've seen those public school test scores."

Fine. But Zeus still isn't going to happen. And in order to ensure harmony within our house, I've adopted the Two-Week Rule. That's how long I'll pretend to consider Stephen's awful names before vetoing them.

january 12th

My mother called to ask what I was doing about a baby shower. It never occurred to me to invite her or any of my other relatives to my shower. In fact, the thought of my family mingling with my friends makes me extremely nervous. The only time it's ever happened was at my wedding, and mercifully everyone was drinking on that occasion.

Now, I may be wrong, but I suspect a full bar isn't customary at baby showers. Especially since the person who'd need a drink the most would be me, and that's *definitely* frowned upon. So not wishing to insult her, I mentioned that a coworker was hosting a "small gathering."

> MOM
> You mean that man Eddie?

How the hell did she know about Eddie?

> ME
> Did Stephen mention him to you?

MOM
No, your sister did. She said he's a pervert.

Nice.

MOM
But back to the subject at hand. I'm getting the sense that you don't want your family at Eddie's shower.

ME
Well —

MOM
No need to apologize.

Apologize?

MOM
I'd be happy to throw a shower for your family members here at the house.

ME
Thanks, Mom. That's really nice of you.

MOM
Now, where are you registered?

Oh, jeez.

ME
Nowhere — yet.

> **MOM**
> Really, Amy. Don't you know how
> important a registry is? It's the only way
> to ensure that you get what you need.
> Although, you don't need half the stuff
> people try to sell you.

So says the woman whose life is ruled by the practical – from her dinners to her dresses, of which she owns three: one for weddings, one for funerals, and one for parent-teacher conferences. The rest of the time it's strictly pants.

> **MOM**
> Trust me. When you were born you had
> two outfits and slept in a drawer for the
> first five weeks.

That explains my flat head.

> **MOM**
> Now, go register somewhere, and I'll call
> you as soon as I've finalized a date.

january 13th

I'm officially in my third trimester. In less than two and a half months we'll be having a child, and so far we've got nothing more than a car seat and the promise of a three-legged crib.

My mother is right. We have to register. Especially with two baby showers coming up. So I insisted that Stephen leave the office early and come to Baby Oasis with me. It's a children's store on the Upper East Side, which, according to the ad in the phone book, offers a complete selection of baby products as well as a knowledgeable staff.

Stephen's initial reaction was that I should go alone, since he knows nothing about baby stuff and I probably know everything. Ha! I should be so lucky. After months of Internet research and failed trips to a variety of stores, I have nothing more than a hodgepodge of informative tidbits and vague notions. Luckily Stephen's tune quickly changed when I began to muse that perhaps *Eddie* would help me out.

And at five o'clock sharp, we were entering the magical land of Baby Oasis.

Baby Oasis is a mom-and-pop store – if mom and pop were Rothschilds. True to its advertisement, they have a fleet of well-trained salespeople. And they offer a complete array of products ranging from butt balm to maternity rocking chairs called gliders. But as Stephen was quick to note, none of it's cheap. They have four-hundred-dollar changing stations and seven-hundred-dollar strollers. I immediately flashed to my gal pals at the Garden of Lauren.

As he made his way down the aisles I could feel Stephen's blood pressure rising. Finally he turned to me and whispered, "Let's get out of here."

We'd been there for less than ten minutes, and our registry form was completely blank.

Refusing to give up, I implored him to relax. Yes, there were lots of expensive things here, but there were also items that were more reasonably priced. I pointed to a bassinet that was marked $150. Stephen balked, claiming that it was nothing more than a basket on a wire frame. For less than twenty bucks he could make the same thing using a plastic laundry basket and a few hangers. And why did we need a bassinet if my father was making us a crib?

At which point a nearby salesperson made the mistake of butting in to say that a baby needed to sleep in a bassinet for the first three months, then the baby could use a crib. Unconvinced, Stephen asked the salesperson why. To which she cheerily responded, "It's cozier."

Stephen wasn't buying it. Turning to me, he began to rant. We were being manipulated by the baby industry, which pressures nervous parents into spending thousands of dollars unnecessarily. If the maternity "glider" had been in a regular rocking chair store, it would have been a third of the price. But put it in a baby setting and suddenly it's worth its weight in gold.

And why did we need a special changing station? After all, it was nothing more than a dresser with contoured top. For a fraction of the price we could glue a piece of foam to a dresser from Goodwill, since spending an additional forty dollars on a changing pad was also insane.

From the corner of my eye I saw the salesperson quietly slink away.

Taking the registry from my hand, Stephen began to scratch things off the list. "Oh, and forget the crib. Your dad's making that for us."

My father's three-legged death-crib? A piece of foam and glue? A laundry basket perched atop a couple of bent hangers? Was he nuts?! There's no way *that* met national safety standards.

How dare he just walk in here and start spouting off like he's got any sort of clue. First of all, save for a few sneak peeks at *BH, BN,* he hasn't done a bit of research. Second, he has yet to do anything in the baby's room. Dingy, filled with boxes, and boasting a window that's completely painted shut, it remains the world's messiest storage room. So when does he envision having the time to *make* a bassinet? Third, while I've got no interest in extorting money from friends and family, the fact remains that the point of a registry is that we don't pay for anything. Other people do. And while I don't think we need a seven-hundred-dollar stroller, we could certainly register for the discounted bassinet priced at $73.50 without falling victim to the evil baby empire. After all, if four people get together to buy it they'll be spending less than $20 each.

But it was no use. Stephen was obsessed with the nefarious intentions of an evil baby empire offering such wicked items as diaper pails and rocking chairs.

Tossing our blank registry on the floor, I stormed out of the store. We would do this some other time.

Like when the kid's in grad school.

january 13th – 2:43 a.m.

You know why men can survive with only a can opener and a cooler? Because they have WIVES.

This is what Lily's doing hanging out under that tree. She's taking a break from her endless responsibilities as wife and mother-to-be.

And that look of awe? It's not about her baby. It's about her husband, who she *cannot believe* is so incredibly useless!

january 14th

My mother called again. At first I thought she was calling to check on my registry progress – none – but I was wrong. It was her annual call to remind me to wish my sister a happy birthday. More than a quarter of a century after the fact, my mother is still racked with guilt about saddling my sister with a birthday that's so close to Christmas. She's convinced that everyone forgets.

Well, not me. At least, not this year. In fact, although it's a few days early, I'd already made plans to celebrate Nicole's birthday tonight. Mostly because I figured she'd still be mourning her breakup with Pablo, but also because I wanted to work the aunt angle. While Anita and Mandy are honorary aunts, Nicole's the real thing. And I want our baby to have a strong sense of family. Especially since Kim won't have a clue, and I suspect Tom will be in a lockdown program for sex offenders.

Besides, now that she lives in the city, Nicole is perfect baby-sitting material. She's trustworthy, conveniently located, and won't charge us beyond the contents of our refrigerator and a few articles of clothing.[81]

With this in mind, I went to Nicole's apartment after work to take her to dinner. And was stunned. The place, located at the better edge of Hell's Kitchen, is a third-floor walk-up in an old tenement building. Sure, it's charming, with its flower boxes and light-filled rooms, but it's the size of a postage stamp, with ceilings so low you can touch them with your fingertips. And the place was filthy.

Here was a woman who once knew her coffee filter and vacuum bag sizes by heart. Now she drinks instant, and judging from the floors, is lucky to sweep. A quick glance at her roommate's disheveled bedroom assured me that

---

[81] Note to self: Have locks installed on all closet doors.

she cared even less for cleanliness than Nicole. Luckily, she wasn't there to verify that in person.

Despite my efforts to appear positive and upbeat, Nicole could sense my shock. Annoyed, she instructed me to ease up. "First you mock my lifestyle with Chet for being too fastidious. Now you mock my lifestyle for being too relaxed. Well, you can't have it both ways. Besides, why do you care?"

"I'm sorry. You're absolutely right. It's just not the best image for a baby-sitter."

Me and my big mouth.

"Who says I'm going to baby-sit?"

I quickly changed the topic to our dinner reservation at a lovely Cuban restaurant called Mojito and made a mental note to myself:

Must work to curry Nicole's interest in baby-sitting.

May need to bribe her with bustier.

january 15th

I've gone from no baby shower to two baby showers. My mother's on February 3 and Eddie's a month later on March 1. My cup runneth over! As I was excitedly entering the dates in my Palm Pilot, I got a phone call from Tangy.

Her New York book-release party is February 2. I've called all the magazines, secured limited news coverage, rented the venue, hired the caterer, finagled free designer clothes,[82] and sent more than two hundred invitations to the city's high-profile celebrities. Of which maybe ten will come. If we're lucky.

---

[82] For her, not me.

Sure, Tangy's a huge television star with oodles of sex appeal, but her book is far from sexy. In fact in the P.R. world it's the furthest thing from sexy – it's drivel pretending to be smart. And even the sight of Tangy in a see-through top and tight leather pants can't make that hot. In short, I've done an outstanding job for a book I would never recommend and a woman I can't stand.

God, I'm good. I only pray that someone at *Focus* notices.

And yet Tangy's still not satisfied. Her latest demand? That I arrange a second book-release party two days later in Los Angeles. The best part? She wants me to attend that one as well.

Don't be fooled. This isn't some sort of compliment. It's just another opportunity for her to abuse me. It's also medically insane. By February 4 I'll be starting my ninth month of pregnancy. According to *BH, BN,* flying in the third trimester, especially late in the third trimester, is emphatically discouraged. Besides, that energy I had back in the second trimester? All gone. So basically I'm running on empty.

The whole thing was ridiculous. So I casually suggested to Mr. Nealy that Eddie go in my place. After all, Eddie's done lots of work in L.A., most recently to publicize Manny Zamon's one-man show. But no. Repeatedly running his hands through his hair, Mr. Nealy shook his head. He needed Eddie here in New York to promote chef Roy "Sizzle" Perkins's new fry pan.

Panicked, I immediately called the Crotch Whisperer's office and asked to speak with a nurse. Unfortunately, she confirmed what *BH, BN* already told me – air travel is discouraged so late in pregnancy. If you go into early labor you could cause an emergency landing, or be forced to give birth thousands of miles away from your doctor.[83] While not illegal, it simply wasn't recommended.

Which meant that ultimately, it was up to me. Great. More responsibility. Isn't having this kid enough?

I wonder what Anita would do.

Who am I kidding? Anita would pack a bag and pilot the plane herself.

january 15th – 7 p.m.

I just got our holiday photos back from the lab, and one of the technicians had the nerve to insert some incredibly fat chick in my place.

Asshole.

january 15th – 10:30 p.m.

It occurs to me that it's been a while, a *long* while, since anyone told me how great I look. In fact, people stopped saying I looked great the minute I started to look pregnant.

So what are we really saying when we tell pregnant women that they look great?

I'm sure many people actually mean it. That the woman looks happy, or healthy, or pretty. But I'm beginning to realize that a lot of times it means that the woman doesn't actually look pregnant. As if being heavy, and tired, and all the other things that happen to our appearance when we're

---

[83] This scenario actually sounded appealing until I realized that Stephen would also be thousands of miles away.

pregnant aren't good. That it's wonderful to have a child but not so wonderful to look the part. Stay slim and perky. Let's marvel at how you still fit into your prepregnancy clothes.

I fully admit that I, too, was guilty of such thoughts. After all, how proud was I to look less pregnant, "better," than that other four-month-pregnant woman at Balanced Breathing. And how often did I boast that I could still wear my jeans?

Only it isn't natural to look the same if you're walking around with another creature inside of you. It'd be like asking someone with a sprained ankle not to limp. Or, more to the point, asking someone who's won the lottery not to shout for joy because it wrinkles their forehead.

Yes, most of the comments I got about looking great were inevitably followed by comments like, "You barely look pregnant." Or "You're so small." Or the unabashedly straightforward, "You haven't gained an ounce!"

Without a doubt, my weight gain has made things more difficult. And certainly I complain about it all the time. But it's wrong to wholly begrudge it. Because unless it's excessive or threatens my health, it's natural. In fact, being pregnant is one of the most natural experiences the female body can have. So isn't it our loss to deny it?

january 16th

Great news. After months of waiting I finally got called for an interview over at *Focus*. Tomorrow!

I also got a call from Gram. She's decided that I should return her book of baby photos. Apparently she feels that Nicole would be a more worthy recipient.

Whatever.

january 17th

Going to *Focus* was like taking a vacation at a really classy resort. Nice facility, intelligent people, not a college T-shirt for miles. And no one seemed the least bit concerned by my pregnancy. On the contrary, they congratulated me and assured me that it would not interfere with employment opportunities. They even *apologized* to me for the delay in organizing interviews, *thanked* me for my sustained interest in the position, and *praised* my résumé.

Pinch me! I've died and gone to the civilized world, where I think I made a *fabulous* impression.

Afterward, I went down to Balanced Breathing, where we spent the first twenty minutes of class chanting *Sat Nam*. I can *Sat Nam* with the best of them, but honestly it drives me insane. I do it to fit in and pass the time.

When class was over I was delighted to find Eddie waiting for me. He does that from time to time if he's in the neighborhood.

And this evening, knowing that Stephen was working late, and seeing no reason to go home to an empty apartment, we went out to dinner. Halfway through the entrée my cell phone rang. It was Stephen. He was home and wondering where I was. When I told him that Eddie and I were having dinner, it was clear that he wasn't pleased.

When I finally got home Stephen was furious. What business did Eddie have picking me up after yoga? Didn't he have anything better to do with his time? Or is seducing me his ultimate goal?

As shocked as I was by Stephen's reaction, I was even more grossed out by his breath. My poor dog nose was getting a direct hit of garlic chicken. I couldn't help but cringe. Which only made Stephen madder.

ME
Eddie's not seducing me. He's just a nice, compassionate person.

I admit the thought that Eddie might be attracted to me has crossed my mind. On more than one occasion. Perhaps many. And that it sort of pleases me. A lot. But is that such a crime? I don't think so. After all, it's nice to have an admirer when you feel so big and clunky. So if Stephen's a little miffed, or even jealous – good.

ME
And what if he is attracted to me? So what?

STEPHEN
So, you're pregnant.

ME
That's right. I'm pregnant. Not *dead*. Is it so crazy to think that someone might think I'm attractive now? That someone could see the woman behind the "bubble butt"?

STEPHEN
Hey, I said I was sorry about that!

january 18th

I was so annoyed by Stephen's reaction to Eddie that I called Anita to bitch. Unfortunately, she wasn't home, so I called Mandy, who had the nerve to agree with Stephen. "Face it,

Amy. There's no reason that man should be so interested in you."

Gee, thanks.

I am completely fed up with defending my relationship with Eddie. Since when is it a crime to be a supportive friend? He's a nice guy. We're pals. If he's a bit attracted to me, who can blame him? I'm a fun, good-looking woman.

Now would everyone please back off?

january 19th

Craving some exercise, but not in the mood for Balanced Breathing, I decided to walk home after work. The sky was clear, the air was crisp, and it wasn't too cold. And as I made my way through Central Park, I ran into Eddie's friend Jillian pushing her infant son in a stroller.

After reintroducing myself, I asked how she was – although judging from the way she looked the answer had to be tired.

> JILLIAN
> I'm great – ever since Cougar came into
> my life.

Cougar? That's the name she was so desperate to protect? Is she insane? With a name like that the kid's practically OB-LIGATED to be a pot smokin' guitarist in a lousy cover band. Start saving bail money now.

> ME
> Cougar? What a great name!

Has Eddie met him yet?

JILLIAN
Who?

ME
Eddie.

JILLIAN
God, no. I haven't seen him since Cougar
was born.

ME
Yeah, I guess you must be pretty busy with
the baby and everything.

JILLIAN
I see you haven't figured it out yet.

ME
What are you talking about?

JILLIAN
Eddie.

ME
What about him?

JILLIAN
He's got a thing for pregnant women.

ME
You mean like an invention?

> JILLIAN
> No, I mean like a *jones*. Pregnant women turn him on. But once you give birth, he couldn't care less.

She shook her head.

> JILLIAN
> It's totally fetishistic.

Oh, God.

january 19th – 11:30 p.m.

I took three showers after my encounter today with Jillian and I still feel gross. Ick. I can't believe I let Eddie touch my stomach!

Eeewe.

I should have known something was horribly wrong with the situation. After all, what normal man would *want* to shop for maternity clothes?

And to think I was his excuse – his "cover" – to hang out at maternity shops, baby stores, and prenatal yoga classes without seeming odd, conspicuous, or in need of intense psychiatric counseling. I feel so used!

But the ultimate insult? He didn't even have the decency to be attracted to *me*. It was my pregnancy that he was hot for. I could have been the village troll for all he cared. The least the bastard could have done is sexualize my *whole* being!

There is no way I can tell ANYONE about this. Not Stephen, or Anita, or Mandy, or my mother. It's far too perverse, and besides, I couldn't possibly handle all the I-told-you-sos.

january 20th

I've spent all day struggling to pull together a last-minute book-release party for Tangy in L.A. It took me three months to plan the one in New York. It's gonna take a miracle to arrange another one by February 4. Sure, we've got a slight advantage since Tangy is a fixture on the L.A. scene, but that still doesn't change the content of her book.

Let's just say the book editor at the L.A. *Times* asked me twice if I was kidding before declining to do a review.

And then there's Eddie. I swear I'll smack him if he tries to rub my stomach once more. I've got to end this friendship *immediately*.

Unfortunately, shaking him won't be that easy. I can break our shopping dates, not mention when I go to yoga, and cut short any discussion of baby names. But how am I going to disinvite him to my baby shower? He's hosting the damn thing!

january 21st

Anita's mole over at *Focus* says they've narrowed their decision to two candidates, and one of them is a Brinkman/Baines employee!

This is why I've been slaving away, sucking up to a woman whose jeans are so tight they've stopped the flow of oxygen to her brain!

Meanwhile, forget birth. Today I witnessed a REAL miracle. A New Yorker gave up a train seat for me. And it was a GUY.

january 22nd

Yip-pee! Stephen and I have chosen a girl's name – Serena. It's beautiful and unusual without being crazy.

Serena Stewart. How euphonic. Even Mandy will approve!

january 23rd

It's official. I now wear underwear the size of a circus tent.

On the plus side, a guy at the grocery store let me jump the checkout line because I'm so pregnant.

january 24th

Margo canceled again. She and all three of her kids are sick. I could hear the entire family moaning in the background during our phone call. It was like the audio track of *One Flew Over the Cuckoo's Nest.*

Figuring she had enough trouble without my complaining, I tried to be supportive. "Look at the bright side. If you're stuck in bed, at least you can read a good book."

Margo's laughter quickly deteriorated into a hacking cough.

"Are you kidding? I'll be waiting hand and foot on the

kids. Trust me, Amy. Once you're a parent, reading becomes one of those forgotten luxuries like sleep, and owning shirts that aren't stained with spit-up, and eating a meal at a leisurely pace, and . . ."

As I listened to Margo detail the realities of her life I had three thoughts. First, where the hell is that husband of hers? Second, she sounds more like a slave than a parent. And third, the media has it all wrong.

This last thought occurred to me as I glanced in the mirror.

We constantly hear stories about the high price of "having it all." The disintegrating marriages, the troubled children, the derailed career. Well, they're all wrong. With a career, a husband, and a baby on the way, I can safely say that the high price of having it all . . .

IS LOOKING LIKE SHIT.

Take Margo, for example. Back when she was a childless bank executive, she wore dry-clean-only suits and tasteful jewelry. Now she wears overalls and granny underwear. Remember the Hanes for Her? And then there's me. Enormous and flatulent. With just enough makeup to maintain a hint of cheekbones.

Well, enough is enough. It's like Mandy said. Pregnancy should never be an excuse to let oneself go. It's time to perk up my appearance. If for no reason other than to feel good about myself.

My first move? Try out that cute Mia Farrow haircut from *Rosemary's Baby*. Sure, I've never had short hair before, but then I've never been shaped like a sphere.

january 25th

I must have been crazy to try this haircut! Mia Farrow
weighed about ten pounds when she wore this style and it
was the 1960s! A whole different millennium! Didn't that
horrible hairdresser know better than to listen to a pregnant
woman? I mean, for God's sake, I look like the fat kid that
nobody wants to play with during recess!

Sobbing and hysterical, I called Mandy the minute I left
the salon. Twenty minutes later we were rendezvousing at
her apartment – me with a scarf wrapped around my head
and Mandy with a bunker full of hair products.

Removing my scarf, I showed her the damage. She
gasped, "That hairdresser should be shot!"

I began to wail all over again. "I just wanted to look nice.
To be soft and sensual and at ease, like Lily."

"Who's Lily?"

"She's my best pregnant friend!" I sobbed some more.
"What's happened to me? I used to be an attractive size-
eight brunette!"

Mandy gently ran a brush through my hair. "Size ten. But
you were definitely attractive."

"Were?!"

"And still are. You're just follicly challenged at the moment."

Pumping a glob of mousse into her hands, she ran it
through my hair. I now looked like a member of The Cure.
At my wit's end, I began babbling on and on about how this
would never happen to Tangy Blair. She was always thin,
and gorgeous, and well groomed.

Mandy scoffed and told me about a magazine that printed
the high school photos of celebrities. Not one of them had

the same nose. I suddenly felt comforted. "And Tangy Blair was in there?"

"No, I think her nose is real. But I'm making a broader point. If it's not a nose job, it's a boob job, or a new hair color. You know darn well that those people are completely manufactured. But you? You're a real person full of vitality and love. So embrace your natural state – because it's beautiful."

Mandy was right. I *am* beautiful. And real. Even more so pregnant. So with a head full of mousse, bobby pins, and styling gel, I gave her a huge hug. Careful not to stain her clothing, she hugged me back – then added, "Just remember that manicures, pedicures, facials, proper haircuts, and the occasional seaweed body wrap can do wonders to enhance that natural state."

Two hours later I walked into my apartment to face Stephen. Although he feigned enthusiasm, it was clear from his expression that at this moment my "natural state" was closer to a natural disaster.

january 26th

After doing an unfavorable double take on my new haircut, the Crotch Whisperer's nurse informed me that from now on I'll have to come in every two weeks for an appointment.

Is she kidding? Doesn't she understand that, in addition to registering, attending two baby showers, hosting a book-release party, and arranging a second one over three thousand miles away, I have to complete the remaining forty-plus items on my Things to Do list?

Apparently not.

Making my visit even more frustrating was the Crotch

Whisperer's silent taunts regarding the baby's sex. Yes, after all these months I'm getting pretty damn good at reading lips. As long as he's not facedown between my legs, I've got a general idea of what the guy's saying. Which is why I was so annoyed when he waved my chart in front of my face and mouthed the words, "Sure you don't want to know the sex?" Trust me, if he wasn't charged with the responsibility of bringing my child safely into this world I would have poked him in the eye with the speculum.

Because, with barely two months left and not a single boy's name, it was a very tempting offer. After all, if we're having a girl, we could just end this name hysteria right now. But no. At this point it was the principle of the thing as much as it was about wanting to be old-fashioned.

Even if my mother dismissively contends that "old-fashioned" just means that something better – like medical science – has been invented since then.

january 27th

My mother's beside herself. In less than a week she's throwing me a baby shower, and I still haven't registered. "What will everyone buy you?"

Who's everyone?

"Mom, this is a really crazy time for me. Work's insane, and there's a chance I'll have to leave town the day after the shower."

"You're seven months pregnant. Where are you going?"

"Closer to eight months, but that's beside the point."

"Well, if you're short on time just go to Baby Bargains. They have everything."

"I've been there, Mom. It's a superstore. Cold, impersonal, unoriginal. It's like choosing a bride from a Russian mail-order catalog."

"Fine, shop wherever you want, but don't take this registering thing too lightly. It's very practical."

Well, *duh*! What does she think I am? An idiot? Why else would I be spending night after night logging onto baby websites, staring at poorly rendered photos with inadequate descriptions? Sure the Sleepy Time crib converts to a toddler bed, but why would I want that? I can't think past my due date, let alone to when the baby starts to toddle.

Would someone please tell me why I waited until now, when I'm completely exhausted, to do this? I should have done it during my energetic second trimester. Oh, wait – I wanted to, but *Stephen* was too busy. That's right. This is all Stephen's fault!

Well, thank God. I may not have a diaper pail, but at least I have someone to blame.

january 28th

I'm completely torn about this trip to L.A.

Professionally, it'd be really bad not to go. After all, *The Damned* is my baby. So to speak. For better or worse I'm personally responsible for introducing it to the world. And both the Crotch Whisperer and *BH, BN* concur that there's no actual medical risk associated with flying. Just the hellish possibility of forcing the emergency landing of a 747.

On the other hand, I'm almost eight months pregnant. I don't want to fly six thousand miles. *In coach*.

This was what I was thinking about when the phone rang. Too tired to get off the sofa, I let Stephen answer it.

Seconds later he appeared with the portable phone in his hand and a look of disgust on his face. "It's Eddie."

He was calling me at night? At home? Was nothing sacred? Was there not a single personal boundary left? Despite the fact that he'd been doing it regularly for the last four months, it suddenly felt incredibly invasive.

So I waved my hands in the air and told Stephen to tell him I wasn't home. Although initially shocked, Stephen quickly recovered and took great joy in giving Eddie the brush-off.

Moments later, he asked why I'd lied to Eddie. Sure, I could have said that Eddie was a sexual deviant with a hankering for pregnant women. And that Stephen and everyone else had been right about the suspicious nature of Eddie's interest in me. And that, yes, I'd been too delusional to know it.

But really? Why go there?

So instead I wrapped my arms around Stephen and lied through my teeth – lovingly explaining that I didn't want Eddie to come between us. And to make Stephen happy, I'd decided to end the friendship. After all, a woman's husband was her first priority, right?

Close enough.

january 29th

> *It's Amy Thomas's baby shower!*
> *Please join the fun*
> *The Mom-to-Be Lounge*
> *At The Joie de Vivre Maternity Shop*
> *156 East 62nd Street*
> *March 1 – 12 noon*
> *A light lunch and beverages will be served.*

It's both brilliant and sick.

Eddie has actually rented out the snack bar at Joie de Vivre, one of New York's most exclusive maternity shops. This means that while hosting a very fancy shower for me, he's guaranteed to rub elbows, *and stomachs,* with tons of pregnant women. Once again, I'm being used for his demented purposes.

I don't know whether to laugh or cry.

january 29th – 4 p.m.

It's official. I'm flying to L.A. on the morning of the 4th and returning on the 5th. That's six thousand miles in twenty-four hours. God help me.

january 30th

It just gets better and better.

Things No One Tells You About Pregnancy
1. No sushi
2. Twenty-four-hour morning sickness
3. Forty weeks (ten months) of pregnancy
4. No aspirin
5. Dog nose
6. "Glow" is sweat
7. Excessive flatulence
8. Heartburn
9. Ungodly constipation
10. CRC (Can't Remember Crap)

11. Public petting
12. Final erosion of personal identity
13. Incontinence
14. Broken capillaries
15. Difficulty breathing

As the baby gets bigger, my air-intake capacity gets smaller. And yet I can't be bitter. With only eight weeks left, I'm already fiercely attached to this oxygen-stealing creature.

After all, it's my baby!

january 31st

After enduring rush-hour traffic, icy sidewalks, a drunk, and two panhandlers, I'm convinced there's no way to raise a child in this city unless you're fabulously wealthy or completely indifferent.

This city is overcrowded, dirty, and, from what I can tell, sorely lacking in acceptable playgrounds.

Don't get me started on the public school system.

Yes, the more I think about it, the more logical the suburbs are beginning to seem. I know that sounds awful. But I don't mean the real suburbs, like where my parents live or where the Stepford Wives are. I mean the hip and funky suburbs. Where the *cool* people go to begin artist colonies and open fantastic multicultural restaurants and form avant-garde theater companies that sell Edamame during intermission and – oh, God!

Who am I kidding?

A burb is a burb is a burb. And Nicole is absolutely right: I AM LAME!

Luckily, my husband's not. Because I arrived home to find a romantic candlelit dinner waiting for me on the table.

And while it was a feat of balance, creativity, and sheer willpower, we finished the evening with some very enjoyable sex.

february 1st

The public petting has really gotten out of control.

In the course of an average day, would you ever stroke a stranger's stomach? Reach across the subway car and pat some guy's tummy? Of course not. And if you did you'd be smacked or arrested. But for some mysterious reason pregnant women are like magnets for random gropes. People just lunge at me without warning. And definitely without asking.

And leading the petting parade is Eddie, who despite my horrible new haircut still pines for me.

Oh, goodie.

february 2nd

I am proud to say that despite all odds, Tangy Blair's New York book launch was a grand success. That's right, the Absolution Bar and Lounge was packed. We had a handful of A-list stars, a smattering of wannabes, and a hefty dose of local has-beens. There were reporters and gossip columnists from the less popular publications. And just enough paparazzi hoping for a shot of Tangy in her see-through shirt to keep the room nicely illuminated with flashbulbs.

And everyone went home with a signed copy of *The Damned*.

Had it not been for Eddie's unrelenting attempts to hang out with me, the event would have been perfect. In spite of the fact that Tangy kept calling me Amanda.

Exhausted and relieved, I arrived home to find Mr. Elbin in the lobby waiting for the elevator. Unwilling to end my glorious evening with an obnoxious crack, I quickly ducked into the stairwell and walked the four flights. Half an hour later I arrived at my apartment door in a pool of sweat.

I swear that man will be the death of me.

february 3rd

I took the day off from work to recover. It was great. After sleeping fifteen hours, I watched some bad TV, then went upstate for my baby shower.

Between all the Tangy hysteria, the Eddie revelation, and the trauma of my new haircut, I'd neglected to consider who'd be at this shower. So it was with great shock and slight trepidation that I arrived at my parents' house to find my mother, Gram, Nicole, Mrs. Stewart, Chuffy, Mrs. Brockton, Kimberly, my cousin Lydia, and three of my mother's friends – two of whom I'd never met before, and one I hadn't seen since I was twelve and she caught me snooping through her makeup drawer when I was baby-sitting for her kids.

Exactly *why* had I said yes to this event?

Seconds later, my cousin Lydia was rushing me with a bear hug. It was the first time I'd seen her since being pregnant, and she couldn't wait to rub my stomach. "You're not nearly as huge as they said you were."

Excuse me? "Who said I was huge?"

I flashed an accusing eye around the room. Curiously everyone avoided my gaze. Lydia immediately dissembled, "Oh, no one in particular. Just folks."

And before I could pursue the matter further, the festivities began. It was an evening of oohs and ahhs as we ate from a mediocre buffet my mother had prepared and I opened presents – my mother giving me a look of exasperation as I unwrapped one nongender-specific baby outfit after another, all of them yellow.[84]

Luckily, my mother bought me a diaper pail, and Lucy was kind enough to send a lovely nursing gown. And then there was Gram – with her sweet face and acid heart – still stewing about our decision not to name the baby Sessy. Unbeknownst to anyone else, it was obvious to my dog nose that the woman *reeked* of steamed broccoli. So pungent was the stink that she must have wiped herself down with the stuff before joining the celebration. Every time she got near me, I was certain I would faint.

Then there was her gift. Opening the package, I was shocked – it was hand-knit and stunning. The kind of thing one would find at Bountiful Mother. And as I pulled it from the box, it just kept coming and coming and coming. "What a beautiful blanket!"

Gram laughed. "Don't be silly, Amy. Blankets don't have neck holes. It's a poncho."

"Oh. You mean to drape over the back of a couch?"

"No, for you to wear."

"But it's huge."

---

[84] Note to self: *Must* register for my next baby shower.

Gram smiled. Patted my belly. And corrected me. "No, dear. It's *enormous.*"

After reminding myself that elder abuse is a crime, I channeled my anger into the consumption of an entire coffee cake.

And so it was. An evening of chitchat, pleasantries, and sublimated fury. And when the coffee cake was finished and the last guest had gone home, my practical mother rifled through the wrapping debris searching for receipts, so that I could return as many yellow outfits as possible.

It was around this time that I began to sense something was wrong with Nicole. She'd been quiet all evening, and though I was fairly certain she was still bumming about Pablo, I wanted to be sure. So when she snuck outside to have a cigarette, I followed her.

After some sensitive sisterly prodding – "Come on! I'd tell *you*!" – Nicole finally came clean. Yes, she was still bummed about Pablo, but there was something else. She'd just heard that Chet and his new wife had had a baby. And, as she was quick to point out, she didn't regret leaving Chet, and she certainly didn't want a baby, but there had been something comforting about coming home every night to someone who loved you.

This from the Bible-thumper of Singledom. I was speechless.

Choking back tears, Nicole dragged hard on her cigarette. "I know you mock my lifestyle, Amy. Except right now it's exactly what I need. But even so, there are plenty of times when being alone just isn't so great."

I thought of how annoyed I'd been with Stephen over these past few months. Of how Anita wants a baby but doesn't want a husband. And of how before I was married I hated when people assumed that being single was the same as being alone. Because it's not. You have family, lovers, and friends. Somewhere between getting married and being envious of Nicole's "exciting" new life I'd managed to forget this. And I'd become a total ass, more interested in mocking Nicole than supporting her. God, I'd been a shitty sister.

Wrapping my arms around Nicole, I held her close. "You're not alone. Because, whether you like it or not, you'll always have me."

With tears streaming down her face, Nicole hugged me back. Then sobbed, "Thanks, Amy. But I'm still not babysitting."

Despite my sister's enduring sense of humor, I couldn't help but think that the next few years were going to be rough on her.

february 4th

As if I wasn't nervous enough about flying, Stephen spent all last night and this morning asking me if I was sure I wanted to take this trip. Well, of course I don't *want* to take this trip. But I feel like I have to. Besides, as I reminded him – and myself – for the hundredth time, it's not medically dangerous. As the Crotch Whisperer's nurse said – it's my decision.[85]

Unfortunately, my blood pressure skyrocketed the minute I arrived at the airport. A white-knuckle flier on the best of days, today was definitely going to be a challenge. Sipping a

---

[85] Which is medical legalese for "We're not responsible if something happens."

cup of herbal tea, I kept reminding myself to breathe and remain calm.

A goal that was seriously challenged when I saw Tangy Blair strut onto my plane – and into First Class. Great. In addition to having more legroom and real silverware, if the plane crashes, all that anyone will ever hear about is how Tangy Blair was aboard.

There is no justice.

That said, everything was fine until forty minutes into the flight, when the stewardesses began to serve breakfast. First my dog nose went off. Whatever was in those tiny trays was definitely not friendly. Then it occurred to me, as I sat jammed in my window seat, that between the meal carts in the aisle and the teenage boy sound asleep next to me, I was TRAPPED. Unable to stand, stretch my legs, go to the bathroom, or breathe. Yes, I could NOT breathe. I simply wasn't getting enough oxygen.

Wasn't the system designed to accommodate those who were oxygenating two? I adjusted the overhead air vents. Nothing. Frantic, I started to pound on the ceiling trying to make one of those little plastic bags fall out. With my blood pressure rising, I began to hyperventilate.

Which was when I felt the kicking inside my stomach.

The baby wanted out! And I lost it.

Good lord! If I was worried about natural childbirth in a hospital, the thought of natural childbirth in row 34, seat E was inconceivable.

So I quickly called for the flight attendant. Although, considering the number of heads that spun around, perhaps it was more of a shriek than a call. Seconds later, flight attendant Kelli, with an *I,* was asking me to lower my voice. But it was no use. Breathing was so difficult that modulating my speaking voice was entirely out of the question. Through gasps I managed to convey to Kelli that I had gone into labor. The kid next to me sprang from his seat. Kelli with an *I* turned sheet white and sprinted down the aisle. I was furious. Weren't these people trained for stuff like this? I couldn't possibly be the first woman to give birth on a plane.

Or could I?!

Moments later Kelli was on the P.A. system, asking if there were any doctors on board. And, suddenly, like a rolling wave of flesh, dozens of hands shot into the air. Certain that I was seeing things, I rubbed my eyes. But no. My eyes had not deceived me, and already a band of men and women was racing my way.

I said a quick prayer of thanks to the gods, the medical community, and the person who invented microwave brownies. I may be thirty thousand feet in the air, but I was about to receive better medical care than my HMO would ever provide.

The next thing I knew I was being dragged from my seat and laid, not on a recliner in First Class, but on the floor of the galley area in the rear of the aircraft alongside the lavatory. The doctors blabbered at each other and stared at me. I was the star of my own *ER* episode. Clutching my stomach, and struggling to control my erratic breathing, I turned to look at the woman who was kneeling by my side checking my pulse. She was neatly dressed and had small wire-rimmed glasses like really smart people wear. I found that comforting. Summoning all my strength, I asked what her specialty was.

Then I asked her again because I was certain she'd just said *bovine*.

"I'm a vet. We're all vets."

I looked up at the group of people who had assembled around me. My sight was getting fuzzy. The group now looked like they had hooves. The woman next to me started to stroke my hand. I began to feel like a German shepherd.

"We're on our way to a seminar on large animal husbandry."

The last thing I remember is gasping for air.

An hour later I came to – still on the floor near the lavatory with Dr. Bovine kneeling by my side. I quickly felt my stomach, wondering if I'd had the baby. Dr. Bovine smiled and calmly explained that I hadn't given birth. On the contrary, I'd simply had a panic attack, which had caused me to pass out. The abdominal pains? Probably Braxton-Hicks contractions, otherwise known as false labor, brought on by anxiety. Or it could have just been gas. In any event, I was fine. Looking around, I caught sight of Kelli serving coffee. She tossed me an icy cold stare of annoyance. It was a good bet that I wouldn't be getting an extra bag of peanuts.

Twenty minutes later they returned me to my seat – in coach. Apparently near-birth experiences don't warrant an upgrade.

february 5th

Last night's launch party went fairly well. We didn't have any press of importance, and there were absolutely no television cameras. But Tangy hardly seemed to notice. She was having far too much fun with her friends to care that the paparazzi were more interested in candid shots of her mingling with other celebrities than in taking home their signed copies of *The Damned*.

By night's end we had 160 copies left over. We'd started with 180.

And despite my horrific flight, my extreme jet lag, and my rampant CRC, which prevented me from remembering anyone's name, I managed to survive the evening unscathed. There was even a humorous moment when I overheard Tangy complaining to friends about some idiot pregnant woman in coach who'd caused a panic on board by almost giving birth. She shook her head. "Those damn spawners!"

If nothing else, I'd succeeded in irritating her, so all in all I'd say it was a worthwhile trip. Even if I was in Los Angeles for less than twenty-four hours and saw nothing but the airport, the pitch-black club where we had the party, and my hotel room.

Determined not to relive my flight experience, I decided to sleep as little as possible. I went to bed late and got up at six this morning, all with the hope of being so exhausted that instead of passing out during the flight home, I'd simply fall asleep. Unfortunately, it was the same flight crew on my return flight as on my inbound flight. So instead of greeting me with a chipper "Good morning and welcome aboard," Kelli and all the gang greeted me with gasps of horror.

Well, what the hell did they expect me to do? *Walk* back to New York?

february 6th

Sound asleep from takeoff to landing, I survived the flight. By the time I arrived home last night I looked like hell, but I was intact. Stephen rubbed my feet, made me dinner, and tucked me into bed.

As a present to myself, I took today off from work. I figured I deserved it after lugging my bulging belly out to L.A. Not to mention the fact that I was entirely too fatigued to deal with Eddie.

At three in the afternoon, Stephen burst through the door, elated. A major medical instrument company has agreed to invest in the development of their new computer program. Short of winning the lottery or successfully completing the project, it's the best thing that could happen.

Two hours later Mr. Spontaneity had rallied ten of our closest friends – and Jon – for a celebratory meal at a barbecue joint in midtown.

And later, as we climbed into bed, Stephen kissed my belly and thanked me for forcing the baby issue.

"You were right. There is no perfect time to have a baby. The perfect time is whenever you decide to do it. I can hardly wait for little Serena or the yet-to-be-named Stewart son to arrive. You are undeniably the most wonderful woman in the world."

He had me at "You were right."

february 7th

I was greeted at work with Eddie's unavoidable bear hug and Mr. Nealy's exuberant congratulations on my job well done – quickly followed by the update that Representative Blanca Fernandez had alienated a group of Italian-Americans by calling them "wops," and that the fifty-two-year-old, bucktoothed, eczema-beset Abe Hamen was eager to boost sagging sales of his massage products by rebranding himself as a sex guru.

And oh, yeah. I now waddle.

But none of this matters. Because my tumultuous affair with Tangy Blair is officially over. With her book release a traumatic thing of the past, she's once again Mr. Nealy's client. Everybody say Amen.

february 8th

Whether calmed by his recent business coup, energized by his newfound comfort level, or simply showing his true colors as Mr. Spontaneity, Stephen suggested that we do our baby registry as soon as possible.

Thrilled, I seized the bull by the horns and brought Stephen to Baby Bargains after work. Sure it's a megasuperstore – cold, impersonal, and generic. But it's one-stop shopping. And extremely practical. No wonder my mother was so pushy about coming here. Armed with a blank registry sheet, I grabbed the first – and only – person we saw with a name tag and insisted that she direct us to the best-selling items in each category. So what if she was the security guard? We were done in thirty minutes, without a single mention of homemade bassinets or the evil baby empire.

february 9th – 4 a.m.

My ever-expanding body has resulted in yet another surprise.

Things No One Tells You About Pregnancy
1. No sushi
2. Twenty-four-hour morning sickness

3. Forty weeks (ten months) of pregnancy
4. No aspirin
5. Dog nose
6. "Glow" is sweat
7. Excessive flatulence
8. Heartburn
9. Ungodly constipation
10. CRC (Can't Remember Crap)
11. Public petting
12. Final erosion of personal identity
13. Incontinence
14. Broken capillaries
15. Difficulty breathing
16. Difficulty sleeping

There's an evil irony at work here: Now that I'm more tired than ever, sleeping has become IMPOSSIBLE. Between my increased girth, my odd shape, and the fact that the baby's head is burrowing into my sciatic nerve, I'm unable to sleep without tossing and turning and getting up. They say it's good practice for when the baby comes, but, let's face it, it pretty much sucks. Your back hurts, your legs ache, and, to top it off, you're constantly peeing.

No wonder Stephen's decided to sleep on the sofa.

february 10th

This boy name is driving me nuts. If only we knew the sex of the child, things would be *sooo* much easier. At first we thought not knowing the sex would make the experience more exciting. Now, in my ninth month, I can assure you that I've had all the excitement I can take.

Besides, who am I kidding? I know this kid's a boy. It's got to be. After all those years spent complaining about men, the gods are definitely gonna challenge me to raise a righteous one of my own.

Me and my big mouth.

february 11th

Since the baby shower invitations have already gone out, and I don't want Eddie further involved in the event, I called Nicole and asked her to casually inform invitees that I'm now registered at Baby Bargains. She graciously said yes.

february 12th

We had our hospital tour today. Electrifying and terrifying. Ah, the two faces of childbirth.

Stephen and I were one of ten couples who are planning on giving birth at Memorial Hospital within the next two months. All different colors and ethnicities, I couldn't help but think we represented the best of New York – a mini-United Nations birthing the next generation. I suddenly got a glimpse of the "big picture." Our baby was a link to the future. Part of the continuum of humanity. An immense wave of hope washed over me. I gave Stephen a big hug.

Our first stop on the tour? The Community Room, where an obstetric anesthesiologist lectured us about drugs. Among other important facts, he explained that the process of having an epidural stopped the brain from realizing that the body was in pain. Or, as he merrily went on to add, "It's like the phone's ringing but no one's home to answer it."

I gasped. Isn't that commonly referred to as *dementia*? I jabbed Stephen in the ribs. "See! That's why I want natural childbirth." Praying I wouldn't cause a scene, Stephen forced a smile and dutifully nodded.

Next stop – the Maternity Ward. Here we were led by a hospital docent who looked like a refugee from a Midwestern church social. The very blond Meredith was sporting pearls, a blue velvet headband, and a lavender twin set. As she began to talk, I couldn't help but marvel at the irony of being led through the maternity ward by a woman who had probably never had sex.

After showing us the check-in desk, the waiting room, the labor and delivery rooms, the recovery rooms, the vending machines, the public phones, and the water fountain, Meredith stopped to ask if we had any questions. A couple of East Indian descent raised their hands. But before they could open their mouths, we were sideswiped by an orderly wheeling a woman from one delivery room into another at breakneck speed. And who could blame him? Drooling and ranting, she was not a happy camper. She took one look at our group of pregnant couples and ominously hissed, "Your day will come! Your day will come!"

Shivers ran down my spine. It was like a scene out of *Carrie*. Not the least bit rattled, Meredith calmly tucked a stray hair under her blue velvet headband and said, "Don't be alarmed. That's just the narcotics speaking."

Stephen turned to Meredith, his voice trembling with fear. "Excuse me, but did you say that's *with* narcotics?"

Meredith smiled. "Yes."

Reaching for my hand, Stephen didn't need to say a word. We were on the same saliva-stained page: I was getting the epidural. Two, if they let me.

february 12th – 10 P.M.

It's official. I'm saying good-bye to natural childbirth and hello to drugs. *BH, BN* assures me that it's okay to have the drugs, that they're no longer dangerous or overly used (at least in most first-world, urban hospitals), and that as long as I communicate my desires to my doctor ahead of time, things will be fine. Party line or not, I'm going with it.

Sure, I'd like to have a natural childbirth. And yes, it's closer to the way nature intended it to be. But let's face it. God's a woman, so in addition to the universe she also created epidurals, Pitocin, and Kit Kat bars. And why create them if she didn't want us to use them – at our own discretion.

Besides, who am I kidding? I'll bitch-slap you for pulling my hair, so how the hell am I gonna get through an unmedicated birth?

> Things to Do
> 1. ~~Find ob/gyn~~
> 2. ~~Get prenatal checkup~~
> 3. ~~Get prenatal vitamins~~
> 4. ~~Find physical exercise~~
> 5. ~~Decide childbirth method~~
> 6. Join childbirth class
> 7. Buy crib
> 8. Buy bassinet
> 9. Buy crib mattress

10. Buy crib bedding
11. Buy changing table
12. Decide cloth or disposable diapers
13. Buy diapers
14. Buy diaper bag
15. ~~Buy diaper pail~~
16. Buy crib mobile
17. Buy layette
18. Buy stroller
19. Buy infant bathtub
20. Buy baby monitor
21. Buy infant swing
22. Buy night-light for baby's room
23. Choose color for baby's room
24. Paint baby's room
25. Buy pacifiers
26. Buy dresser for baby's clothes
27. Buy infant-size hangers
28. Create medical emergency kit
29. Prepare emergency phone lists
30. ~~Decide nursing or formula~~
31. Buy nursing supplies or formula supplies
32. If nursing, decide to rent or buy breast pump
33. If nursing, buy nursing bras
34. If nursing, buy nipple cream
35. Decide on legal guardian
36. Prepare wills
37. Plan estate
38. Create college fund
39. ~~Begin Kegel exercises~~

40. Buy first-year memorabilia scrapbook

41. ~~Decide whether to learn gender~~

42. Choose name(s)

43. ~~Choose hospital~~

44. ~~Take tour of hospital maternity ward~~

45. Find pediatrician

46. ~~Appoint someone to organize baby shower~~

47. ~~Make invite list for baby shower~~

48. ~~Register for baby shower~~

49. Buy thank-you notes for baby shower

50. Select birth music

51. ~~Prepare for appropriate religious ceremony~~

52. ~~Book venue for religious ceremony~~

53. ~~Arrange for priest, rabbi, or *mohel*, etc.~~

54. ~~Buy baby's outfit for religious ceremony~~

55. ~~Buy maternity clothes~~

56. ~~Decide who will be in delivery room with you~~

57. Prepare baby announcements

58. Prepare overnight bag for hospital

59. Make birth plan

60. ~~Schedule maternity leave~~

61. Make phone list for announcing baby's birth

62. Buy baby's take-home-from-hospital outfit

63. Decide on postbirth child care

february 13th

I spent all morning feeling guilty about abandoning natural childbirth and sprinting to the narcotics counter. So after convincing Abe Hamen that "sex guru" may not be the best way to rebrand himself, I called Anita and told her all about the women in my prenatal yoga class with their fleecy lambskins and their ironclad determination to birth un-aided. After mocking me mercilessly for going to Balanced Breathing – and for keeping it a secret – Anita scolded me for allowing others to shame me about my birthing choice. As she reminded me, this is my body, my labor. "Hell, in a perfect world most women would give birth in a lounge chair, drinking wine, and watching a George Clooney movie."

I suddenly felt better. Anita was right. This is my preg-nancy, my baby, my body. I need to have this child in a way that I'm comfortable with.

Although right now that means hiring a surrogate mother.

february 13th – 8 p.m.

I arrived home to find a message on my answering machine from Mandy regarding my baby registry. Apparently she'd sooner give herself a home-permanent than step foot in Baby Bargains.

Guess she won't be getting me that nifty baby wipes warmer.

february 14th

Today was Valentine's Day.

In an effort to pamper myself I went to Balanced Breathing after work and got an extra treat – a former patron returned to class with her adorable baby girl. Rachel was four-months old and cute as a button. We all cooed over her, every one of us with the same joyful thought running through our mind: "Soon *I'll* have this!"

Then, halfway through the class Rachel started to cry. And wail. Then shriek. Her piercing tones shattered our chorus of *Sat Nam,* chilling me to the bone. I cautiously opened my eyes and saw that we were all cringing. Every one of us with the same horrific thought running through our mind: "Soon *I'll* have this!"

Afterward, as I was walking down the stairs, I caught sight of Eddie hanging out by the building's entrance – chatting up a bunch of pregnant women, asking about their due dates, discussing ginger teas. I was shocked. I'd been out of the office for most of the day overseeing a photo shoot for Glyniss O'Maley. There was no way Eddie could have known I was coming to Balanced Breathing. There was only one explanation: The guy was stalking me. Desperate not to be anywhere near Eddie on Valentine's Day, I did the only sensible thing I could think of – I hid in the bathroom until he left.

This unforeseen event, which I couldn't possibly mention to Stephen, caused me to arrive home late. Which meant that I only had ten minutes to look fabulous for our romantic Valentine's Day dinner. I quickly rifled through the closet and discovered that I was now too big to fit into any of my "fancy" maternity clothes, including the special-occasion dress that I'd gotten on sale at Bountiful Mother.

Stephen came into the bedroom and asked me to hurry up. I quickly explained that unless geodesic domes now came in fashion colors, I was unable to clothe myself for a nice evening out. Searching through the closet, Stephen pulled out a pair of black pregnancy pants and an extra-large green cardigan. Essentially the same outfit I'd been wearing to work for the last week. But preggers can't be choosers, and as Stephen was quick to point out we had a dinner reservation in less than ten minutes. I completed the ensemble with one of my many decorative scarves, and we were out the door five minutes later.

But not to the pretty little French place around the corner, as I had been led to believe. Oh, no. My super, fantastic husband surprised me with a delicious meal at Estrella, an extremely hot restaurant down in Tribeca. Very trendy. Very hard to get into. Apparently Stephen made the reservation six months ago! How's that for romantic!

It was a wonderful evening, made perfect by the knowledge that next Valentine's Day . . .

We'll have a BABY!

february 15th

Because she's a great friend, and she's tired of hearing me complain about my aches and fears, Mandy bought me a day pass to her gym so that I could relax in the Jacuzzi spa. It was an incredibly thoughtful gift. Even if I couldn't take advantage of it.

> Things No One Tells You About Pregnancy
> 1. No sushi

2. Twenty-four-hour morning sickness
3. Forty weeks (ten months) of pregnancy
4. No aspirin
5. Dog nose
6. "Glow" is sweat
7. Excessive flatulence
8. Heartburn
9. Ungodly constipation
10. CRC (Can't Remember Crap)
11. Public petting
12. Final erosion of personal identity
13. Incontinence
14. Broken capillaries
15. Difficulty breathing
16. Difficulty sleeping
17. No hot tubs

After spending hours scrounging for an outfit that would be socially acceptable – and physically possible – for a pregnant woman to wear in a public Jacuzzi[86] I arrived to the hot tub's warm and bubbling edge to find a notice posted on the wall: due to extremely high water temperatures, the use of spa tubs is prohibited to pregnant women.

I spent the next forty-five minutes drowning my sorrows in the juice bar next door.

february 16th – 3:47 a.m.

It suddenly occurs to me that I keep hearing about how the doctor cuts the umbilical cord at the baby's navel.

---

[86] Because there's no way I was investing in a maternity swimsuit.

But what happens to the other end?!

Is it on some kind of pulley? Do I just wheel it back inside of me like a fishing rod?

How can I be a month from my due date and not know the answer to this question?!

february 16th

I've come to realize that there are two categories of expectant fathers: those whose impending fatherhood causes them to panic and hide, and those whose impending fatherhood brings them closer to their family. Clearly Stephen has gone from the first to the second. Which is wonderful. It's what I've been wishing for. Except he's gone *so* far into the second category that he's created a third: those who try to take over the process.

Careful what you wish for.

That's right. Mr. Spontaneity's sudden participation has become really annoying. Thanks to his sudden obsession with Internet research, I'm now expected to walk three miles a day and bide my time for twenty minutes each night as he chats to my stomach. Yes, he's learned that parents are encouraged to talk to the baby inside the womb. In this way the baby will recognize and be comforted by the sound of those voices at birth. Touching. Except why the baby needs to hear about binary computer code is completely beyond me.

Luckily, he did have an answer to my late-night panic about the umbilical cord: the other end is attached to the placenta, which is expelled from my body after the baby's born.

Whoa. *That's* a relief. Sure beats wheeling it back inside me.

february 17th

My old friend Bianca Larsen called today to say she'd received the invitation to my baby shower, but that she wouldn't be able to make it because *she's* due a week before that. I couldn't believe it. I know I've been busy, but how could Bianca have been pregnant for the last nine months without my even knowing about it?

With all due respect to Lily, it would have been much nicer to have a real-life pregnant friend during this experience.

february 18th

Stephen called me at work today, panicked. Apparently Martin, his procreation junkie coworker, had been touting the benefits of birthing classes when Stephen realized that we haven't even signed up for one.

I swear I meant to do that months ago. After all, it's #6 on my Things to Do list. But somehow it fell through the cracks. Like so many other things I've meant to do. So I gave Stephen carte blanche. Call around, do some research, knock yourself out. Just tell me where to show up.

february 19th

I ran into an old work acquaintance this afternoon. Years ago, Lizzie and I were copyeditors at *Round-Up*. She went on to a series of crummy jobs at other magazines, while I stayed around to become associate editor of a magazine that eventually folded into oblivion.

We all make our choices.

But today Lizzie was beside herself with joy. She'd just landed an amazing job at *Time* magazine. Not only does she get good health benefits, a decent salary, and the opportunity to write, but she also gets to travel *around the world*.

It sounded amazing. And in the middle of raving about it, she suddenly stopped and apologized to me. Embarrassed by the fact that she was boasting about her fabulous new job while being aware, through the grapevine, that I was still looking for meaningful employment.

I immediately told her not to worry. I was thrilled for her and quite happy for myself.

And I meant it. Sure, had it been last year I would have killed for that job at *Time*. But not anymore. In just over a month I'm going to have a baby. And despite the aches, pains, and excessive urination, I wouldn't change that for all the jobs in the world. And yes, I'm still crossing my fingers, toes, and eyes for that elusive position at *Focus*. But that's in midtown Manhattan. Not Nairobi.

Without a doubt, I still plan to make a career for myself. Only now it'll be a career that accommodates a family.

february 20th

Tonight was our first birthing class.

Call me a prude, but lying on the ground with my legs splayed open while simulating "pushing from my vaginal floor" would be odd enough in the privacy of my own home. But to do it in a hospital conference room along with seven other couples was beyond weird. Thank goodness I

303

wore pants.

Our instructor, Nancy, an R.N. from the maternity ward, was very brass tacks about the entire thing. None of Pippa's lavender oil or chanting. And I was grateful for her helpful information – the physical changes during delivery, the different stages of labor,[87] the methods of breathing to help manage pain . . .

But seriously, folks, I was *panting* in public!

february 21st

Stephen has agreed to choose birthing music for the delivery – #50 on my Things to Do list. As the music coordinator in our family, he alphabetizes our CDs and programs our radio stations into the stereo. He even chose our wedding band, and they were great. So, needless to say, I'm thrilled that he's handling the music for this event.

Meanwhile, my legs look like tree trunks and my wedding ring is cutting off my circulation.

When were they going to mention the bloating?

> Things No One Tells You About Pregnancy
> 1. No sushi
> 2. Twenty-four-hour morning sickness
> 3. Forty weeks (ten months) of pregnancy
> 4. No aspirin
> 5. Dog nose

---

[87] Informally known as Ouch, Yikes, and Holy Shit!

6. "Glow" is sweat
7. Excessive flatulence
8. Heartburn
9. Ungodly constipation
10. CRC (Can't Remember Crap)
11. Public petting
12. Final erosion of personal identity
13. Incontinence
14. Broken capillaries
15. Difficulty breathing
16. Difficulty sleeping
17. No hot tubs
18. Spongelike water retention

february 22nd

Anita called this evening, completely depressed. Her second encounter with #119 was unsuccessful. She's still not pregnant. In an effort to cheer her up, I offered to take her to dinner or to a film. But she declined. Uncertain of what to do, I offered her the only bit of wisdom that I could think of – that she shouldn't worry, because it took me three tries to conceive.

And that was with a live man.

february 23rd – 11 p.m.

Mrs. Stewart and her paramour Roger came over for dinner tonight. They've recently decided to live together, so it was a sort of unofficial "welcome to the family" meal that I was serving.[88] But it was also an opportunity for me to prove that my kids won't be raised on Chinese takeout.

I spent three days planning a great home-cooked meal. A highly ambitious act, as I have an ugly personal history with food preparation – a history with genetic origins, since I come from a long line of women who specialize in frozen meals, canned soups, and anything that can be made in a microwave.

But after hours of slaving, everything was beautiful. From the place settings to the flowers to my exquisite chicken pot pie prepared *en croûte* in an enameled casserole dish. And amid coos of approval I proudly carried it to the dining table in my newly purchased suede oven mitts.

And that is precisely when I lost my grip, and the burning hot casserole dish fell from my hands and tumbled onto Roger's legs. Suddenly the coos of approval turned to gasps of horror (Mrs. Stewart's) and yelps of pain (Roger's) as my steaming chicken pot pie and piping hot casserole dish seared through his pants and began to burn his flesh.

Minutes later Roger, Mrs. Stewart, and Stephen were in a taxicab racing for Mount Sinai Hospital – leaving me behind to wallow in mortification and splattered bits of chicken.

Yes, it seems my spongelike water retention has a nasty consequence.

Things No One Tells You About Pregnancy
1. No sushi
2. Twenty-four-hour morning sickness

---

[88] That's right. At thirty-two I've become so staid and fuddy-duddy that *I'm* making a family dinner for my mother-in-law who's living in sin. Next I'll be embroidering a sampler for Chuffy.

3. Forty weeks (ten months) of pregnancy
4. No aspirin
5. Dog nose
6. "Glow" is sweat
7. Excessive flatulence
8. Heartburn
9. Ungodly constipation
10. CRC (Can't Remember Crap)
11. Public petting
12. Final erosion of personal identity
13. Incontinence
14. Broken capillaries
15. Difficulty breathing
16. Difficulty sleeping
17. No hot tubs
18. Spongelike water retention
19. Clumsiness

I'm now a disaster waiting to happen. This explains why so many pregnant women fall in their third trimester – the bloating caused by water retention makes it impossible to accurately find balance.

Although, to be honest, I can't help but think this latest culinary disaster is related to my antagonistic relationship with the "female arts."

february 24th

God bless my stoner coworker Stella. She's convinced Mr. Nealy that she needs additional help at Councilman

Hastings's weekend summit with a group of influential financial contributors. To that end, Mr. Nealy has instructed Eddie to assist. Which means that come March 1 while I'm at Joie de Vivre enjoying my baby shower, Eddie will be buffing his nails in a midtown conference room! He was positively devastated.

And the day just got better from there. I arrived home to discover that Stephen had cleaned and freshly painted the storage closet an incredible rainbow of beautiful colors. He even pried open the window.

Who knew it was the nicest view in the apartment?

february 25th

With Eddie out of the picture, I needed someone to host my shower. Although Anita's been incredibly supportive of my pregnancy it didn't feel right to ask her, since she's still struggling to get pregnant herself. And we all know about Mandy's threshold for baby-related activities. So I asked Nicole, who immediately agreed to step in for Eddie. Especially once I explained that everything had been paid for.

Meanwhile, my visits to the Crotch Whisperer have become a weekly event. Which is good, since the closer I get to my due date, the more regular checkups offer me a sense of comfort. Or at least they would offer me a sense of comfort if I could understand what the guy was saying.

For the last few months, I've gotten by with my enhanced lipreading skills, the audible voice of his testy nurse, and the ever-popular sneak-a-peek-at-my-chart-when-he-leaves-the-room method. But now we're in the big leagues. We're using terms like "engagement" and "lightening," which lead me to think the time for guesswork is OVER.

february 26th

I haven't heard boo about the *Focus* job. According to Anita's mole, the hire's going to happen. It's just slow. Well, that's grand, but don't these people know that I'm going on maternity leave in less than a month and I need to know now?

february 27th

Tonight was our second, and final, birthing class. After further discussing breathing techniques, we watched a video that showed both vaginal and cesarean births in intimate detail.

Leaving me with one question: Who are the women that volunteer for these films?

february 28th

Sat Nam and *sayonara* to the lambskins and navel rings, the auras and the paintbrushes in the butts – with a raging Things to Do list and a baby due in a month, today was my last prenatal yoga class. Besides, I'm tired of hiding in the bathroom to dodge Eddie.

Plus, they've basically frozen me out ever since I mentioned that I wasn't going to use cloth diapers. That's right, I don't like carrying shitty diapers around in my purse. Sue me. Judging from their reaction, you would have thought I was a child molester.

They probably would have stoned me if they knew I plan on having a son circumcised.

march 1st

Fat, swollen, and beset with CRC, I attended my shower today. After all these crazy months it was a luxury to spend a whole afternoon with my girlfriends. Especially at a swanky place like Joie de Vivre, whose snack shop is closer to a first-class lounge than a doughnut hut – huge comfy chairs, gourmet food, and people to clean up after you.

In total there were twelve of us. The perfect size for a relaxing afternoon spent stuffing our faces and opening presents. And oh, boy, did we get presents! My entire registry must have been cleared out.

Misty, whom I invited since she'd been excluded from the family shower out of deference to Mrs. Stewart, gave us our entire layette – which turns out to be the basic clothing and blanket needs for a newborn child. Everything from one-piece outfits and sleeping gowns to receiving blankets and towels.

You learn something every day.

Still unwilling to go to Baby Bargains, Mandy gave me an Ab-Master to get my stomach back in shape after the birth, and some fancy French cream – or rather *crème* – to help reduce my stretch marks.

Even though she couldn't attend – because she'd given birth to a baby girl only a week earlier – Bianca Larsen sent a first-year memories book and a rattle.

Anita gave me a bassinet, a box of thank-you notes, and a bottle of champagne for after the delivery. But, to be honest, I was more appreciative of her presence than her presents. After her recent failed attempt with #119, I would have completely understood if she hadn't felt like celebrating my pregnancy. But she did, and I was immensely grateful.

In fact, I was touched by how many of my incredibly busy friends managed to take time out of their lives to help celebrate our baby.

Margo came, although she had to leave early to pick her daughter up from tumbling class. And though I didn't have the heart to tell her she had gum in her hair, I did thank her for the case of nipple cream. When I asked her exactly what it was for, she patted my hand and said, "Just trust me."

Suzy Parks even brought her son Lucas with her. Absolutely adorable, he's a perfect replica of her. Now *that's* power. With my luck, our kid will defy all genetic sense and end up looking like Chuffy.

But the best gift of all was feeling like my baby would have a loving community of friends to welcome him/her into the world. And for this we toasted Eddie, with the lemonade and finger sandwiches that he'd paid for.

And while he wasn't able to make it in person, he let his presence be known by sending a few gifts – an electric breast pump, and a book extolling the benefits of large families.

march 1st – 8 p.m.

I spent two hours showing Stephen all the wonderful gifts we'd gotten at the shower. And it was during those two hours that I got another, unexpected, gift as we stumbled upon a boy's name that we both like: Jasper.

Jasper or Serena. After nine months, our search is over!

Things to Do
1. Find ob/gyn
2. Get prenatal checkup
3. Get prenatal vitamins
4. Find physical exercise
5. Decide childbirth method
6. Join childbirth class
7. Buy crib
8. Buy bassinet
9. Buy crib mattress
10. Buy crib bedding
11. Buy changing table
12. Decide cloth or disposable diapers
13. Buy diapers
14. Buy diaper bag
15. Buy diaper pail
16. Buy crib mobile
17. Buy layette
18. Buy stroller
19. Buy infant bathtub
20. Buy baby monitor
21. Buy infant swing
22. Buy night-light for baby's room
23. Choose color for baby's room
24. Paint baby's room
25. Buy pacifiers
26. Buy dresser for baby's clothes
27. Buy infant-size hangers

28. Create medical emergency kit
29. Prepare emergency phone lists
30. ~~Decide nursing or formula~~
31. ~~Buy nursing supplies or formula supplies~~
32. ~~If nursing, decide to rent or buy breast pump~~
33. ~~If nursing, buy nursing bras~~
34. ~~If nursing, buy nipple cream~~
35. Decide on legal guardian
36. Prepare wills
37. Plan estate
38. Create college fund
39. ~~Begin Kegel exercises~~
40. ~~Buy first-year memorabilia scrapbook~~
41. ~~Decide whether to learn gender~~
42. ~~Choose name(s)~~
43. ~~Choose hospital~~
44. ~~Take tour of hospital maternity ward~~
45. Find pediatrician
46. ~~Appoint someone to organize baby shower~~
47. ~~Make invite list for baby shower~~
48. ~~Register for baby shower~~
49. ~~Buy thank-you notes for baby shower~~
50. Select birth music
51. ~~Prepare for appropriate religious ceremony~~
52. ~~Book venue for religious ceremony~~
53. ~~Arrange for priest, rabbi, or *mehel*, etc.~~
54. ~~Buy baby's outfit for religious ceremony~~
55. ~~Buy maternity clothes~~
56. ~~Decide who will be in delivery room with you~~

57. Prepare baby announcements
58. Prepare overnight bag for hospital
59. Make birth plan
60. ~~Schedule maternity leave~~
61. Make phone list for announcing baby's birth
62. Buy baby's take-home-from-hospital outfit
63. Decide on postbirth child care

march 2nd

Sometime around three A.M. I started to feel funny. Well, not so much funny as uncomfortable. And in pain. But it didn't feel like labor. So I looked at *BH, BN,* only to learn that judging from my symptoms I might be experiencing something called eclampsia. Which wasn't good. After pacing the floor wondering whether to call the Crotch Whisperer, the emergency room, or my mother,[89] we finally left the apartment and were waiting outside the Crotch Whisperer's office when the nurse arrived to unlock the door at seven-thirty A.M. Panic-stricken, we told her that I had eclampsia. She looked at us, a mix of pity and annoyance on her face.

"Did you read *Baby How, Baby Now?*"

My heart stopped. "Yes. Religiously. OK, I missed last month and part of this month, but I've been really busy. I swear, like CRAZY busy, which isn't to say that I've prioritized my work over the baby. Oh, no. It's just that it got a little out of control and – "

She shook her head. "This makes me so mad."

I reached for Stephen's hand. "I *swear* I meant to keep

---

[89] We were desperate, OK?

current."

"That book is the biggest piece of alarmist shit ever to hit the store."

Excuse me?

"Too many misleading statements, not enough details. Trust me. If I had a dime for every hysterical woman that came running through our doors after reading that book, I'd have a tummy tuck and a vacation home in the south of France."

I suddenly flashed back to our earlier false alarms.

"But it's been around for generations! It's a *best-seller*."

"So was *Jaws*, but we still go swimming, don't we?"

march 2nd – 8 p.m.

I had every intention of going home and destroying *Baby How, Baby Now*. But Stephen beat me to it. After three terrifying false alarms, he'd had all he could take. He marched into the apartment, grabbed the book, and headed out the door to the incinerator.

And as he got ready to toss it down the chute, it occurred to me that Lily probably wasn't even pregnant. After all, God knows how long she'd been standing under that tree, and yet her ankles weren't even swollen. Not to mention the fact that she still had a waist.

No, Lily, that little minx, was just some gal with a pillow shoved under her shirt. Part of the whole *Baby How, Baby Now* charade. Scaring women for generations. Maybe a hired gun, or perhaps the author herself, perpetrating the ultimate hoax upon unsuspecting women with heightened hormonal levels.

Which is why I stopped Stephen mid-toss and demanded to have the honor. Stephen handed me the book and stormed back to our apartment. Moments later *Baby How, Baby Now,* the source of sleepless nights and terror-filled hours, was gone for good. And to think I actually bought it in HARDCOVER!

And as I turned around to exit the garbage room, I saw Mr. Elbin, flashing a triumphant smile. "That was *recyclable.*"

march 3rd

Mrs. Stewart and Roger have broken up. At first I was concerned that it had something to do with my scalding-hot chicken pot pie that left him with multiple third-degree burns below the waist. But it turns out the cause is pure canine.

Chuffy, to be exact.

As tolerant as Roger is, he refuses to live with Chuffy. In addition to being uncomfortable with Mrs. Stewart's particularly intimate relationship with the dog, it turns out Roger is allergic to Chuffy's dander. In short, it was him or Chuffy.

Mrs. Stewart chose Chuffy.

march 4th

I had the misfortune of riding the elevator this evening with Mr. Elbin. Bracing myself, I waited for some witty insult. Instead he asked if we'd chosen a name for the baby. I proudly informed him, yes. Serena for a girl and Jasper for a boy. Stepping off the elevator, he smiled. "I'm flattered."

"Why?"

"Because that's my name."

By the time Stephen arrived home from work, I was halfway through a dozen glazed donuts. "Jasper's no good."

I thought Stephen was going to cry. "Why not?"

"Because it's Mr. Elbin's name, and that's entirely too much bad karma to stick on a child."

"Who's Mr. Elbin?"

"You know. That guy next door."

Stephen stared blankly.

"You know who I mean. Tall, fifties, blue eyes, black heart."

He shook his head. "Nope, don't know him."

"You mean to tell me that while I end up in the elevator, the hallway, the bodega, and the garbage room with him almost every week, you've never even seen this guy?"

Stephen shrugged. "Guess so."

And there it was. Either Mr. Elbin's a figment of my imagination, or he's stalking me. Either way it's terrifying.

march 5th

Lucy died last night.

march 9th

My mother called to say that Lucy's funeral was beautiful. Lots of friends, flowers, and, as per a request in her will, a swing band and sherry. Less than three weeks from my due date, there was no way I could fly to Wisconsin for the event. And to be honest, I'm glad. This way I can pretend it never happened.

march 11th

Lucy's death has hit me like a ton of bricks. I go to work, come home, and just crawl into bed. I no longer care what I look like, or that I'm wearing clothes that could double as theatrical backdrops. All I know is that I'm about to have a baby who will never meet my precious Lucy.

And Lucy will never meet my baby.

I can tell Stephen's worried about me. On a daily basis, he tries to bring a smile to my face with a dish of ice cream or a container of sesame noodles. But I'm just not interested. All I can do is lie here and cry.

I keep reminding myself that there's a balance at work here. Someone enters this world, someone leaves it. It's a continual cycle that just keeps spinning.

Except there are some people you wish could live forever.

march 16th

After reading in the newspaper that Tangy Blair's set to star as a welfare mother in an upcoming miniseries, I opened the mail to find a birth announcement from Bianca Larsen.

Apparently her seven-pound, two-ounce baby girl is named *Serena*.

She stole our baby name!

The nerve! I'm certain that I told her I'd chosen that name during our phone conversation last month! I should have known better. At her wedding, a month before mine, Bianca stole our processional song. Once a thief, always a thief.

Positively livid, I called Mandy. Who laughed.

> MANDY
> For goodness' sake, Amy. Calm down. It's not like it's a pair of Ferragamo pumps.

I momentarily missed Eddie.

> ME
> You don't get it. Names are impossible!

> MANDY
> I have one word for you.

> ME
> Please don't let it be *Sessy*.

> MANDY
> Shoes.

> ME
> What?

> MANDY
> As in wedding shoes. Your inability to decide on a baby's name is just your way of distracting yourself from the terrifying fact that in less than two weeks something the size of a Fendi handbag will come out of a hole the size of a Chanel compact.

Okay, maybe it wasn't the nicest way to put it, but she was making sense. I spent nine months before my wedding frantically searching for shoes, only to end up with the very first pair I ever tried on. In short, worrying about wedding shoes was a hell of a lot easier than worrying about the fact that I was actually getting married. And here I was again, spending nine months frantically searching for a baby name. Yes, it might definitely be a distraction . . .

But I *still* don't have a name!

march 18th

Only eleven more days to finish organizing the baby's room, tie up all the loose ends at work, and figure out how to use this breast pump . . . the cones go *where*? This is called kamikaze nesting. Everybody better get out of my way.

Luckily Stephen's decided on our birthing music, although he refuses to tell me what it is. He wants it to be a surprise. Like we haven't had enough of those already.

Another bit of good news is that Margo gave me the name of her pediatrician. He speaks English, was educated at an accredited medical institution, and takes our insurance. Sure, it'd be great to meet him, check out his offices, and vet him with the A.M.A. But did I mention I'm having a baby in eleven days?

So Dr. Frederick Q. Hickman it is.

Things to Do
1. Find ob/gyn
2. Get prenatal checkup
3. Get prenatal vitamins

4. Find physical exercise
5. Decide childbirth method
6. Join childbirth class
7. Buy crib
8. Buy bassinet
9. Buy crib mattress
10. Buy crib bedding
11. Buy changing table
12. Decide cloth or disposable diapers
13. Buy diapers
14. Buy diaper bag
15. Buy diaper pail
16. Buy crib mobile
17. Buy layette
18. Buy stroller
19. Buy infant bathtub
20. Buy baby monitor
21. Buy infant swing
22. Buy night-light for baby's room
23. Choose color for baby's room
24. Paint baby's room
25. Buy pacifiers
26. Buy dresser for baby's clothes
27. Buy infant-size hangers
28. Create medical emergency kit
29. Prepare emergency phone lists
30. Decide nursing or formula
31. Buy nursing supplies or formula supplies
32. If nursing, decide to rent or buy breast pump
33. If nursing, buy nursing bras

34. ~~If nursing, buy nipple cream~~
35. Decide on legal guardian
36. Prepare wills
37. Plan estate
38. Create college fund
39. ~~Begin Kegel exercises~~
40. ~~Buy first-year memorabilia scrapbook~~
41. ~~Decide whether to learn gender~~
42. ~~Choose name(s)~~
43. ~~Choose hospital~~
44. ~~Take tour of hospital maternity ward~~
45. ~~Find pediatrician~~
46. ~~Appoint someone to organize baby shower~~
47. ~~Make invite list for baby shower~~
48. ~~Register for baby shower~~
49. ~~Buy thank-you notes for baby shower~~
50. ~~Select birth music~~
51. ~~Prepare for appropriate religious ceremony~~
52. ~~Book venue for religious ceremony~~
53. ~~Arrange for priest, rabbi, or *mohel,* etc.~~
54. ~~Buy baby's outfit for religious ceremony~~
55. ~~Buy maternity clothes~~
56. ~~Decide who will be in delivery room with you~~
57. Prepare baby announcements
58. Prepare overnight bag for hospital
59. Make birth plan
60. ~~Schedule maternity leave~~
61. Make phone list for announcing baby's birth

62. Buy baby's take-home-from-hospital outfit

63. Decide on postbirth child care

march 19th

Today at work I spent twenty minutes listening to Stella – with her bloodshot eyes and trendy cut jeans – tell me how tired she is of devoting her writing skills to the mindless work at Brinkman/Baines.

Oh, yeah? Join the club, Junior Miss.

But before I could feign interest in her plight, Eddie accosted me. "Remember, call me the minute you go into labor, and I'll be there in a flash to hold your hand and massage your shoulders."

Sure. Like *that's* gonna happen.

"Of course, Eddie. Wouldn't have it any other way."

march 20th

According to the Crotch Whisperer's chart, I'm at "zero station." Which means close, but no cigar.

Doesn't anyone understand how incredibly nervous I am about giving birth? And how indescribably excited I am to meet my baby? Come on, folks, let's hurry it up!

Unfortunately the Whisperer's nurse has informed me that it's not uncommon for first pregnancies to go late. Sometimes delivering as much as *two weeks* past the due date.

How nice.

Top Twenty Things
No One Tells You About Pregnancy
1. No sushi
2. Twenty-four-hour morning sickness
3. Forty weeks (ten months) of pregnancy
4. No aspirin
5. Dog nose
6. "Glow" is sweat
7. Excessive flatulence
8. Heartburn
9. Ungodly constipation
10. CRC (Can't Remember Crap)
11. Public petting
12. Final erosion of personal identity
13. Incontinence
14. Broken capillaries
15. Difficulty breathing
16. Difficulty sleeping
17. No hot tubs
18. Spongelike water retention
19. Clumsiness
20. "Due date" is a figure of speech

march 21st

How is a control freak like me supposed to cope with an in-exact due date? Doesn't anyone understand that I need to plan? To schedule? To control!

march 22nd

Tangy Blair's dopus-opus has actually made a best-seller list. Not *The New York Times* best-seller list, but a best-seller list all the same.

And yes, in the real world this makes me responsible for the mass promotion of an ill-conceived, narrow-minded text written by a complete jerk. But in the wonderful world of P.R., it makes me a hero.

march 23rd

This evening Stephen and I prepared a list of people to call once the baby is born. All thirty-seven of them.

We also packed our bag for the hospital, following some guidelines that Stephen found on the Internet. Judging by the size of the suitcase, you'd think we were taking a three-week vacation.

march 24th

Things to Do list #59: Prepare birth plan.

I know they mean make a detailed account for the Crotch Whisperer of how I would like my birth to be handled . . . Drugs, no drugs, blah, blah, blah.

Well, I'm cutting to the chase:

Amy's Birth Plan
Short.
Painless.

march 25th

I am *sooo* ready to give birth to this child.

The hell with my fear of childbirth. Bring it on, baby, bring it on!

march 26th

My maternity leave started today.

Mandy and Jon came over on their way to dinner to say hello. Jon wasn't in the apartment one minute before he started giving us a hard time about not having any names.

> JON
> If you can't manage to decide on a name, I
> suppose you could give the kid a sign, like
> Prince had.

Yeah, Jon. I've got a sign. See this middle finger?

Later in the evening, Anita left me a very nice message while I was sitting on the toilet trying to take a crap.

> ANITA
> I'm sending you positive thoughts. If it's
> an easy delivery, you owe me. If it's rough,
> you can blame your grandmother.

march 27th

I feel like I've been pregnant since the dawn of time.

march 28th

In less than two days I'm going to be a mother for the rest of my life!

One day it's nine[90] months and then suddenly it's *tomorrow*!

march 29th – 3:05 a.m.

Unable to sleep, I've spent the last three hours watching reruns of bad 1980s sitcoms on cable TV. All of them about families. And while I understand that these people aren't real, and that their homes have been made by production designers and set decorators, it does appear that good, responsible parents keep a list of emergency phone numbers on the refrigerator door.

Stephen and I have a list of our favorite beers.

march 29th

The phone's been ringing nonstop. Everyone wants to know if we've had the baby yet.

Are they insane?

Are they trying to make *me* insane?

Don't they know that over half of first-time pregnancies go late? That due dates are inexact? And that if the baby were here we'd have e-mailed or called them, and that if they keep tying up my phone line we won't be able to order

---

[90] TEN.

out for Chinese food?!

After forty weeks of running around, scrambling to get ready for this baby, here I am with nothing to do. With nothing scheduled for the next eight weeks – sitting on my sofa with my pants half zipped, reading *People* magazine, and thinking about how much I miss Lucy.

march 30th

Well, my due date came. And went.

I'm now convinced I'll be pregnant FOREVER.

march 31st

What the hell am I doing? I should be at work being productive. Instead I'm wasting away my maternity leave. The longer I wait, the more insane I begin to feel. I swear that damn suitcase is mocking me!

And the phone calls! "Did you have the baby yet?"

Trust me, I check every fifteen minutes to make sure the baby's head or hand isn't dangling out between my legs.

Stephen finally had to put an outgoing message on the answering machine: "No. Now stop calling."

And of course everyone's got some "trick" to induce this birth. Eat something spicy. Walk up three flights of stairs. Have sex with your husband.

That last one's a hoot. Are they kidding? At this point it's physically impossible for him to be on top of me, and it'd be manslaughter for me to mount him. It's all lunacy. If they told me to get a full-body massage and eat a box of chocolates, I might listen. But the rest of the advice? Forget it.

Meanwhile I've been reviewing my Things to Do list and have decided not to do anything. That's right. Screw it. Especially since most of the outstanding items are ridiculous. An emergency phone list? Here it is: 911. A will? The baby will get everything. The big-screen TV, my studded bustier, and our horrible plaid sofa. Planning our estate? Let's wait until we have one. Ditto for the college fund.

As for the issue of guardianship? We still haven't resolved it. Clearly we have no stable, responsible, age-appropriate person in our family. This leaves us with only one solution.

We will NEVER die.

april 1st

Okay, I know I've been bitching about not giving birth, but for the next twenty-four hours I'm keeping my legs firmly crossed because there's NO WAY I'm giving birth to a child on April Fools' Day.

Hell, I'll epoxy my knees together if I have to.

april 4th

What a long, strange, wonderful trip it's been. . . .

On the evening of April 1, Kimberly invited herself over for dinner after a particularly stressful appointment with a gastroenterologist here in the city. To punish her, I ordered a large ham-anchovy-and-pineapple pizza.

True to form, she spent the entire evening questioning how three people could exist in such a tiny apartment, why we didn't have a slipcover for our atrocious sofa, and whether or not she should go back to school to become a psychologist. Now there's a grand idea. Who better to dole out compassion than the Queen of Sensitivity herself?

Oh, please.

Whether it was shock, fury, or amusement over this suggestion I'll never know. But seconds later, I was sure I'd pissed myself. Turns out my water had broken. With labor imminent I sucked down Stephen's beer. Kim gasped. So I sucked down hers as well.

With contractions starting, Stephen called the Crotch Whisperer while Kim ran screaming to the bathroom in search of some Tylenol – for herself. Both nervous and excited, I thought back to birthing class and tried to remember what I was supposed to do. The word "WALK" sprang to mind, so I did. Around and around our 650-square-foot apartment, all the while thinking that after all these months I was actually about to have a baby. NOW. Despite the fact that the contractions were already pretty damn strong, the whole thing didn't seem real.

Stephen hung up the phone. As soon as the contractions were five minutes apart, we were supposed to go to the hospital. Setting the timer on his watch and slipping his keys and wallet into his pocket, I could tell he was trying to remain calm and rational. Like a good little computer programmer. Except he'd accidentally taken my wallet and the laundry room key. I silently thanked God that he didn't have to operate heavy machinery.

Within a half hour my contractions had advanced to five minutes apart. Stephen and I both knew this was fast. Stephen called the doctor. I slipped on my shoes. Grabbing my suitcase, we headed out the door – yelling a quick good-bye to Kim, who had inexplicably locked herself in the bathroom without a word.

Thankfully it was nine-thirty P.M., so getting a taxi was easy. Unfortunately, getting across Central Park to the hospital was not.

Unbeknownst to us, a car had broken down in the Eighty-sixth Street transverse, which meant that crosstown traffic was down to one lane. By the time we realized what was going on, it was too late to turn back. And for the next thirty minutes we were in stop-and-go traffic behind a bus whose exhaust levels far exceeded national emissions standards. So much for my well-timed test runs.

Between the traffic, my increasingly painful contractions – currently four minutes apart – and my refusal to give birth on April Fools' Day, I suddenly remembered that we still didn't have any names. Sensing my alarm, Stephen reminded me to breathe. And relax. Attempting to calm me, he suggested I focus on a soothing location.

I thought of a Balinese beach. And of the candy factories in Hershey, Pennsylvania.

When we finally arrived at the hospital Stephen paid the taxi driver, then almost forgot to get our suitcase out of the trunk. Clutching my stomach, we made our way to the maternity ward, where we happily surrendered to the experience of others. With impressive efficiency we were checked in, and the Crotch Whisperer was notified of our arrival. I was quickly examined by a resident, declared very close to delivering, then placed in a wheelchair, and taken to a labor room. All the while Stephen was right alongside me, lugging my eighty-pound suitcase.

It was eleven o'clock. Only an hour until April 2.

Could I make it?

This was what raced through my mind as I was wheeled down the hall – until I happened to catch sight of Eddie on the other side of the check-in window.

How did he know I was here? Had he slapped a homing device on me during one of his thousand belly rubs? Did he have an inside connection at the hospital admitting department?

Panicked, but not wanting to upset Stephen, I reached up, yanked the orderly down to eye level, and quietly instructed him to alert security *not* to allow that guy with the man-purse and the really nice tan into the maternity ward. He was a wanted criminal. His crime of choice? Kidnapping.

The orderly eyed Eddie, then dutifully nodded his head.

After helping me into the hospital bed, Stephen revealed his much-anticipated musical selections for the birth:

"Little Creatures" by the Talking Heads.

"Alive and Kicking" by Simple Minds.

"Born in the U.S.A." by Bruce Springsteen?!

THIS was how he wanted to welcome our baby? With synthesizers and guitar solos? But Stephen couldn't understand my displeasure. "It's thematically perfect. And it's music from our youth. It's nostalgic!"

We were giving birth to our child. Bringing another life into this world. Did he really think it was necessary to search elsewhere for a nostalgic moment?

But before we could discuss it further, Eddie burst breathlessly into the room. "Sorry it took me so long to get here, but some crazy security guard insisted I was a kidnapper!"

Stephen was speechless. So I did the talking. "How'd you ⌐e here?"

⌐our apartment to see how you were doing.

Your sister-in-law told me where you were. Did I miss anything?"

And just when I thought Stephen was about to tackle him to the ground, a couple of nurses walked into the room and gasped. The taller of the two, who looked like a member of the W.N.B.A., menacingly snapped, "You again? I told you the next time you stepped foot in this maternity ward I was calling the police!" Stephen and I watched in shock as she lunged for the phone and Eddie bolted out the door, toppling a garbage can and a chair on his way out.

Satisfied by his exit, the nurse hung up the phone and shook her head. "Freak."

I was about to agree when a huge contraction grabbed hold of my body. I shuddered in pain. Seconds later the room was filled with people, and I was hooked up to all sorts of machines, beeping and ringing and buzzing.

Already looking exhausted, the Crotch Whisperer appeared, dressed in surgical scrubs and rubber gloves. I thought back to those high school birthing films. After a quick examination he nodded to the nurses and said something inaudible. Suddenly everyone was looking at me. I looked at Stephen. He shrugged helplessly.

The smaller nurse pulled down her mask. "The doctor would like you to push."

Push? *Already?!* I looked at the clock and panicked. It was 11:45 P.M. I started to babble, "I can't. We have to wait because it's April Fools' Day and I can't possibly give birth for at least another fifteen minutes, and – "

And that's when the Crotch Whisperer turned to the nurse and with complete exasperation said, "Good lord, this woman's a pain in the ass!"

I was stunned. It was the first audible thing he'd ever said.

But there was no time to marvel. Or be offended. My contractions were coming one after another and I was in excruciating pain. I turned to the nurses, sensing they'd be more sympathetic than the Whisperer. "When do I get the drugs?"

Some machine beeped louder.

"No time for drugs. The baby's coming *now*."

And sure enough I felt an enormous surge of pressure ripple through my body. Bigger and stronger than any of the contractions I'd felt before. Terrified, I did the only thing I could think of.

"SAT NAM!"

It was one of the quickest deliveries they had ever seen. And seconds after it was over, it was a complete blur to me. I remember *incredible* pain. And people telling me to push. And Stephen urging me to use the breathing techniques from birthing class. And someone asking why I kept saying *Sat Nam* and what the hell did it mean. And then suddenly there was a cry.

The most wonderful cry I'd ever heard.

My entire body relaxed. I caught my breath and looked up. With tears of joy streaming down his face, Stephen was cradling our child. Gently handing me the baby, he softly whispered, "It's a girl."

She was so small and delicate. And yet miraculously so full of life. And as I gazed into her tender face I immediately knew her name. She wasn't a Madison or a Serena.

This beautiful baby was a Lucy.

Now, three days later, we're back home with Lucy, and paperwork that, thanks to a twenty-dollar bill, says she was born on April 2 at 12:01 A.M. And though she's only been with us a few days, I can't remember life without her.

Especially since we're surrounded by tons of her *stuff*. While we were at the hospital, my incredibly thoughtful mother came to our apartment, did inventory on our baby supplies, and filled in the blanks. We now own everything that's practical. Proving once again that neither God nor the Devil is in the details. Just my mom.

Among the many new things we have is my father's triangular crib. Finally finished, it's not nearly as scary as I thought it would be. In fact, it actually seems quite safe – if a bit odd. Let's just call it "unique." Luckily, my mother figured out a way to use standard rectangular sheets in it. Although, where they found a triangular mattress I'll never know.

And we're still receiving gifts! Pablo sent a bouquet of flowers, and Abe Hamen sent a basket of his citrus-scented massage oils. True to his reputation, I haven't heard a peep from Eddie. He didn't even sign the card I got from Brinkman/Baines. Which is great. Except I still want to cry when I think of how often I let him touch my belly.

Although it's not nearly as upsetting as thinking about how much I would have loved to introduce our little Lucy to big Lucy. Big Lucy would have loved her namesake's splash of light brown hair, her sparkling brown eyes, and her father's little smile that I swear lists to the left.

Two momentous life events happening at the same time has been overwhelming, to say the least. My only solace is looking at little Lucy and knowing that a part of big Lucy lives on in her.

Of course, Gram is near-apoplectic that after all her campaigning we named the baby after Lucy instead of her. Or Sessy. Whoever that is. It's clear from the way she says the baby's name that she thinks big Lucy scooped her in the end.

I just laugh. Because that's what Lucy would have done. In fact I bet Lucy's somewhere right now laughing her butt off about Gram's irritation. I certainly hope so.

The second best thing to happen these past few days is that Anita learned she's pregnant. Seems the third time was a charm with #119. And even though I don't really understand her desire to be a single mom, it's clear that Anita's given more thought to the decision to have a child than any married person I know. So I offered her my congratulations and all of my maternity clothes. But she passed – politely mentioning that she intends to stay fashionable. Ha! I said that, too. But who knows? Maybe she'll pull it off. After all, this is Anita we're talking about.

Oh, and she also gave me big news about the job at *Focus*. They've decided to hire a Brinkman/Baines employee – Stella. Seems the whole time I was vying for the job, so was my stoner coworker Stella. And while I'm certain that I'll eventually be disturbed about this development, at the moment, I couldn't care less. Because having given birth, I'm convinced I can achieve anything.

As for all the odd physical changes that accompanied my pregnancy? Most of them have gone away. Certainly my dog nose has significantly decreased. Although I'm still glowing. But it's not sweat. It's love. And perhaps a drop or two of leaky breast milk catching the light.

They say April is the cruelest month. Well, not for me. Sure, it's got a day of fools and lots of showers, but to me it will forever be the month of Lucy. And though I still don't know what makes a good mother, or a perfect parent, one thing is certain: As I hold my daughter tightly in my arms, I'm overwhelmed by the desire never, ever, to let go.

Top ~~Twenty~~ 21 Things
No One Tells You About Pregnancy
1. No sushi
2. Twenty-four-hour morning sickness
3. Forty weeks (ten months) of pregnancy
4. No aspirin
5. Dog nose
6. "Glow" is sweat
7. Excessive flatulence
8. Heartburn
9. Ungodly constipation
10. CRC (Can't Remember Crap)
11. Public petting
12. Final erosion of personal identity
13. Incontinence
14. Broken capillaries
15. Difficulty breathing
16. Difficulty sleeping
17. No hot tubs
18. Spongelike water retention
19. Clumsiness
20. "Due date" is a figure of speech
21. It's worth it.